MW01193258

THE
MAGICIAN
OF
TIGER
CASTLE

BOOKS BY LOUIS SACHAR

⋛◇⋚

Holes
Small Steps

Fuzzy Mud
The Cardturner
Dogs Don't Tell Jokes
The Boy Who Lost His Face
There's a Boy in the Girls' Bathroom
Sixth Grade Secrets
Someday Angeline

WAYSIDE SCHOOL

Sideways Stories from Wayside School
Wayside School Is Falling Down
Wayside School Gets a Little Stranger
Wayside School Beneath the Cloud of Doom
Sideways Arithmetic from Wayside School
More Sideways Arithmetic from Wayside School

MARVIN REDPOST

Kidnapped at Birth?
Why Pick on Me?
Is He a Girl?
Alone in His Teacher's House
Class President
A Flying Birthday Cake?
Super Fast, Out of Control
A Magic Crystal?

THE
MAGICIAN
OF
TIGER
CASTLE

Louis Sachar

Ace
New York

ACE

Published by Berkley

An imprint of Penguin Random House LLC

1745 Broadway, New York, NY 10019

penguinrandomhouse.com

Book design by Daniel Brount

Export edition ISBN: 9780593956748

Library of Congress Cataloging-in-Publication Data

Names: Sachar, Louis, 1954- author.
Title: The magician of tiger castle / Louis Sachar.
Description: New York: Ace, 2025.
Identifiers: LCCN 2024043343 (print) | LCCN 2024043344 (ebook) |
ISBN 9780593952306 (hardcover) | ISBN 9780593952313 (ebook)
Subjects: LCGFT: Fantasy fiction. | Novels.
Classification: LCC PS3569.A226 M34 2025 (print) | LCC PS3569.A226 (ebook) |
DDC 813/.54—dc23/eng/20240927
LC record available at https://lccn.loc.gov/2024043343
LC ebook record available at https://lccn.loc.gov/2024043344

Printed in the United States of America
1st Printing

The authorized representative in the EU for product safety and compliance is
Penguin Random House Ireland, Morrison Chambers, 32 Nassau Street,
Dublin D02 YH68, Ireland, https://eu-contact.penguin.ie.

To the Cool Breezers

THE
MAGICIAN
OF
TIGER
CASTLE

PART ONE

TAMPERINGS

1

HOMECOMING

So here I sit, dressed like a typical American tourist, sipping a cappuccino at an outdoor table in an authentic medieval village. I can see the turrets of Tiger Castle in the distance, silhouetted against the red morning sky. I break off a piece of my almond croissant and place it inside the front pouch of my hoodie.

My hands are bruised, and I think I may have sprained my left wrist. The street here is paved with cobblestones, all of different shapes and sizes. In places, there are significant gaps between the stones. I doubt I was the first person to stumble and fall. My dignity suffered the greatest harm.

I suppose the street is kept like this for authenticity, but five hundred years ago there wouldn't have been coffee, or chocolate. Only the *popolo grasso*, or "fat people," could afford such luxuries. The *popolo minuto*—"little people"—ate mostly bread, ale, and whatever greens they managed to grow.

Also, a shop wasn't a separate entity then, but part of the crafts-man's home. A craftsman worked in the front room, and the family slept together in the back room. (Only the *popolo grasso* could afford privacy.) The craftsman would lower his shutter outward toward the street to create a display table for his wares.

These cobblestones could well be the original stones, but five hundred years ago, the spaces between the stones were regularly refilled with a claylike dirt. After a heavy rain, we'd have to strap wooden planks to the bottoms of our shoes to keep the mud off.

I TOOK A TOUR OF TIGER CASTLE YESTERDAY. ACCORDING TO OUR tour guide, the tigers are well cared for and are fed a scientific blend of meat and nutritional supplements. In 1523, the tigers ate live animals, including goats, pigs, sheep, horses, and, of course, the occasional human.

It wasn't called Tiger Castle then, but simply the Castle, or perhaps the Esquavetian Castle. The kingdom of Esquaveta no longer exists.

As our tour guide led us along the winding corridors and up and down the stairs, she told tales of some of the people who had lived there. There was the Whispering King, a man so powerful he only needed to whisper. She also spoke of a treacherous queen who killed one king to marry another. And she related the tragic tale of a beautiful princess who was abducted on her wedding night and murdered.

I was disappointed that she never mentioned the great magician Anatole, but I suppose it was to be expected. History isn't written by the conquered. Besides, these days magicians are regarded as nothing more than entertaining tricksters. In the 1500s, science and magic were virtually indistinguishable. Gunpowder was created out of animal dung. Was that magic or science? If sand could be turned into glass, why couldn't it also be turned into gold?

I was surprised to see the enormous glass elephant. Considering how many times the castle had been conquered, I would have thought it had long been shattered.

The guide pointed out the entrance to a secret passageway, but to everyone's disappointment, we weren't allowed to venture in. She claimed it was too dangerous.

Everyone's worried about lawsuits these days. If I could make it through the passage, then surely the others on the tour could have too. I was probably the least agile of our group.

The tour guide also led us down to the dungeon, where she switched off the lights—yes, there's electricity now—and she made us experience thirty seconds of total darkness. She spoke of a prisoner who'd been locked in the dungeon for one hundred years! She described this prisoner as a kind of holy man.

I'M DRINKING COFFEE NOW, BUT I USED TO BE A TEA DRINKER; some might even call me a tea snob, though I prefer the term *connoisseur.* After just one sip, I could have told you not only the variety of the tea but where it was grown, at what altitude, and possibly what wildflowers had been in the vicinity.

I think my acute sense of smell and of taste had a lot to do with my success. Intuition also played a part, but really, intuition is little more than paying attention to the world around you. While I may not have known why I made the choices I made, the knowledge was somewhere inside me.

Sadly, while my other faculties have remained intact, my senses of smell and taste have been greatly diminished. Only strong and bitter flavors can get through to me now. I prefer an onion to a fig. And, alas, I've had to switch from tea to espresso.

THE FIRST TIGER

I WAS THERE WHEN THE first tiger was delivered to the castle. It arrived by horse-drawn cart. Two knights in full regalia rode along beside it, carrying the red, green, and black banner of Oxatania. In the sixteenth century, knights were only used for spectacle. Gunpowder had rendered them obsolete for warfare.

The tiger was inside an iron-and-wood box, with only a small slot for food. The box reeked after the three-day journey from Oxatania. Who knows how long it had been kept inside it before that? In 1523 kings and queens didn't concern themselves about the humane treatment of animals. To be fair, they weren't overly concerned about the humane treatment of humans either.

The tiger was a gift in anticipation of the upcoming wedding between Princess Tullia of Esquaveta and Prince Dalrympl of Oxatania. The marriage had been arranged twelve years earlier, when the princess was only three.

I had been in my workshop, dissecting beetles, when I was

startled by a tug on my tunic. "I'm betrothed, Natto!" the three-year-old princess had proudly told me.

She couldn't pronounce the *L* in *Anatole*.

There was no door to the archway that separated my workshop from the castle corridor, but I'd hung two curtains made of beads and shells on either side of it. These not only added to my mystique as court magician, they warned me if anyone was coming. Princess Tullia, however, had a way of slipping through the curtains without making a sound, often startling me.

"Congratulations!" I replied. "Who's the lucky man?"

Her face scrunched up in confusion. *What man was I talking about?*

Since then, gifts had been sent back and forth between the two kingdoms. At first these were simple tokens of friendship, but as the wedding date drew closer, the gifts became increasingly extravagant, as each king tried to outdo the other.

When the tiger arrived, the wedding was only six months away. Once the Oxatanian knights had departed, King Sandro raised his hands to the heavens and bellowed, "What am I supposed to do with it?"

Queen Corinna, who had a predilection toward the unusual and exotic, suggested that the tiger be served at the wedding banquet. The kitchen steward immediately protested. He warned that tiger meat might be tough and stringy. In addition, the king worried that the Oxatanians might be insulted if we butchered their most generous gift.

An even bigger problem than what to do with it was how to reciprocate. That task fell to Dittierri, the king's regent. I took secret pleasure in seeing the regent's anguish as he fretted over finding the perfect gift.

But I had problems of my own. The day before the arrival of the tiger, twenty-two sacks of black sand had been brought to me from Iceland.

Xavier, the finance minister, had been with me when the sacks were hauled into my workshop. He was younger than me, with fiery red hair, but the pressures of his job had taken a toll. He had bags under his eyes and had developed a facial tic.

According to him, the kingdom of Esquaveta was on the verge of bankruptcy. All wages would have to be cut by half. A number of soldiers had already deserted.

We couldn't squeeze out any more taxes from the *popolo minuto*. As it was, all land, crops, and livestock were considered the property of the king. If an ox or horse died, the peasant who had tended the animal was forced to compensate the king for his loss. Similarly, if that peasant died, his family had to compensate the king for the loss of a worker.

These were dangerous times. We didn't dare let the French to the north or the Italian city-states to the south learn of our vulnerability. Even the pope maintained a mercenary army and was always looking to expand the Papal States.

We just needed to make it through the wedding, which would first be preceded by a lavish banquet, and then a weeklong festival. The marriage between Princess Tullia and Prince Dalrympl had been dubbed "the wedding of the century."

The wedding was more than a marriage between two people. It would be the union of two kingdoms.

We sophisticated Esquavetians had always looked down upon the crude and boorish Oxatanians. The stereotypical Oxatanian oaf was often the butt of our jokes. But the truth was, we desperately needed their fearsome army and their efficient economy.

———

INSIDE MY WORKSHOP, XAVIER SEEMED MORE LIKE A SHIPPING clerk than the finance minister, making careful note as each sack of black sand was unloaded. There was a nervous excitement in his manner, giving me the sense that in his mind, each sack was already filled with gold.

I cautioned Xavier that whatever gold I *might* be able to produce would necessarily weigh less than the sand. He shrugged off my concern, saying there was plenty more sand on the black beach of Iceland.

In hindsight, I should never have agreed to take on this project. My expertise was in the living world: plants, bugs, sea life, and animals. I had never applied my magic to rocks and minerals.

3

DITTIERRI

MY APPEARANCE WAS ROUGHLY the same then as it is now. I was forty years old, with a bit of a paunch and no hair. By today's standards, I suppose I'd be considered short and dumpy, but in the sixteenth century the average height for a man was about five feet, seven inches. I was only three or four inches below that. A healthy plumpness was a sign of prosperity, as well as a hedge against famine.

By *no hair*, I'm not referring just to my head. My entire body was, and is, bald.

This was an unintended consequence of an early experiment, conducted long before I came to the castle. Who knows, it may have helped me get the job. What king wants an ordinary-looking magician?

I had been trying to find a way to limit human perspiration. Keep in mind my especially keen sense of smell and the fact that in the sixteenth century people didn't bathe as often as they do today.

I wasn't so much offended by natural human odor as I was by the sickly-sweet powders and oils people used to try to mask it.

In a way, it could be said my experiments were successful. In addition to my hair loss, I also lost the capacity to sweat.

IT WAS DITTIERRI WHO FIRST ENCOURAGED MY SAND EXPERI-ments. Initially, I used common white sand. I spent months trying to find the necessary additives and catalysts to transform it into gold. Molecules and atoms were unknown, and I had thought, not unreasonably, that a tiny grain of sand was the basic building block for everything else.

Saffron came closest to providing the color I wanted, but ounce for ounce, saffron was more expensive than gold, so what would be the point of that?

Inspiration struck when I learned of the black beach in Iceland. Instead of trying to *add* to white sand, I would *subtract* from black!

Dittierri supported me there too, and he authorized the shipment. The regent couldn't lose. If I succeeded, he'd reap the benefits. And if I failed, my court status would fall even further than it already had.

The regent had resented me ever since I was first summoned to the castle, eighteen years earlier, when King Sandro was suffering from the "strangling sickness." When I first saw him, he lay in bed, his sheets wet with sweat, and was desperately gasping for breath. Dittierri told anyone who would listen to him that I was a fraud, and even after the king recovered, he insisted that the king would have survived with or without my intervention.

The regent's slander was mostly ignored, at least during my first decade at the castle, as I successfully treated courtiers for various ailments, mostly minor, but some quite serious. However, I'd recently suffered a long string of what others might call *failures*. I prefer *temporary setbacks*. Regardless, at the time the tiger was delivered, my court status had fallen considerably.

I needed the black sand to rehabilitate my reputation.

ABOUT A WEEK LATER, DITTIERRI SPECIFICALLY SOUGHT ME OUT and excitedly told me he'd found the perfect reciprocal gift. I had been sitting on a bench by the fishpond, contemplating the black sand problem.

"A life-size elephant, Anatole, made entirely of glass." He said it would be presented to the prince at the banquet, then eagerly awaited my reaction.

This was the first time he'd ever asked my opinion about anything. Perhaps my stature had fallen so low that he no longer viewed me as a threat. Either that, or he thought I was the only one diabolical enough to appreciate his genius.

Dittierri had a long face and pointed chin, and just the thin outline of a beard. It was almost as if an artist had drawn the beard on his face but hadn't gotten around to coloring it in yet.

I agreed a glass elephant sounded impressive. "But how will they ever manage to transport it back to Oxatania?"

"That will be his problem." He smiled. "It's *his* elephant!"

Just as the tiger was our problem.

FOUR AND A HALF MONTHS LATER, THE SAND WAS STILL BLACK. I listened to the pings of the shovels and pickaxes banging against the dirt. It had been going on for months, along with the grunts and curses of the soldiers digging the moat, and their occasional bursts of laughter. *How did anyone expect me to concentrate on my work amid such noise?*

It was a tactic of modern warfare to pack explosives against the base of a castle's protective wall. The moat was being dug all around the wall, which circled the castle complex. King Sandro laughed as he described the frightened enemy soldier who, while loading the explosives, turns around to see a tiger curiously watching him.

I had laughed too, but I don't think I was the only one with doubts and fears. Gregor, the engineer in charge of the moat, had assured everyone that it would be sufficiently deep, with steep sides. But what did he know about the leaping and climbing abilities of tigers?

In the meantime, Gregor had also constructed several more boxlike structures, allowing the tiger to freely move from one to the next. The tiger could be locked inside any one of these boxes, so the others could be cleaned.

I STARED HELPLESSLY AT THE MOUND OF SAND. I HAD ONLY agreed to *try* to turn it into gold, but by then, Dittierri had managed to twist my reluctant willingness *to try* into a *guarantee of success*. Unless inspiration struck soon, I doubted I would still be a member of the king's court by the time the moat was completed.

I was so consumed with my own worries that I had only been vaguely aware of the new apprentice scribe, Pito. I knew that the royal scribe, Voltharo, had been having difficulties. In fact, before I got so involved with the sand, I'd been experimenting with treatments for Voltharo's shakes and hand cramps.

But then, less than six weeks before the wedding of the century, an even bigger problem arose, one that made all other concerns seem trivial in comparison. Princess Tullia announced that she refused to marry Prince Dalrympl. She'd fallen in love with the new apprentice scribe.

Pito was immediately locked in the dungeon. And, happily for me, the king told me to set aside the sand experiments.

Instead I was given a new task. I had a little more than a month to save the marriage, and thereby the kingdom, and, of course, my career.

4

PRINCESS TULLIA

PRINCESS TULLIA HAD BEEN born defective.

Her biggest defect was being born a princess. King Sandro needed an heir, and that meant a prince.

Dittierri had tried to blame me for that too, even though the potion I had given Queen Corinna was solely for morning sickness. I never claimed otherwise, but I had only been at the castle for about two years then and was not yet fully aware of Dittierri's propensity to twist the truth.

Princess Tullia's other defect was her eyes. Her left eye was brown, and the right one was blue.

When she was young, she liked to visit me in my workshop and play with the mice I used for my experiments. Her brown eye always seemed to be in deep contemplation of something or other, while her blue one sparkled with joy. She charmed me.

But this was during the Renaissance, and there were well-understood standards of art and beauty. Perspective and symmetry were essential.

Tullia was asymmetrical.

AS SHE GREW UP, OF COURSE, SHE CAME TO UNDERSTAND WHAT it meant to be betrothed, and accepted it as her duty even though Prince Dalrympl was more than twenty years older. "Love is for poets, Anatole," she told me with the haughty authority of a thirteen-year-old who believes she fully understands the way of the world. "Only peasants can afford to marry for love. For merchants and traders, it is just another business contract. And for royalty, it is an alliance."

That was two years before Pito came to the castle.

INSIDE MY WORKSHOP, I BREWED A KIND OF TEA FROM THE POW-dered wings of the African moon moth. From what I'd been told, Tullia had been in a constant state of hysteria since Pito had been locked in the dungeon. I added galingale and turmeric to the tea. When she was young, we had tea parties in my workshop. While I sipped some rare and fine variety, she especially enjoyed anything made with galingale and turmeric.

I removed a urine glass from a cabinet. In the sixteenth century, any physician worth his salt kept a ready supply of urine glasses. It was a symbol of the profession, much like the stethoscope is today. I owned more than a dozen, as I had a propensity to drop things.

I could diagnose most diseases simply by the color and odor of my patient's urine. I'd find a cure by mixing various ingredients with the urine and then observing the changes. I was able to detect twenty-four distinct shades of yellow.

It wasn't Princess Tullia's urine I needed, however, but her tears.

With a goblet of moon moth tea in one hand and the urine glass in the other, I carefully stepped around the pile of black sand

and then walked backward, pushing through the twin curtains of beads and shells.

The princess's chambers were on the third floor. I took the back staircase, the one mostly used by servants. I was in no mood to run into any courtiers or courtesans, who, of late, often greeted me with snide remarks and looks of either contempt or pity.

I knocked on the door to the princess's chambers with my elbow. The moment Tullia's handmaiden, Marta, opened it, I realized I should have made some moon moth tea for her as well. Marta immediately let loose with a barrage of incoherent complaints that I could barely follow as she switched from one incomplete thought to another.

I sidestepped around her and entered Tullia's drawing room. Two chairs had been overturned, and the drapes from the large bay window lay in a heap on the floor. Shards of pottery and broken glass also littered the floor. There was no sign of the princess.

I followed Marta's eyes to a closed door. "I finally got her to bed," she said, with a sense of relief. "Don't disturb her!" she shouted as I placed my hand on the doorknob.

Holding the urine glass in the crook of my elbow, I entered the inner chamber.

The princess was tied to her bed. A strip of red satin was tied over her mouth. Her eyes were wide open. I could see hopelessness in the brown one, but the blue one shone with determination.

I set the goblet and urine glass on a bed stand, and, bracing myself for a storm of fire and fury, I removed her gag. Instead, all I got was a tightly controlled "I'm glad you're here, Anatole. I was hoping you'd come."

I'd started on the ropes when Marta shouted, "No!" and pulled my arm back.

The princess's maidservant was considerably stronger than me.

"You can leave, Marta," said the princess. "Anatole and I need to talk in private."

"But you haven't slept in—"

"Get out!" shouted Tullia.

Marta let go of my arm and backed toward the door. "If you knew what I've been through . . ." she said to me.

"Out the other door too!" ordered the princess.

"But I'm not supposed to . . ." Marta started, then fled the bed-chamber. A moment later I heard the other door open and slam shut.

I finished untying the ropes, then offered Tullia the goblet.

She took a small sip and smiled. "Galingale and turmeric," she said. "Like old times."

"African moon moth wings too," I said, not wanting to deceive her. "For your nerves."

"Good, I need to think clearly," she said. "We haven't much time. They've locked Pito in the dungeon."

"I know."

"You have to get him out of there!"

I didn't know what she expected me to do. For one thing, Harwell, the keeper of the dungeon, may not have been an actual giant, but he was the largest human I'd ever seen. I couldn't even take on Marta.

"You can easily sneak past Harwell," the princess said. "He can't hear."

That part was true. The prison guard was deaf.

"The dungeon door will still be locked," I pointed out.

"You can steal Harwell's keys. He won't notice. Cast a spell on him, if you have to! Then you can give Pito a potion to make him invisible."

Unlike Dittierri, Tullia believed there were no limits to my magic.

I told her I knew of no invisibility potions, and that I didn't cast spells.

The princess frowned, but was not ready to give up.

"Surely, you can give Harwell something to knock him out. Then help Pito escape."

I gently explained that even if I came up with some sort of reason why Harwell should drink a potion, I wouldn't be able to communicate it to him. Besides, if Pito escaped, leaving Harwell unconscious in the dungeon, there would be little doubt as to who was responsible.

Tullia clutched my arm. "Pito did nothing wrong!" she exclaimed, shaking it. "It's my fault he's down there!"

I could see terror in her blue eye, and only sadness in the brown.

I told her she shouldn't blame herself. "It takes two people to have . . ." I began, putting it as delicately as I could, "a romantic rendezvous."

I could feel my face redden as I said those words. In some ways, Tullia was like a daughter to me, and it was difficult for me to talk about such things.

"What Pito did to you would have been . . . untoward," I continued, "even if you weren't a princess. You've promised yourself to another." I avoided saying she was betrothed, since that word had become something of a private joke between us.

"Pito did nothing to me! There was no *romantic rendezvous*, as you call it. Although, I did wish he would be a little more . . . *untoward.*" Her blue eye twinkled.

"All we did was read together," she continued. "And only because I told him it was a duty of the apprentice scribe to teach me English."

She explained that they would meet every day in the library, and read to each other from *Utopia,* a book written by an Englishman named Thomas More. Utopia was a mythical island somewhere off the coast of South America. Everyone was equal there. "No kings. No queens. And *no princesses!*" she pointedly added. And nobody owned anything on the island of Utopia. Everything was shared, so there was no need for fences or locks on the doors.

These were radical ideas, but they didn't explain why Pito had been put in the dungeon.

"I also made him read to me from another book," Tullia admitted.

She said it was a collection of Italian love poetry. "I'd close my eyes and pretend the words were his, meant only for me.

"Some of those poems were very *untoward,*" she added. Her blue eye twinkled again, even as tears fell from the brown one.

"I love him, Natto! You have to save him."

I pressed the urine glass against her face, collecting her tears, first from the brown eye, and then also from the blue.

"I have a plan," I assured her.

5

LUIGI

ACK IN MY WORKSHOP, I transferred Tullia's tears into a vial and sealed it with a cork. I hadn't lied to her. If everything went as I hoped, Pito would be set free, and the wedding of the century would still take place, solidifying our alliance with Oxatania.

I set the vial on a shelf. Before I could get started, however, I needed the king's approval.

To a modern observer, even without the mounds of white and black sand, my workshop would have seemed cluttered and disorganized. My shelves and cabinets were crammed with tools, tins, and more than a hundred earthenware jars, none of which were labeled. They didn't have to be. I knew what was where.

The earthenware jars were flanged at the top. This allowed for a piece of cloth or parchment, waxed or unwaxed depending on the jar's contents, to be easily tied over them. The jars were concave in the middle, which made them easy to grasp. I rarely dropped a jar.

My tallow candles emitted the rancid smell of burning animal fat, but I'd become accustomed to it, so it didn't interfere with my experiments. I could discern other unique odors from the smell of burning tallow.

In other parts of the castle, the candles were made from scented olive oil, but my experiments required me to burn through a great deal of candles. That I was allotted only tallow was an indication of the kingdom's plummeting finances, as well as my plummeting court status.

I don't think I would have been able to work in a modern-day sterile, brightly lit laboratory, where ultra-precise instruments can make measurements down to one millionth of a nanogram. I relied more on feel and instinct than precise measurements.

The accuracy of my measuring devices varied depending on the skill of the craftsmen who made them. Unlike in the twenty-first century, where even the machines are made by other machines, everything in the sixteenth century was handmade. Every pot, goblet, chess piece, fork, or shoe was unique. It was said that sailors could recognize their home ports by the distinct tones of the bells ringing in the church tower.

I SUPPOSED THAT MY SEVENTEEN MICE ALSO CONTRIBUTED TO the foul odor. The mice were in two cages. Sixteen were kept in one cage.

The other held Luigi.

As a rule, I didn't give the mice names. When conducting experiments, it is important to remain detached and objective. Princess Tullia had named Luigi.

Luigi was seven years old, so Tullia would have been about eight at the time. Most mice only live to be two or three.

An elaborate obstacle course extended from Luigi's cage, complete with tubes, tunnels, spinning wheels, swinging bridges, and a maze. I'd yet to observe any diminishment of Luigi's strength, agility, stamina, or memory.

In hindsight, I wish I had tested for taste and smell.

My curtains clattered, and I turned to see Ian, the young page, come through the archway. Ian was Dittierri's nephew, and though only ten years old, he'd already perfected his uncle's haughty sneer.

"Your presence is requested in the regency," he announced.

Despite the nicety of the language, it wasn't a request.

Without even a glance at Luigi's giant obstacle course, Ian did an about-face and marched out through the archway. I ask you, what normal ten-year-old boy wouldn't have been intrigued by something like that?

When Tullia was his age, she'd begged me to build an even larger one for her.

6

POPPY TEARS

UNFORTUNATELY, IT WAS QUEEN Corinna and not King Sandro who was waiting for me in the regency. Dittierri was at his very large desk, and the scribe, Voltharo, was at a smaller one.

I knelt before the queen. She had a crescent-shaped scar on her right cheek. People said it enhanced rather than detracted from her beauty, but they would have to say that, wouldn't they?

Sixteen years earlier she had been clawed by a sable she had kept as a pet. Shortly afterward she had a neck warmer made from its fur.

I'd treated her wound with an ointment of my own concoction and had to lean close to apply it. Unlike her daughter's, the queen's eyes were neither brown nor blue but a startling green. As I dabbed her wound, I suggested she might want to consider a different type of pet. "Perhaps a dog?"

She laughed quietly, then said she "abhors all things ordinary."

She placed a finger on my head and slowly moved it down my

forehead, over my nose and mouth, stopping at my chin. "You're not an ordinary man, are you, Anatole?"

I was unable to speak.

Her finger continued down my neck. "Is it true you have no hair, *anywhere?*"

I backed away, trying to keep my voice steady, as I advised her to avoid touching her face for several hours. On my way to the door, I stumbled over a rug, banged my knee against a low table, and had to grab on to a wall sconce to keep from falling.

THERE WAS A LADY OF THE COURT, ANGELICA, MUCH ADMIRED for her charm and wit. Sometime after my encounter with the queen, I overheard her talking to a small group of courtiers and courtesans. She quipped that "a woman may forgive a man who made an unwanted advance, but not the man who missed his chance."

I don't know if Angelica knew about my encounter with the queen, but that sentiment aptly described the queen's disdain for me over the ensuing years.

I was still on my knees before her, as she had not yet granted me permission to rise. She stared contemptuously. "I presume that somewhere amid your chaotic jumble of bugs and plants, you have an adequate supply of poppy tears?"

I confirmed I had a sack of seed pods, but quickly added that I had an idea for a new potion, which would be more effective and less harmful.

"A new potion?" she questioned. "The wedding is just a month away!"

I said that I believed I had enough time to develop the potion.

"And what about your *unintended consequences?*" Dittierri asked snidely.

The queen laughed and said, "The prince would be most disappointed if the princess lost all her hair."

Voltharo also laughed, which was very unprofessional. A scribe is supposed to remain as unobtrusive as a piece of furniture.

I assured the queen that the potion would be well tested before I gave it to the princess.

"We can't risk it," Queen Corinna decreed. "You will begin the regimen of poppy tears immediately. And gradually increase the dosage each day until the banquet. The princess will suffer no harm, and her compliance will be assured."

That was true, if you define *unharmed* and *compliance* as a willingness to do absolutely anything to get just one more taste of the poppy.

I listened to Voltharo's quill scratch against parchment, recording the queen's edict. A quick glance revealed the unsteadiness of the elderly scribe's hand.

"There's a spy!" King Sandro bellowed, entering the regency.

He stepped past me and said he'd just come from a meeting with the Oxatanian ambassador. "Prince Dalrympl knows all about the princess and Pito. Get up, Anatole! I nearly stepped on you."

I bowed my head to the queen as I rose.

The king went on to say that the prince was still willing to proceed with the wedding, but he set out two conditions. First, Pito was to be executed at the banquet. And second, the princess must watch. The prince also prescribed when the execution was to take place. After the main meal but "before dessert."

The king turned to me. "So, what have you come up with, Anatole?"

The queen was glaring at me.

I told the king that I planned a regimen of poppy tears, beginning with a small amount today and gradually increasing the dosage every day up until the banquet. "The poppy will give her the serenity to understand and accept her duty."

He scowled, well aware of what the poppy would do.

In all my time at the castle, I never heard either him or the queen refer to their daughter as *Tullia*. She was always *the princess*. For her part, Tullia never called them *Mother* or *Father*. They were *the queen* and *the king*.

"I suppose that's the only way," the king said. "But I'm disappointed in you, Anatole. It doesn't take a magician to administer poppy tears. I was hoping you would have come up with a more creative solution."

I said I did have an idea for a potion, but the queen, in her wisdom, understood the urgency of starting the poppy regimen at once.

"I'd like to hear your other idea," said the king.

I suppressed a smile. "A memory potion," I told him. "It will erase all memories of Pito from her mind."

A scoff came from Dittierri, but it was immediately stifled by the king's glance.

"So she won't know him at all?" the king asked me.

I told him it would be as if the two of them had never met.

He rubbed his chin as he slowly nodded. "Well, it will still be disturbing for the princess to witness a beheading. But if she doesn't know who the poor lad is . . . How long will it take you to prepare the potion?"

"Two weeks," I confidently answered. "Three at the most. Maybe three and a half."

There was still a little more than a month until the wedding, but really, I needed to give the potion to Tullia before the banquet, which would take place one week earlier.

I explained to King Sandro that I wanted to experiment first on the prisoner, Pito. Once I safely and effectively erased all memories of the princess from his mind, then I would administer it to the princess.

The king nodded and said, "I'll arrange it with Harwell."

Voltharo's hand trembled as his quill scraped the parchment.

7

PITO

AN ESSENTIAL ELEMENT FOR any love potion is a personal identifier. Or else the one who drinks it might fall in love with *anybody*.

Other, lesser magicians have been known to employ fingernail clippings or bits of hair as their personal identifiers. In my opinion, their potions lacked a certain spirituality. What they created would be more accurately called *lust potions*.

I used tears.

I'd collected enough tears from Tullia to run a month's worth of experiments on the prisoner. Once the potion was perfected, I'd need only a single tear from Pito.

Not any tear would suffice. I couldn't, for example, arrange for Harwell to torture him until he wept. It had to be a *heartfelt* tear.

Yes, my goal was not to create a love potion but what might be regarded as the opposite of one. Opposites, however, tend to have more similarities than you might imagine.

My memory potion wouldn't be entirely new. I was aware of

two different potions that induced memory loss, but they couldn't pinpoint specific memories. I might just as well hit Tullia on the head with a hammer. My plan was to combine certain elements from these amnesia-inducing potions with elements from a love potion.

Despite the urgency, I would need to proceed with care. If the first potion I gave the prisoner erased too much of his mind, he'd be useless for subsequent experiments.

URINE GLASS IN HAND, I MET HARWELL AT THE TOP OF THE DUNgeon stairs. First and foremost, I needed to collect Pito's heartfelt tear before he'd forgotten Tullia.

I watched Harwell untie the key from his belt and then unlock the stone door. The lock hardly seemed necessary. The door was so massive, Harwell was probably the only one in the castle with the strength to open it.

Besides being the keeper of the dungeon, the brute was also the executioner. He was well suited for that job, as he couldn't hear screams or cries for mercy.

He swung open the door, seemingly without effort. I grabbed a candle from a wall sconce and followed him down the steep and narrow staircase, also constructed of stone. He held a candle as well. Though he was two steps below me, our heads were level with one another.

I wondered if Harwell had any notion as to why I was there. I could feel the temperature drop as we descended. The air smelled musty. We continued lower and lower, and I was already dreading the climb back up.

I wasn't accustomed to physical exertion. It wasn't just laziness. Because of my inability to perspire, exercise was dangerous for me.

I'd become overheated, which would lead to dizziness and possibly fainting.

There was an iron door at the bottom of the stairs. Harwell unlocked it, then held it open for me. I took a breath to steady my nerves and entered the dungeon.

I gestured to Harwell to remain outside. I needed to gain the prisoner's trust, and it wouldn't help to have his executioner hovering nearby.

The prisoner was sitting against the far wall. He shielded his eyes from my candle as I came toward him. I heard Harwell's plodding footsteps behind me. Once again, I gestured for him to stay back.

A length of chain was connected on one end to a bolt in the wall, and on the other to a shackle clamped around the prisoner's left ankle. I saw a bucket a couple of meters off to the side, presumably as far as the chain would stretch. From the smell, the bucket needed emptying.

I eased myself down onto the hard dirt in front of him.

"Hello, Pito," I said.

"Hello, friend," he replied.

That was a good start. While I needed to remain detached and objective, I would also need his cooperation.

I started to tell him my name, but he just smiled and said, "Everyone in the kingdom knows who you are."

If he was trying to flatter me, it worked.

Harwell suddenly plopped down next to me. I glared at him, but his expression was blank.

Pito didn't seem bothered by his presence. Perhaps he didn't know he was to be executed.

"I'm here to help you," I said.

"Don't," he replied.

"You don't want my help?"

"Don't give me false hope. I'm well aware . . ." He glanced at Harwell. "My fate may be beyond my control. But only I can control how I meet it."

I'd been told that Pito was seventeen years old, but three days in the dungeon had drained any sign of youthfulness. In the flickering candlelight, I could see his dark eyes and sunken cheeks. I could also see why Tullia might have been attracted to him. He had the soulful look of a suffering poet. There was also a hint of goofiness to his smile.

"I saw the princess," I told him. "She blames herself for your predicament."

"I am responsible for my actions."

"So you agree you acted inappropriately?"

He cast his eyes downward. "If she says I did, I did."

"She didn't say that. Others are saying it."

"I have no control over what other people think or say."

I studied the young man across from me. Ever since I spoke to Tullia, something had been bothering me, but in my zeal for my new potion, I'd chosen to ignore it. Though she'd unabashedly asserted her love for Pito, she had also confided that he didn't return that love.

And if he didn't love her, then my experiments would be inconclusive at best. Even if I erased every memory of Tullia from his mind, it wouldn't prove anything! It's one thing to erase the memory of someone you merely *know*, but quite another to erase the memory of someone you *love*.

I needed to find out. "The fact is," I said, "the princess wishes your behavior had been less appropriate."

He didn't seem to comprehend what I was suggesting.

"She's in love with you."

He stared back at me, wide-eyed. He seemed genuinely surprised. "That's impossible."

"Are you in love with her?"

He seemed confused. His eyes went from me to Harwell, and then to his bucket, before returning to me. "How could I be?" he asked.

And with that, my experiments were over before they began. I sighed. Of course, he couldn't be in love with her. This was Esquaveta, not the island of Utopia.

I tried to rise, but it was difficult with a candle in one hand and my urine glass in the other.

"How is she?" he asked.

"I gave her some moon moth tea to calm her hysteria," I said.

She hadn't been hysterical when I saw her, but for some reason I felt the need to exaggerate my own importance.

"Moon moth tea," he quietly repeated.

"She refuses to marry the Oxatanian prince," I told him. "I am to begin a regimen of poppy tears, in order to change her mind."

"Her eyes," he whispered.

I stared at him.

"The way the blue one sparkles when she looks at you. The poppy will dull that light. And when I gaze at her brown one," he continued, "it's like I've wandered into a dark and mysterious cavern."

I could see a bit of moisture in his eyes, glistening in the candlelight.

"You are in love with her?"

"How could I *not* be?"

I pressed the urine glass against his face and captured one heartfelt tear.

8

DAISIES

I TRANSFERRED PITO'S TEAR TO a vial using a pipette that consisted of a glass tube attached to a sheep's bladder. I corked the vial and then, as an extra precaution, sealed it with wax.

I took it outside to my root cellar. While the area outside my workshop was open to anyone, it was relatively hidden from view, tucked in a corner between my workshop and a turret. There was a large iron stove that I used mostly for boiling water for my tea.

The root cellar was between the stove and the turret. I'd had it dug shortly after I first came to the castle, and nobody ever used it except for me. I presumed that everyone else had long since forgotten about it.

I kept the hatch covered in a layer of sand and also kept two full sacks of sand on top of it. At least the sand had been good for something!

I dragged the sacks to the side and kicked away sand until the handle was exposed. Then I raised the hatch and climbed down the ladder. The cellar maintained a cool temperature even in the heat of summer.

My root cellar contained more than just rutabagas. It was where I kept things that might otherwise spoil. This included the tin with the letter *L* scratched on one side. *L* for *Luigi.*

I placed the vial on a shelf behind a jar of yak's blood. I wasn't so much worried about it spoiling. The salt in Pito's tear would prevent that, and this was October, so the temperature wasn't oppressive. But there had been times, when caught in the exuberance of a potion, I'd gotten careless. I thought it best to keep Pito's tear safely out of the way until I was ready for it.

I looked around for what else I might need and decided on a length of eel skin and the egg sac from a wolf spider. Then I climbed up the ladder, covered the hatch with sand, and dragged the sacks back on top of it.

WHEN I WENT ON THE TOUR OF THE CASTLE, THERE WERE ONLY native plants and trees in the garden. I'm sure that too was done for the sake of authenticity. But that definitely didn't represent how my garden looked in 1523.

The great Esquavetian explorer Mario Cuvio shared my interest in plants and bugs and brought back numerous clippings and seeds from all around the world. He knew I would be especially interested in the insects and plant life found in the New World.

"Think of it, Anatole," he once said to me. "Entire civilizations separated from us since the beginning of time. Just imagine all we can learn from them!"

YOU MAY HAVE HEARD ABOUT THE SPANISH EXPLORER PONCE DE León and his search for the fountain of youth. I suspect he envisioned crystal blue water and frolicking virgins.

Ponce de León would have been better advised to wade through the murky, snake-infested swamps of Florida. That was where Cuvio collected the nuts, reeds, dried dragonflies, alligator organs, snake venom, and everything else that went into the Luigi potion. Cuvio had learned of the swamp from native doctors, who used the water to treat a variety of ailments associated with old age.

For now, however, I needed nothing so exotic. I had a jar full of dried daisy petals in my workshop, but despite the lateness of the season, I searched my garden hoping to find some that were still fresh.

THEN, JUST AS NOW, MOST PEOPLE REGARDED THE ROSE AS THE flower of *amore*, but there is no magic in rose petals. Take my advice. If you want to woo someone—or whatever people call it nowadays—give them daisies.

For a love potion, I use an odd number of daisy petals. *She loves me. She loves me not. She loves me.* You scoff, but like Ponce de León's fountain of youth, most folklore has some basis in reality.

BACK IN MY WORKSHOP, I CAREFULLY EXTRACTED THE SCALES from the length of eel skin. Unlike fish scales, eel scales aren't on the surface but are embedded within the skin.

I put the scales into a clay pot and added fourteen freshly picked daisy petals. For this potion, I wanted an even number. *He loves me not.*

I recorded everything in my logbook, for which I'd devised my own set of cryptic symbols. This wasn't so much for security. Words alone couldn't describe my methodology or the quality of the ingredients. Only symbols could capture the smell and intensity of color, the feel and the essence.

I removed the cork from Tullia's vial and, using my pipette, added this final ingredient to the clay pot. Then I attached the pot to stiff metal wires and suspended it over an array of candles. The placement of each candle, along with its size and shape, was also recorded in my logbook.

I would need to get up many times in the night to change the candles. Different candles needed to be replaced at different times. All that would have to be recorded as well.

As each candle burned lower, the temperature inside the pot would also slowly lower. When a candle is replaced, the temperature rises a little bit.

A potion is alive. The gentle rising and falling of temperature is how it breathes. If a potion boils, it dies.

9

BABETTE

T HE NEXT MORNING, HARWELL had already opened the heavy stone door when I met him atop the dungeon stairs. I held two goblets. One was for the prisoner, and the other contained dragon pearl tea, for me.

What with changing the candles and, even more, the anticipation of having to do so, I hadn't slept much. I desperately needed my morning tea, but I decided to wait until I was in the dungeon with Pito. He was more likely to drink from his goblet while I drank from mine.

Harwell's face gave no hint of recognition or even acknowledgment when I approached. But he must have noticed that my hands were full, because he took two candles from the wall sconce before starting down. He held both candles in the same hand, separated by one of his large fingers.

"HELLO, FRIEND," PITO ONCE AGAIN GREETED ME AS I STOOD BEfore him.

I was still standing, because I was trying to figure out how to get into a sitting position without spilling either goblet. I carefully sank to one knee, set Pito's on the hard dirt, and then brought down my other knee and set my goblet on the other side. I slipped my knees out from under me and plopped down the rest of the way, nearly toppling over backward as I did so. Fortunately, I regained my balance, and with it my dignity.

I could detect just a hint of a smile on Pito's face. I made certain which goblet was which, then held out the one meant for him.

He didn't take it. "How about you drink from this one, and I'll drink from yours?" he suggested.

He obviously knew my reputation.

I didn't lie to him. "I'm experimenting with a new potion," I admitted, "to save the princess from the poppy."

I didn't mention that it might save him as well. He didn't want false hope.

To my annoyance, Harwell sat next to me. I glared at him, but the big brute was oblivious.

Pito took the goblet. "So you're experimenting on me?" he asked. "Since I'm going to die anyway." He glanced at Harwell.

I didn't deny it.

"What will it do to me?"

"I can't tell you that."

I couldn't. If I revealed the purpose of the potion, then even if he didn't try to resist the effects, the knowledge alone could add a protective layer to his memories of her. It would be like telling someone not to think about a purple goat.

He slowly brought the goblet to his lips, then took a long drink.

I took a much-needed drink of tea and let its warmth linger in my mouth before swallowing.

Dragon pearl tea was so named because the tea leaves are wrapped into balls, which tighten as they dry. As the tea steeps, these pearls slowly unfurl, releasing a rich complexity of flavors.

I took another sip and watched with satisfaction as Pito did the same.

"It tastes like apricots," he said.

I hadn't used apricots. Perhaps he was tasting the combination of fennel seed, cucumber, and nutmeg.

"Have you ever been in love?" he asked abruptly.

I was taken aback, and might have rebuked him for asking such an insolent question, but I realized that he wasn't the one who was asking. It was the daisies.

"Once," I admitted. I could feel my stomach tighten. "I was about your age," I said.

That was more than two decades ago, but the pain had never gone away.

Pito smiled and said, "I hope she wasn't a princess."

"No. She tatted lace."

"What was her name?"

I took a deep breath. It had been a long time since I had spoken her name. "Babette."

Pito turned to Harwell. "Have you ever been in love?" he asked his executioner.

Harwell's expression remained blank.

Pito giggled.

I was relieved Pito had shifted his attention away from me. Harwell was still holding the two candles between his fingers, and I reached over and took one.

"Was Babette pretty?" Pito asked.

The question shook me, and it took a few seconds to regain my composure.

"She had beautiful fingers," I said, "delicate but strong, like her lace."

"That's nice," Pito said.

I told him that when I watched her work, it was like watching a spider spin an elaborate web.

"I hope you didn't tell her that!" he said with a laugh.

"She knew, coming from me, it was high praise," I assured him.

Babette was well aware of my fascination with plants and bugs. We'd take walks in the forest, and I'd point out various plants and insects and explain their medicinal properties. *The oil from those seed pods cures itchy toes. If you mash up this root it can relieve constipation.*

Pito laughed again as he poked fun at my method of courtship.

As I continued to speak about Babette, I felt myself becoming more at ease. It was as if all my tightly bound memories and emotions were gently unfurling, like the leaves of my dragon pearl tea.

Maybe it also had something to do with the darkness of the dungeon. I suppose Pito's imminent execution could have been a factor as well. I knew that whatever I said would die with him.

"I had hair then," I said, which for some reason Pito also found to be funny.

I also had a flat stomach, and, according to Babette, a "mischievous twinkle" in my eye.

"Did you kiss her?" he asked.

I explained that I was shy, and pointed out that Babette was only fifteen.

"Like Tullia," Pito said.

His words jarred me out of my reverie. I felt the stab of disappointment at his mention of her name. I had to remind myself that it would have been foolish to expect him to have already forgotten her.

I returned to Babette.

Once a month, an open-air market sprang up around the cathedral. Babette would gather up all her lace, and we'd walk there together. We had to leave early in the morning, since the journey took about forty-five minutes.

Those were always my happiest forty-five minutes of the entire month.

"Just walking next to her," I said to the darkness. "That was enough for me."

"I know what you mean," said Pito.

I would tell her about the different trees and bushes. Much of my knowledge came from my grandmother, but at seventeen, I'd already begun experimenting on my own too.

Babette broke off a twig from an alder tree and asked me, "What does this one do?"

There were two leaves on the twig, and as far as I knew, they had no magical properties.

But that wasn't what I said to Babette.

"Oh, be very careful with those," I warned Babette, quite possibly with a mischievous twinkle in my eye. "If you bite into the leaf, you will have an uncontrollable urge to kiss the first person you see."

Babette pulled off the leaves and handed one to me.

I had been carrying her basket of lace, and I set it on the forest floor.

Babette swept a lock of hair away from her face as we stood

close, holding our leaves, and gazed into each other's eyes. Then, at the same time, we bit into our leaves.

"What happened?" Pito asked eagerly.

"It was our first kiss," I told him. "And our last."

I abruptly stood up, taking both goblets, and headed toward the dungeon door. My eyes had filled with heartfelt tears.

Harwell, who may have been lost in his own thoughts, if he had any, took a moment to scramble to his feet and come after me.

10

VOCAL CORDS

B ACK IN MY WORKSHOP, forcing all thoughts of Babette out of my mind, I returned to work. Detached and objective, I recorded the results of the experiment.

I didn't regard the fact that the prisoner still remembered Tullia as a setback. I had managed to reach the section of Pito's mind that focused on love. I'd caused an otherwise serious person to giggle like a child. He had also called her *Tullia*, I noted, and not *the princess*.

It was a good first step, but the potion needed to be modified. I lessened the ratio of daisy petals to eel scales, and I altered the arrangements of the candles. As a general rule, when working on a new potion, I never made too many modifications at once. Otherwise, I had no way of determining which modification caused what. Even worse, there was the possibility that one modification might cancel out another. But given that the banquet was now less than four weeks away, I had to take shortcuts.

One thing that Pito said had struck a chord.

Although it was too late in the year for fresh apricots, the root cellar contained three jars of apricots preserved in vinegar. I retrieved one of the jars, untied the string around its waxed parchment lid, and, using copper tongs, removed one apricot.

I cut off three thin slices and added them to the clay pot. I put what was left of the apricot back into the vinegar and retied the lid. I didn't return the jar to the cellar but kept it on a shelf where it would be more handy.

Would I have thought of using apricots if Pito hadn't commented on the taste? Maybe. Eventually. It is hard to know how ideas occur to me. I just know that Pito said the potion tasted like apricots, and it resonated.

I added another of Tullia's tears to the pot and lit the candles beneath it.

"HELLO, FRIEND," PITO GREETED ME IN THE MORNING. I'D HAD another night of little sleep.

Now that our routine was established, I was able to hand him his goblet before I attempted to sit down, thereby avoiding making a spectacle of myself. Harwell sat beside me, but Pito didn't seem bothered by his presence, and so I accepted it too. In fact, if it weren't for the occasional snort, I might have forgotten he was there.

Pito drank the modified potion while I enjoyed my tea, which had come from India's Brahmaputra River valley. It had an earthy flavor, reminiscent of mushrooms, with a light and flowery aftertaste.

This time I was determined to let him do most of the talking. Anything he said could prove illuminating, but I was particularly interested in testing his memory. I began by asking about his childhood.

If anything, it seemed the potion had enhanced his memories. I was inundated with an endless stream of highly specific details, with no distinction as to what was significant and what wasn't.

There was none of the giddiness of the previous day. He spoke without any emotion. He described the death of his younger brother in the same tone he used to explain the process of making ink out of walnut husks.

He betrayed not even a hint of either sadness or resentment when he told me that when he was seven years old, his parents sent him away to apprentice with a scribe in the city. His work started before sunrise and wasn't complete until well after sundown. In the beginning his apprenticeship duties were secondary to his work as a servant. These included cleaning the cottage, emptying the chamber pots, and doing the laundry.

Pito droned on at great length about everything that the master scribe expected from him. Parchment was made from the hides of either goats or sheep. Vellum was produced from oxen or aurochs. It was Pito's responsibility to butcher and skin these animals. He'd have to treat the hides with harsh chemicals that burned his skin, then scrape all the hair away. The parchment or vellum would naturally curl back to its original shape, so he had to tack the finished product to the writing table.

Customers brought in legal documents to the scrivener's shop for copying. Students sometimes brought entire textbooks. Even before Pito learned to read, he became adept at copying the individual letters.

When he turned eleven, the master scribe decided it would be beneficial to teach his apprentice to read, but he was surprised to discover that Pito already knew how. He'd taught himself.

———

I HAVE TRIED TO PRESENT ALL THIS IN A COHERENT AND INTER-esting manner, but as I mentioned, Pito's telling consisted of an endless stream of details. He was able to recite, word for word, the first legal document he'd ever copied.

After two successive nights of little sleep, I was having trouble staying awake. I felt myself starting to drift off when suddenly Pito's voice cracked and then, inexplicably, squeaked.

We both laughed.

When he tried to continue, he had the voice of a young child.

We both laughed again, and even his laughter was a child's laugh.

I glanced at Harwell, but the brute had no clue as to why we were laughing. Nor did he seem the least bit curious.

"What was in that potion?" the childish voice asked me.

I could only shrug.

I SUPPOSE A TWENTY-FIRST-CENTURY PSYCHOLOGIST MIGHT SAY that Pito's memories of his childhood were so strong they had evoked a physical manifestation. The psychologist would stress the trauma he suffered from being separated from his family, as well as the fact that he'd been subjected to slavelike labor at such a young age. His suppressed emotions were released in his childish voice.

But as this was more than three hundred years before Freud, such concepts were beyond me. I assumed the change to his vocal cords was an unintended consequence of the potion.

I suggested he rest his voice for a while, and took advantage of the opportunity to leave and get back to work.

11

THE JEWELED KNIFE

I WON'T LOOK AWAY!" PRINCESS Tullia asserted.

Startled, I almost knocked over the jar of apricots.

Once again, she had silently slipped through the two curtains, and I'd been unaware she had been standing right behind me.

"Did you know he's to be executed at the wedding banquet?" she asked.

I didn't answer.

"Prince Dalrympl insists upon it! I hate him! And I hate the king and queen for acquiescing."

If I admitted I knew about the execution, she might include me among the acquiescers.

"So you will attend the banquet after all?" I asked.

"For Pito," she said. "When the time comes, I will look right at him. The last thing he sees will be my eternal love."

She turned her back to me and took a few steps away. "Did you know, on my twelfth birthday, the prince sent me a jeweled knife? Rubies, emeralds, and onyxes, the colors of Oxatania."

She faced me again, her brown eye deep in sad contemplation, while her blue one flashed determination. "After Pito is dead," she said, "I will stand, remove the knife from beneath my gown . . . and thrust it between my breasts."

I watched, horrified, as she held an imaginary knife with both hands and plunged it into her heart.

"Pito won't be executed," I said, my voice shaking. I looked toward the clay pot.

"A potion?" she asked.

"It will save Pito," I told her.

Both eyes lit up. "How? What will it do? Will it make him invisible?"

"I can't tell you," I said. "Otherwise, it won't work. You just have to trust me."

Her brown eye became what Pito had called a mysterious cavern. The blue one was a bottomless lake.

"I trust you, Natto."

She walked over to the mouse cages and warmly greeted Luigi. And when my aged mouse pressed his nose between the slats, Tullia bent forward and kissed it.

I wondered if she realized how long Luigi had been with me. But then again, most people don't know the expected life span of a mouse.

I KNOW WHAT YOU'RE THINKING. WHY COULDN'T I JUST GIVE THE Luigi potion to Pito? Wouldn't that save him?

The potion only affected the aging process. Even assuming it would be effective on humans, which was a huge assumption, it wouldn't protect Pito's neck from Harwell's axe, any more than it would protect Luigi from the sharp claws of a cat.

12

THE RELEASE OF
THE TIGER

I TOOK TO BRINGING MY entire pot of tea down to the dungeon with me, instead of just one goblet. The prisoner's voice had returned to normal, but I wanted to have something handy to soothe his vocal cords, in case it happened again.

I'd been mostly encouraged by the results from those first two experiments. The first triggered giddy thoughts of love from a young man who at an early age had learned to keep a tight hold on his emotions. And while the second potion seemed to have enhanced and sharpened his memories rather than diminish them, none of those memories had included Princess Tullia.

The brain is a bucket of memories. If some memories expand, others, by necessity, must spill out. It's a physical law of nature.

The potions had yet to strike the center of the target, but they were in the vicinity.

The third iteration caused the prisoner to hum incessantly. Perhaps I would have gleaned something positive out of that too, if I hadn't found it so annoying. I kept reminding him to drink his tea, hoping that might put an end to it, but as soon as he'd put down his goblet, he'd start up again. It was the same simple melody, over and over again.

He hardly seemed to notice the tea. He might as well have been drinking water. I didn't expect him to be a connoisseur like me, but considering that since his confinement he'd eaten nothing but a watery bean soup and stale bread, one would expect some expression of appreciation, or at least acknowledgment.

Later that same day, back in my workshop, I kept catching myself humming that same annoying melody.

And even now, five hundred years later, I can hear the tune inside my head. It no longer annoys me but rather elicits feelings of nostalgia.

A MORE PROMISING RESULT CAME TWO DAYS AFTER THAT, WHEN to the prisoner's dismay he couldn't recall the Greek alphabet. This wasn't just trivia, like forgetting the names of the planets—unless the one who couldn't remember was named Galileo or Copernicus.

The Renaissance was a time of renewed interest in the art and philosophy of the ancient Greeks and Romans. When Pito was in his early teens, he had copied a number of those ancient texts. By then, he told me, many of the master scribe's customers were requesting that his apprentice do the work they needed. Not only had Pito taught himself to read, he also had taught himself to read Latin and ancient Greek.

I was impressed but not surprised. There was a reason that someone from such humble beginnings had been brought to the castle.

In fact, I began to suspect that it might be the elderly scribe Voltharo who had started the vile gossip about Pito and Princess Tullia. Managing the royal library was one of Voltharo's duties. He would have seen them reading together. Voltharo surely recognized Pito's talent, and he would have also recognized the threat it posed.

There was no point in mentioning my conjecture to the prisoner. His mind might dwell excessively on what did and did not take place in the library and reinforce those memories.

THE DAY CAME FOR THE TIGER TO BE RELEASED INTO THE MOAT. The event had garnered almost as much excitement and anticipation as the wedding of the century.

I had hoped to be there early so as to get a good view, but first I needed to get everything into the clay pot and carefully record it all in my logbook. That required patience.

Unfortunately, in my haste to attach the wires, I knocked over a jar of aspic, which in turn knocked over one containing pigeon eggs. They both crashed to the floor.

Lest you get the impression I'm completely inept, allow me to point out that it took quick reactions and agility to save the clay pot. Keep in mind, too, that I'd hardly slept for a week.

I was staring down at the gooey mess when I heard the blare of the crumhorns. I quickly covered it with sand, then hurried outside.

King Sandro was in the midst of his oratory when I reached the bridge. Gregor the engineer stood next to him. On the other side of Gregor was the tiger cage, and beyond that a large wooden structure with ropes, pulleys, hooks, and two cranks.

In addition to overseeing the construction of the moat, Gregor had also refashioned the gate so that it could be lowered to form a bridge. Two large spools of heavy cable were on my side of the bridge, each spool manned by two soldiers.

I could see only a small portion of the throngs on the other side of the bridge. Most were hidden by the wall. I couldn't see into the moat.

Dittierri and Queen Corinna were also on the bridge. Princess Tullia wasn't interested, apparently.

When the oratory concluded, Gregor attached two hooks to the tiger cage, one on the top and one to a latch in the front. Four guards stepped forward, each taking a corner of the cage. They helped raise it up as Gregor turned a crank.

The guards let go, and the cage swung out over the moat, rocking back and forth. I could hear the collective gasps coming from the other side of the wall.

Gregor cranked in the reverse direction, and the cage slowly lowered. I was unable to see when it reached the ground but heard the cheers of those watching.

King Sandro glanced in my direction and motioned for me to come onto the bridge. I took a few tentative steps and went just far enough so that if I strained my neck, I could see the cage down in the moat. I was afraid to get too close to the edge.

Gregor turned another crank, and there was a great roar as the cage door dropped open. The roar came from the crowds, not the tiger. The tiger hadn't made a sound.

Admittedly, I felt envious of the attention Gregor was getting, especially when the king warmly placed a hand on his shoulder. *That could be me*, I told myself, *once my potion is perfected*.

I heard a scream and turned to see a man falling into the moat. Considering the number of people pressing close to the edge, it was surprising others hadn't also fallen. I could only hope, for his sake, that the fall killed him before the tiger did.

Gregor maneuvered a rope over and above the fallen man. He

suddenly sprang up and grabbed it. We all cheered as Gregor cranked him up to safety.

All the while, the tiger never emerged from its cage.

Ten minutes later, it still hadn't.

Nor twenty minutes after that. The people began to grumble.

After a while those who had fought their way to the front began to leave. Others took their place, looked down awhile, then also left.

They'd come from miles away and might have lost two or possibly three days' worth of wages, just to glimpse the tiger and hear it roar.

I heard more expressions of displeasure and outright contempt coming from the *popolo grasso* than from the *popolo minuto*. That wasn't surprising. The latter were better accustomed to disappointment.

Not everyone was disgruntled. I saw a woman wearing a green veil leave on the arm of a gentleman.

IN THE CAFÉ, I SIP MY CAPPUCCINO. I BREAK OFF A SMALL PIECE of croissant and place it in the front pouch of my hoodie. There are now six tigers in the moat. A plexiglass barrier surrounds the circumference, which is probably more than a mile. Viewing platforms extend over the moat in several places.

That first tiger hadn't died. I was to later learn that it finally emerged from its cage shortly after sundown, some six hours after the cage door was opened.

I can empathize. It took me much longer than that to emerge from mine.

13

IN THE DUNGEON

ODD AS IT MIGHT seem, the mornings I spent with the prisoner in the dungeon became the most enjoyable part of my day. Along with the pot of tea, I sometimes also brought cucumbers and cheese. Harwell helped me carry it all.

Cucumbers then didn't look like those you find in modern supermarkets. They were twisted into all sorts of shapes, some of which Pito found amusing. They came in different colors too, including some with yellow and green stripes, and others that were purple like an eggplant.

Down in the dungeon, I could say things to Pito that I never dared say aboveground. He invariably offered an insightful and interesting perspective. It was a shame I couldn't tell him about the potion. I wouldn't have been surprised if he came up with a useful suggestion.

Pito was also the only one I ever told about my Luigi experiments.

"If a mouse could live to the age of seven," I said, "a man might live to be a hundred and fifty!"

He said he wouldn't want to live that long, which was interesting, I thought, coming from someone awaiting execution.

"But you won't be old," I pointed out. "By all objective measurements, Luigi hasn't aged."

He said that the cosmos, and everything in it, was in a constant state of change. "You're not the same person you were when you entered the dungeon. And the dungeon is not the same place."

He explained that if we didn't age, we wouldn't change, and, in effect, we would be out of step with the cosmos. To him, death would be just another incremental change. He believed his essence would continue to undergo more changes throughout eternity.

I could only nod and sip my tea. I didn't understand, then, what it meant to be out of step with the cosmos.

"Will you tell me what happened with Babette?" he asked. "If it's not too painful."

I considered a moment, then blew out my candle. I waved the candle in Harwell's face until he got the idea and extinguished his candle too.

It would be easier in the dark.

BABETTE AND I WERE STILL UNDER THE SPELL OF OUR MAGICAL kiss as we continued our way to the market. We had held hands for a while, but the baskets of lace were too bulky to carry with just one arm.

Other vendors were already setting up their wares when we arrived, and Babette was peeved that all the best spots were already taken. Textiles were sold on the north end of the cathedral. Meat and vegetables were sold on the south side, and wine and other spirits were sold inside.

I located a rickety table that nobody else had wanted and moved it to the only available space, behind a display of fancy hats. "No one will see me here!" Babette complained, but then she smiled at me and said, "I'm glad we . . . stopped."

SURPRISINGLY, IT WASN'T PAIN I WAS FEELING IN THE DUNGEON as I told this to Pito, but relief, and even a kind of warmth. I'd suppressed these memories for such a long time, I'd forgotten her smile, and the love that shone in her eyes.

SHE NEEDN'T HAVE BEEN WORRIED ABOUT THE LOCATION OF HER stall. Her customers specifically sought her out. Tailors and dressmakers used her lace to adorn the clothes they made for the *popolo grasso*. Some commoners, too, were willing to pay a florin or two to add a bit of flair to the clothes they made for themselves. Babette kept trying to shoo me away, saying I was interfering with business, but I knew from the look in her eyes and the laughter in her voice that she was happy to have me loitering about.

Everything changed when a nobleman came through the market. He wore a sable surcoat, which was something like a vest. The sleeves of his shirt were purple. A sword hung from his belt.

All the vendors immediately began straightening up their stalls, making sure that only their best merchandise was on display. "He's looking this way," Babette whispered. "Go!"

This time, I knew she meant it. Still, I wasn't about to scurry away like a scared rabbit. I took my time and casually sauntered away. For just a brief moment, I found myself face-to-face with the nobleman.

THOUGH I REFER TO HIM AS A NOBLEMAN, HE WAS ABOUT MY AGE.
He had stringy blond hair and a jutting chin. He and his two companions had been laughing, but when I crossed his path, the laughter ceased. He glared at me with cold blue eyes.

That was how I remembered it when I described the encounter
to Pito, and how I remember it now, but my memory may have
been tainted by what followed. Perhaps he only gave me a quick
glance.

In the dungeon, I simply said, "He wore the purple," and Pito
understood his nobility.

Esquaveta had strict sumptuary laws. Only the noble class was
allowed to wear purple. A violation could result in a large fine, or
even death.

For the *popolo minuto*, this was mostly irrelevant. Their clothes
were usually the natural color of the flax or wool, or if they did dye
their clothes, it was either rust or brown. Other dyes were too
costly, and purple was the most expensive.

During the Dark Ages, only royalty could afford purple, but
with the Renaissance came the rise of the *popolo grasso*. Some of
these merchants and traders became richer than kings and took to
wearing fine clothing. Kings enacted sumptuary laws so that the
nobility could distinguish themselves from mere businessmen. Specific types of fur, sable for instance, were also restricted to only
nobles.

Other sumptuary laws required Muslims and Jews to wear special markers, so that good Christians wouldn't be "tricked into
marriage." For the same reason, certain women were required to
wear a green veil during daylight, lest unsuspecting gentlemen mis-
takenly believe them to be respectable.

———

SO, AS THE YOUNG NOBLE AND HIS COMPANIONS WENT TO BABETTE'S table, I went to the closest stall and pretended to be looking for a hat. I didn't trust him. From the way he carefully examined each piece of lace, one might have thought he was a dressmaker! Meanwhile Babette looked on nervously. She smiled whenever he glanced at her.

The lace came in different shapes and patterns. I watched as the noble picked out one shaped like a flower. "Exquisite," he said, as he showed it to his companions.

Babette beamed, but from my vantage point, I could see they weren't looking *at* the lace. They were looking through it, at the exquisite lace maker.

The noble took Babette's hand in his and set some coins inside it.

"Oh, that is too much!" she exclaimed, and tried to give some of the coins back to him, but he assured her it was well worth the price.

She thanked him with a curtsy.

"My boots are caked with mud," he said, then tried to hand the piece of lace back to her.

Babette didn't understand.

"It rained last night," he said. "The ground is muddy."

"You want me to clean your boot?"

"If you would be so kind."

His companions laughed. And then when Babette said she wouldn't do it, they dragged her out from behind her stall and forced her to her knees.

AND WHAT DID I DO? DID I BOLDLY COME FORWARD TO DEFEND her honor? Or did I cowardly remain behind the hats and watch her humiliation?

"There was nothing you could have done," Pito consoled me.

"You would have stepped up," I said.

"And look where am I now," he said.

HER KNEES IN THE MUD, BABETTE TRIED TO CLEAN THE BOOT, BUT
the lace was too delicate and tore into tatters. The noble's companions grabbed more lace from her stall and threw it down at her.

She scooped up her month of hard work and clutched it close
to her breasts. "No!" she whispered.

The noble drew his sword and ordered her to finish the job, and
when she didn't move, his sword came down.

IT WASN'T UNTIL AFTER THE NOBLE AND HIS FRIENDS HAD EN-
tered the cathedral, presumably to purchase liquor, that I came to
Babette's aid. She had a gash the length of her forearm.

Lace was no more effective as a bandage than it was for cleaning boots. One of the other vendors provided a greasy rag, which I
used to stop the bleeding.

As I held her upright, we began the long journey back to her
home. She stumbled most of the way, and even lost consciousness
a couple of times, but I kept her moving and finally managed to
reach her cottage. There, I left her in the care of her grandmother,
while I went back to the forest to gather what I needed.

I returned a short while later with angelica root, three different
varieties of nettle, and a mushroom-like fungus called *chaga*, which
grew from damaged tree bark. Babette was asleep. All color had
drained from her face. Her breathing was harsh and erratic.

Her grandmother had replaced the bandage with a fresh one.
When I removed it, I saw that a yellow-green crust had formed over
the gash. There was a putrid odor. I applied a poultice made from
the items I'd collected.

"I'D BEEN STUDYING BREAD MOLD," I TOLD PITO, "BUT HAD ONLY run a few preliminary experiments."

Babette would have to be my first test case. And somehow, I would have to remain detached and objective. I prepared a pot of bread mold soup.

FOR TWO DAYS BABETTE WAS TOO WEAK EVEN TO LIFT THE SPOON, and others had to help feed her. But on the third day, she was strong enough to complain about the awful taste!

And when I entered her cottage on the fifth day, I had to duck the flying ladle she'd hurled toward me.

Babette was laughing. Her cheeks were the color of peaches. "When we get married, I'll do the cooking!" she asserted.

Oh, how my heart soared!

14

A TWENTY-FIRST-CENTURY
WARNING

CAUTION: DON'T EAT MOLDY *bread. Side effects include vomiting, diarrhea, stomach cramps, trouble breathing, paralysis, and death.*

Such a warning wouldn't have been necessary in the sixteenth century. Evidently, it's now required.

In 1523 we were well aware of life's precariousness. It wasn't only the threat of war, famine, or plague. We had to remain alert at all times, and if someone failed to exercise basic common sense, they had no one to blame but themself. Today if someone does something foolish, such as eating moldy bread with no knowledge of the particular type of mold or how to safely prepare it, they expect others to be responsible for their stupidity.

Besides, antibiotics are now readily available. According to the history texts, the first antibiotic, penicillin, was discovered by the esteemed Scottish physician and scientist Alexander Fleming.

In 1928, he synthesized penicillin from bread mold.

Do you think any of these texts mention the work I'd done four centuries earlier?

I don't even rate a footnote!

But then, after all, I wasn't a highly esteemed physician and scientist. I was a mere magician, a purveyor of hocus-pocus.

SIX YEARS AFTER THAT FIRST POT OF BREAD MOLD SOUP, MY REP-utation as a physician was known throughout Esquaveta. When King Sandro suffered from the strangling sickness, I was summoned to the castle.

By then, I had neither my hair nor my mischievous twinkle.

By then, I also knew that the king would need to ingest the soup for a full two weeks, even after his symptoms had disappeared. All remnants of the evil spirits had to be thoroughly destroyed. Otherwise, they would return, more powerful than ever.

It wasn't the initial infection but the relapse that killed Babette.

15

DELAY

I N THE DARK DUNGEON it felt as if my eyes were coated in tar. I
was sobbing when I finished telling Pito about Babette.

There were no matches to relight our candles. In 1523 fire
was started by striking flint against a piece of iron.

To leave the dungeon I had to hold on to the back of Harwell's
tunic as I trailed behind him. When he stopped to unlock the iron
door, my nose smashed against his broad back.

The door at the top of the stairs had been left ajar, so light returned once the iron door opened. Harwell had become accustomed
to my slow pace up the stairs and moved slowly too. He kept turning
around to make sure I was still with him. I suppose he thought me
clumsy, and he knew he wouldn't be able to hear me fall.

I RETURNED TO MY WORKSHOP AND MADE TWO SMALL MODIFICA-
tions to the potion and one that was more drastic. I added the
teardrop, arranged the candles in the shape of a crescent, and suspended the pot above them.

The more drastic change involved the addition of a kind of slime mold commonly called *dog vomit*. The name comes from its appearance, and it is not smelly or repugnant in any way. It grows on dead and decaying trees and can be found in abundance after a heavy rain. I grew some in a jar in my cellar.

I used it in an ointment for warts. It could eradicate the wart entirely, without damaging any of the healthy skin around it.

In the same way, I thought it might aid in the removal of specific memories without damaging others. I increased the number of daisy petals to bring those memories closer to the surface.

I WAS FULL OF HOPE AS I DESCENDED THE STONE STEPS, MY POT of tea in one hand and the newly modified potion in the other. Even before I reached the prisoner, however, I could see in the flickering light of Harwell's candles that something was wrong.

I took one of the candles and held it close to Pito's face, which was splotched with large red welts. I examined his hands and feet too, and they were also covered.

"Must have been the cucumber," he said, and smiled his goofy smile.

Alas, I had no choice. I dumped the potion into the bucket that served as his chamber pot. I used the goblet to collect a urine sample from him. I couldn't conduct any more tests until all traces of the rash were gone.

Nonetheless, I continued my daily visits to the dungeon. Harwell was expecting me, and I didn't want to upset the routine. That was the reason I told myself, but the truth was, I enjoyed my visits with Pito.

I also didn't want to call attention to this setback. The banquet was only two weeks away, three until the wedding, and I worried that if Queen Corinna or Dittierri learned of the delay, they might convince the king to put an end to my experiments altogether and start the poppy tears.

PITO WAS ONLY JOKING, OF COURSE, WHEN HE SAID HIS RASH WAS caused by the cucumbers. We both knew it came from the potion he'd taken the day before. Still, as a precaution, I stopped bringing cucumbers and instead brought him cheese, fresh pears, and dried figs along with the tea.

I also brought down two board games: Twelve Men's Morris and queen's chess. Queen's chess is now universally recognized as just plain chess, but the expanded movement of the queen had been a recent innovation. Previously, the queen could only move one square in any direction. With the innovation, she became the most powerful piece on the board. No doubt, the change was inspired, or perhaps ordered, by a real-life queen.

I considered myself to be a very capable chess player, and I even have had occasional flashes of brilliance, but Pito beat me every game. Of course, he was younger than me and had only known the queen's chess variant. Much of my experience and strategy was based on the antiquated version of the game.

While he readily enjoyed the fruit and cheese, I was dismayed he never seemed to share my appreciation for tea. I tried explaining to him how the shape of the tea leaf can affect flavor, but he just didn't seem to get it. One time, I must have been watching him too intently as he sipped, because he immediately swallowed and declared, "Very tasty!"

I sighed. He might just as well have described a Michelangelo painting as "Very colorful!"

Twelve Men's Morris is somewhat similar to the Japanese game

Go. I fared somewhat better at that, although it too was a challenge. To beat Pito, it was necessary to think four or even five moves ahead. I was trying to do that when my concentration was interrupted by Harwell banging a tin cup against the ground. He stopped when I glared at him, but when I turned my attention back to the board, he started up again.

"I think he would like some tea," Pito said.

I looked curiously at Harwell. His expression remained blank as he extended his dented cup toward me.

I turned back to Pito. "You don't mind?"

"Why should I?"

I filled his executioner's cup.

16

BREAKTHROUGH

I STOOD OUT BY MY stove and examined four vials of the urine in sunlight. I'd collected a sample from Pito each day, and as I studied the most recent, I could detect no trace of the potion that had caused his rash.

The delay, while frustrating, hadn't been all bad. I'd been able to catch up on my sleep. I felt clearheaded and could see things from a fresh perspective. Once again, I prepared the potion with the dog vomit slime mold.

When Harwell met me at the top of the stairs the next morning, I noticed his tin cup tied to his belt. At least somebody appreciated my tea!

"Hello, friend," Pito greeted me as I sat down.

The welts were gone from his face and hands. I handed him the goblet.

"Back to work," he said, and drank it down.

I poured myself a cup of tea, then filled Harwell's.

YES, THE POSSIBILITY OF GIVING HARWELL SOMETHING OTHER than tea occurred to me. After all, that was what Tullia had asked me to do. My mind pondered a number of poisons and sleeping powders. Harwell was an exceptionally large man. Whatever I gave him would have to be an awfully big dose.

I wondered if he'd be suspicious if I didn't drink the same "tea" that I gave to him. Was his mind capable of such thought? Perhaps I should take a pre-antidote first, so we could both drink from the same pot.

But even as I considered all this, I knew I would never do it. I was still the same coward who had failed to defend Babette.

I set up the chess pieces while Pito finished the potion and Harwell loudly slurped from his tin cup. At first, the game seemed no different from the other games we'd played. Though I was holding my own, I expected that at any moment Pito would soon turn whatever small advantage he had into a slow and relentless attack that would overwhelm me. I had been so accustomed to losing that it took me a while to realize that I was the one with the advantage.

If I hadn't been so pleased with myself, I might have noted the effect the potion was having on his cognitive abilities. Instead, I attributed it to my own brilliance. When I heard Pito muttering to himself, I took it as confirmation of that brilliance.

As his mutterings became louder, however, I realized that his mind wasn't on our game. He was reciting poetry.

Though his tone was emotionless and flat, the words that flowed forth were full of passion. These were Italian love poems. *Amore* was being glorified not just for its spiritual aspect but also for the physical pleasure, which, at times, was graphically described.

Some of those poems were very untoward, Tullia had said.

It was a little unsettling. I suppose a part of me still thought of Tullia as the little girl who played with mice. I had to remind myself to be detached and objective.

Pito went on for what must have been more than an hour. He probably recited more than forty poems, though it was difficult to tell when one poem ended and another began. There was no pause between the poems.

When I asked him how he managed to commit so many poems to memory, he seemed confused.

As a test, I said I wanted to hear the poem about the milkmaid again.

"I don't understand what you're asking."

"The girl in the barn," I said. "Her bare feet."

He was as oblivious as Harwell. Once the words had left his mouth, they were gone.

17

WAITING FOR
INSPIRATION

MORE OFTEN THAN NOT, when I'd been working on a potion for some time, the answer I'd been seeking would come to me in a flash, usually at night while I was sleeping. Sometimes I'd be dreaming about the potion, and I'd see myself add grasshopper spiracles, say, to the clay pot. Or other times, I could be dreaming about something that seemingly had nothing to do with the potion when I'd abruptly wake up and exclaim, "Caraway seeds!"

With only sixteen days left before the wedding, nine before the banquet, I desperately needed that flash of inspiration to strike soon. I felt an increasing sense of urgency, both for Pito's sake and also Tullia's. She said she trusted me, but I suspected she still planned to bring her jeweled knife to the banquet. I tried to keep my mind relaxed. Urgency and desperation made my work more difficult.

I knew I was close. The recitation of the erotic poetry and the immediate memory loss had clearly been a major breakthrough. I just needed the final piece of the puzzle.

But the breakthrough also had a negative effect. I became fearful of making too drastic a modification. I added a bit more dog vomit slime. I adjusted the ratio of eel scales to daisy petals. I rearranged the array of candles.

Nine days became eight. Eight became seven.

I got little sleep, changing candles, making notations in my logbook, and then anxiously awaiting the next time I'd need to change a candle.

How can inspiration strike me while I'm sleeping *if I don't sleep?*

I became plagued by doubts.

That was nothing new. I was well aware that there was always self-doubt when I was working on a potion. That self-awareness helped me ignore the doubts and persevere.

But this time my doubts weren't just about the ultimate success of the potion. I questioned the very purpose of it.

I had convinced myself that the potion was best for Tullia, but was it?

My own memory of Babette was full of pain, regret, and shame, but it also enriched my life. I wouldn't want it erased. And to forget Babette would be a betrayal.

I would have liked to hear Pito's insights about this, and what any of his Greek and Roman philosophers might have written on the subject. But this was the one topic I couldn't discuss with the prisoner.

SEVEN DAYS BECAME SIX, AND THERE MAY OR MAY NOT HAVE BEEN another positive development. Pito asked me to bring a mirror on my next visit. He said he'd forgotten what he looked like.

I don't know if that should be credited to the potion. It may have been a natural result of living in a dark dungeon for close to a month.

Six days became five. Five days became four. I adjusted the array of candles. I added an extra slice of apricot.

Every time I lay down on my mattress and closed my eyes, I pleaded for inspiration to strike. But inspiration is a fickle and elusive lover. The more you want her, the more you need her, the more you chase her away.

18

FOLLY

WHAT CAME TO ME in the night was something entirely different. Unable to fall asleep, I contrived an elaborate plan for Pito's escape.

I knew this was fantasy. For one thing, it would require courage and bold action on my part. It was just a way to take my mind off my own failures.

The idea involved re-creating a potion I'd previously given to Pito, except instead of using daisies, I would substitute butterfly pea petals. The pea petals are blue. I would also add dried blueberry skins.

I'd gotten the dried blueberries from Mario Cuvio, who brought them back from the New World. They came from a village the local people called *Kanata*.

According to Cuvio, the taste of the blueberry was more sublime than any berry grown in this part of the world. However, for my purposes, I was more interested in the color than the taste.

My fantasy also involved the use of corpse flower petals, but not as a part of the potion.

The corpse flower is an interesting plant. Other flowers emit sweet aromas to attract birds, bees, and other insects. As the birds and insects drink the flower's nectar, they unintentionally aid in pollination, enabling the plant to reproduce. The new plants grow more flowers, and so forth.

The corpse flower smells like the rotting carcass of a dead animal. It attracts flies and maggots, also for pollination.

I lay awake indulging my fantasy, pretending I could be courageous.

FOUR DAYS BECAME THREE.

I brought a small mirror to the dungeon as Pito had requested, and he studied his features in the candlelight.

He drank the latest potion. The only modification I made was the size and shape of one candle.

His mind seemed as sharp as ever. I saw no sign of memory loss. He beat me at queen's chess rather easily, although in my defense, I was distracted. I was still imagining the daring escape plan I had dreamed up the night before.

WHEN I RETURNED FROM THE DUNGEON, I FOUND THE PAGE IAN waiting outside the archway. My presence was requested in the regency.

We passed Xavier and Gregor on our way there, but they seemed to deliberately avoid eye contact. I assumed the king wanted an update on my progress, what with the banquet only three days away. I would tell him about the prisoner's poetry recitation but thought it best to omit the erotic nature of the poems. I would need to speak confidently, assuring him that success was just a day or two away, but not too confidently. Best to leave a little wiggle room.

As it turned out, I never got to say any of that.

"Your folly is over," Queen Corinna declared the moment I entered the regency. The king stood silently next to her. Dittierri smiled smugly from his desk.

"How soon can you prepare the first batch of poppy tears?" the queen asked.

I was stunned. "But the banquet is still three days away," I protested.

"That wasn't what the queen asked you," said King Sandro.

"It's time for the princess to behave like a princess," said Queen Corinna.

I lowered my head, and told her that the first dose of poppy tears could be ready by morning.

Voltharo's hand was shaking so hard, I doubted the words he wrote were legible.

"You tried, Anatole," King Sandro said, somewhat sympathetically. "After Pito recited those poems, I thought you were close, but it was false hope. Perhaps if you had more time . . ." His voice trailed off.

I LEFT THE REGENCY DEFEATED. I THOUGHT I HAD THREE MORE days! I felt so devastated I hardly noted the king's use of the words *false hope*, Pito's words. I also didn't wonder how he knew about the poetry recitation.

"Three more days!" I complained, coming down the back stairs, causing two servants to turn their heads.

If I'd known that this morning's potion would be the last, I might have tried something more drastic than merely changing the size and shape of just one candle! But deep down, I also knew that three more days wouldn't have made a difference. Or ten. I'd run out of ideas.

Down in my root cellar, I took a long look at the jar of blueberry skins. Then I took the one containing the seed pods from the opium poppy and ascended the ladder.

Poppy tears were derived not from the seeds but from a dried milky substance on the insides of the pods. Using a dull knife, I scraped it out of each pod and put it in a copper pot.

Unlike a potion, the poppy tears would need to boil. There was no danger of destroying them. Opium was a sledgehammer. It was neither delicate nor subtle.

As the poppy tears boiled, I brewed some moon moth tea to help me fall asleep. I tried to take comfort in the knowledge that Tullia's mind would be so dulled, she'd feel nothing as she watched Pito's beheading.

The moon moth tea was of little help. I lay awake all night, tossing and turning. I needed to talk to someone, and odd as it may seem, Pito was my only friend.

I didn't know if Harwell would still allow me to see him, now that my folly was over. But maybe nobody had told him. I didn't even know how anyone communicated anything to him.

I brewed a pot of tea and took it along with two goblets to the top of the dungeon stairs. Harwell was nowhere to be seen.

"I thought I had three more days," I said to the massive stone door, but then realized it wasn't all the way shut.

I set down the tea and goblets. I pulled on the handle with both hands as I pressed my feet against the adjacent wall. The door opened a little more, and I was able to squeeze through the opening.

The only light came from above. I had forgotten to take a candle.

I knew this was still more of my folly. It would be too much to expect that the iron door was unlocked too. Not to mention the fact that Harwell could return at any moment, notice the open door, and shut it, locking me in here.

Well, if I was trapped down here, I thought, then at least I wouldn't be able to administer the poppy tears.

The stairs made several turns on the way down, and with each one, the light dimmed further. When I reached the bottom, I couldn't even see the iron door and had to feel for it. I found the handle and pulled on it, but of course it was locked.

"Three more days!" I shouted, and pounded on the door with the side of my fist. Then I sat down on the bottom step and covered my face in my hands.

Light filtered through the gaps between my fingers. I looked up to see Harwell holding a candle, standing in the open doorway.

I stood up. He held the door as I entered the dungeon.

"No goblet?" Pito asked as I approached.

I had left the tea and goblets at the top of the stairs.

"My experiments are over," I quietly replied.

Harwell sat back down. The Twelve Men's Morris board had been set up between the two of them. It seemed I'd interrupted their game.

"Did they lead to a successful result?" Pito asked me.

"No."

"I'm sorry, my friend."

"I thought I had three more days," I told him.

Harwell made a move, and then Pito instantly responded.

They were playing Six Men's Morris, a less complex version of the game, often played by children.

While Harwell was pondering his next move, Pito explained

that he'd heard the banging on the door. He said he was able to convey this to Harwell by pointing at the door while knocking on the ground with his fist.

"I'm supposed to give Tullia poppy tears this morning," I told him.

"A waste of your talent," said Pito. "Like having Michelangelo paint the barn."

That seemed like an odd response, but I couldn't disagree with the sentiment.

Harwell chose his move, and then Pito responded, almost instantaneously. It seemed to me that he was being a bit unkind. He could, at the very least, pretend to have to think for more than a second.

But then again, in two days Harwell would bring an axe down upon his neck.

"May I ask you a question?" Pito asked.

I imagined he was curious as to the purpose of the experiments, and I realized I had no reason to keep it secret any longer.

"I don't wish to intrude where I don't belong," he began. "You clearly care a great deal for her, and I don't want to add to your pain, but who is Tullia?"

19

REPLICATION

IN MY EXCITEMENT, I ran up the stone stairway. My body temperature rose to a dangerous level. Halfway up I became dizzy and nearly fainted. I had to sit until it returned to normal. I rested my face against the cold stone wall.

Harwell, who must have been surprised to see me move so quickly, came up behind me. He looked at me a moment, then stepped completely over me and continued up the stairs.

Although I said that I'd only changed the size and shape of one candle, it was really a little more than that. I had also changed the time it was replaced and used a different-sized candle to replace it.

Thinking back, I realized it was genius.

As my temperature slowly lowered, so did my excitement. The king had ordered poppy tears. Did I dare defy him?

It would take another day to prepare the potion for Tullia. And it might not have been only that particular candle substitution that made the difference. It could have been the combination of everything I'd given him over the past few weeks.

There was also the problem of figuring out how to account for Pito's and Tullia's different and unique physiologies. Besides the obvious differences of sex and weight, many other hidden factors might cause the potion to be ineffective on Tullia, or worse, lead to unintended consequences.

I considered asking for an audience with King Sandro. Tullia was his daughter, after all, and he'd always seemed reluctant to give her opium. I could apprise him of the latest development and let him make the decision.

But to speak to the king, I'd have to go through his regent. In my mind I could see Dittierri sneering at me, his face framed in that thin outline of a beard. He might never pass on my request to the king. Or worse, he might twist my words into a confession of treason.

To my astonishment Harwell came back down the stairs, holding one of the goblets, which he handed to me. He'd found it along with my teapot at the top of the stairs and poured me a cup.

ONCE MY BODY TEMPERATURE COOLED, I RETURNED TO THE workshop, got a leather glove from my sleeping alcove, and went outside. I lifted the copper pot off the stove and dumped out its contents.

A short time later, when I knocked on the door to Tullia's chambers, the goblet in my hand contained nothing more than African moon moth tea with a little galingale and turmeric. *Michelangelo does not paint barns!*

Marta had been expecting me. She had a somber expression, and I struck a similar pose.

"Is that . . ." she started.

I nodded, then requested that she leave while I see the princess.

She was hesitant.

"The princess will feel a warm sense of well-being," I assured her. "And then she will fall asleep."

Marta hesitated a moment longer, then stepped out as I entered.

"Why should I go to sleep?" Tullia shouted at me from the table. A plate of eggs and fish lay in front of her. "I haven't even finished breakfast!"

"To save Pito," I answered.

While I couldn't mention the memory potion, I did tell her about the poppy tears. "To ensure your compliance." I assured her that only moon moth tea was in the goblet. "You have to pretend it's the poppy."

"How will that save Pito?"

"I can't tell you."

She stared at me a long moment, then took a sip of tea, swooned, and clunked her head on the table.

It was the worst acting I'd ever seen.

She raised her head and giggled.

INSIDE MY WORKSHOP I CAREFULLY STUDIED THE MOST RECENT entry in the logbook. I measured carefully, relying not on instinct or my inherent genius but on exactly what was written before me.

I decided that any attempt to account for their different physiologies would be guesswork and likely to do more harm than good. Tullia would get exactly what I'd given Pito.

When everything else was in the pot, I went outside, dragged the sacks of sand off the hatch, and went down into the cellar. Pito's vial was where I'd put it, behind the jar of yak's blood.

Back inside, I scraped away the wax, removed the cork, and then poured his heartfelt tear into the pot.

I checked and double-checked the diagram in the logbook as I arranged the candles. Unfortunately, I had difficulty making out some of my notations regarding when and how they should be changed in the night. I'd been half asleep when I entered those details, and to be honest, I hadn't taken great care. I hadn't recognized my own genius at the time.

I did my best to decipher the squiggles, then rewrote the instructions for later.

I took extra care in connecting the pot to the wires. I didn't dare drop it.

I lit the candles.

The clock in my alcove was powered by weights on a chain. It wasn't accurate by today's standards, but it didn't have to be, just as long as the inaccuracies were consistent from one night to the next.

I lay in bed with my eyes open.

20

SMOKE PACKETS

I N THE MORNING, I filled the goblet close to the brim and carried it through the curtained archway, careful to not allow even one drop to spill. I continued down the long corridor, then turned and headed up the back staircase.

Two more turns brought me to the princess's chambers, and the goblet was still full. Holding it steady in my right hand, I knocked on the door with my left.

"Is that Anatole?" Tullia called out when Marta opened the door. "I need some of his special tea, desperately!"

Scowling, Marta let me in. The scowl was not aimed at me but at the poppy tears. Evidently, Tullia's acting had fooled her.

"I must have it now!" Tullia desperately demanded from the sofa, even as the twinkle in her blue eye revealed her delight in our little conspiracy.

Some of the potion sloshed out of the goblet when she took it, and I admonished her to be careful not to spill even one drop.

She looked at me curiously. *What did it matter? It wasn't real.*

She took a drink but then stopped abruptly. Something was different. It didn't taste like the brew I'd given her the night before. She looked at me with alarm.

"It's good for you," I told her.

She obediently finished the goblet.

AFTER THAT, THERE WAS NOTHING TO DO BUT WAIT. I PASSED THE time stuffing smoke packets with corpse flower petals.

In periods of plague, physicians wore hooded masks with large birdlike beaks while tending to their patients. They'd fill these beaks with sweet-smelling flowers, such as gardenias or jasmine. They believed the sweet smells would protect them from the evil spirits.

Nowadays, when people talk of the plague, they call it the Black Death. We never called it that, although we would sometimes refer to it as the Blue Death. The faces of the dying would be covered in large blue welts called buboes.

Physicians, wearing their beaked masks for protection, would lance the buboes with hot pokers, as a way to release the evil spirits from those infected. The well-educated people of today might scoff at that term, but what difference does it make whether they're called evil spirits, germs, or viruses?

I wonder how many of these well-educated scoffers even know what a virus is?

Germ, virus, or evil spirit, the patient invariably died, often taking the rest of their family with them, and probably the doctor too. If a member of the clergy had come to guide the suffering soul into the afterlife, he would soon join them there as well.

In the middle of the fourteenth century, during a period of less than two years, the bubonic plague killed more than half the population of Esquaveta. It had returned roughly every thirty years since to cause more suffering and death. The last time it swept through the kingdom had been when I was an infant.

We were ten years overdue.

This may have been the reason why, despite all my setbacks, I was still employed at the castle. While I never outright promised the king that I could save him from the plague, I never dissuaded him from that notion.

My method, as of yet untested, involved the corpse flower. It seemed to me it would be more effective against evil spirits than the sweet smells of jasmine or gardenia. Instead of stuffing the petals into a mask, which only protected the nose, I planned to create a shield of foul-smelling smoke.

"WHAT IS THAT DISGUSTING ODOR?" TULLIA ASKED.

Startled, I spilled the packet I was holding.

Once again, she had noiselessly slipped through my curtains.

"Being a poppy slave is boring," she complained.

I refilled the packet.

Tullia held her nose. "Is that for your Pito experiment?"

I spilled it again as my head jerked toward her. I stammered incoherently.

"Marta told me you were experimenting on Pito!"

I kept my mouth shut, wondering exactly what Marta had said or what she even knew. My experiments had been a closely guarded secret.

Whatever Marta had told her, Tullia didn't seem too angry. She merely laughed at my discombobulation, then headed to Luigi.

"How can you stand the smell, Luigi?" she asked my very old mouse.

She petted the tip of Luigi's nose, then turned her attention to the other cage, which housed my other sixteen mice. She leaned close and asked, "So, which one's Pito?"

21

THE GREATEST MAGICIAN
IN ALL THE LAND

I WAS STILL STUFFING SMOKE packets when Xavier came to the workshop. Evidently, he'd heard that my experiments, whatever they were, had come to an end, and was hoping I would return to the black sand.

"The banquet will bankrupt us!" he complained. His face was almost as red as his beard. "And then the festival . . ." He threw up his hands in consternation.

He'd been predicting imminent bankruptcy for more than a year now, but even if it was true this time, I didn't know what he expected me to do about it. The banquet was tomorrow.

The finance minister stared at me a moment, then looked disdainfully around my workshop. "How can you work here?" He asked me if, in the nearly twenty years I'd been living in the castle, I'd ever once cleaned the place.

Holding my temper, I quietly explained that while it might look like disorder to him, everything was carefully arranged. "And I've only been at the castle eighteen years, not twenty."

"So you're waiting until twenty to clean up?"

"Servants do that," I said.

"From what I hear, the servants refuse to come in here."

That wasn't true. I didn't want servants disrupting my sanctum. We had an agreement. I left my laundry, chamber pot, and greasy dishes in the archway, and in turn they left fresh clothing, the washed pot, and my meals.

Xavier picked up a fistful of black sand and let it sift through his fingers. "Do you know how much it cost to transport this here?"

I started to explain the necessity of proceeding slowly, without making too many modifications all at once, and about how every setback is revealing. His eyes suddenly lit up, as the expression on his face changed from despair to hope. "What's that?"

He was pointing to a small mound of white sand that was coated in some kind of yellow crust.

I bent down and rubbed the sand between my fingers.

"Is it . . . ?" the finance minister asked, struggling to contain his excitement.

"Pigeon eggs," I told him, remembering the jar I'd broken the day the tiger was released. I had never quite gotten around to cleaning it up.

His disdainful expression returned. "No wonder all your experiments fail!"

That made me mad. I told him that magic required more than just adding and subtracting numbers.

He took offense at that, saying that I had no idea what it took to keep this castle functioning.

"If you're so smart," I asked him, "why is the kingdom on the verge of bankruptcy?"

Glaring back at me, he said, "It doesn't take a great magician to give the princess poppy tears!"

"I'm not giving her poppy tears!" I shouted back at him.

Xavier stared at me, more curious than angry. I think we both regretted our words. He turned and left through the archway.

LESS THAN AN HOUR LATER, I WAS BACK IN THE REGENCY, STANDING before the king and queen, while Voltharo read aloud from the royal record.

Your folly is over. Anatole will begin the opium regimen immediately.

My legs were trembling. I didn't know if Xavier had betrayed me or if someone else had overheard our argument. It was rumored that the king had spies throughout the castle.

"Did you comply?" Dittierri asked, seated at his desk. "Or did you defy the king's order?"

"I prepared the poppy tears, as suggested," I said.

"It was not a suggestion," said the queen.

"Did you comply, or did you defy?" Dittierri repeated.

I directed my answer to King Sandro. "It was not intended as an act of defiance."

"You brought a goblet to her chambers this morning," said Dittierri. "What was inside it?"

It took great effort to stop shaking. I tried to explain about the potion, but my words were incoherent, even to me. I think I might have said that Michelangelo wouldn't have enough paint for an entire barn.

"What was inside the goblet, Anatole?" asked Queen Corinna.

My voice cracked as I said, "The memory potion."

King Sandro stepped toward me. For a moment I thought he would strike me, but he strode past and continued on out the door.

It seemed he was leaving my fate to the queen. The fact that I'd saved his life would not be a consideration.

I remained standing there for what felt like a long time. The queen said nothing. Dittierri smirked at me. I was afraid I might faint if I didn't sit down soon.

"She thinks Pito's a mouse!" King Sandro announced, coming back inside. "She doesn't know who is in the dungeon!"

He jovially slapped my back as he passed, but my legs gave way and I collapsed on the floor.

The king smiled at me as he helped me back up. "Voltharo, put this in the record. 'Anatole is the greatest magician in all the land!'"

Dittierri was no longer smirking.

It took the elderly scribe a moment. He was as surprised as the rest of us. I watched him dip his quill and then write the king's words.

My confidence continued to grow as I listened to King Sandro relate the details of his conversation with the princess. *Of course she plans to marry Prince Dalrympl. She couldn't understand why I would question her on that.*

It was not my place to give advice unless asked to do so, but I had told Tullia the potions would save Pito, and whether she remembered that promise or not, I would not betray her. "If I may be bold, Your Highness," I began, "there is no longer any justification for Pito's execution, or even his imprisonment."

The king glared at me, but I pressed on. "She doesn't know him. He doesn't know her. Neither of them would even know why he was being executed."

"No justification?" questioned the king. "I decreed it. Isn't that justification enough?"

I bowed my head and apologized for my poor choice of words. Dittierri's smirk returned.

"Pito's actions, whether he remembers them or not, were an insult to the princess, to me, to Queen Corinna, and to all of Esquaveta." The king's tone softened. "I understand, Anatole, for the purpose of your experiments, it was necessary for you to form a kind of friendship with the prisoner. But even if, for your sake, I was willing to spare his life, Prince Dalrympl insists on witnessing the beheading. The wedding cannot take place without it."

"I understand, Your Highness."

"I didn't ask for your understanding. Thanks to you, the princess will marry the prince, and we are all grateful. With good fortune, she will soon bear him a son."

"How unfortunate that is left to fortune," quipped Dittierri.

Not even the queen smiled at his petty remark. I had saved the marriage and the kingdom. Nothing Dittierri could say could take away from the fact that I was the greatest magician in all the land! It had been inscribed in the royal record.

THAT DOCUMENT MOST LIKELY STILL EXISTS TODAY. PARCHMENT, made from animal hide, doesn't deteriorate like paper. It is probably squirrelled away in the dusty archives of some museum. Just because scholars and historians have chosen to ignore it doesn't diminish its importance. Rather, it reveals the biases and ignorance of these so-called experts!

22

THE BANQUET

O N THE MORNING OF the banquet, Harwell led me down the stone stairs to the dungeon. King Sandro agreed that I could see the prisoner one last time. I brought neither the teapot nor the goblets but just a clear glass containing a blue liquid.

"Remarkable," Pito said, when I held the candle close to the glass so he could see the color.

I told him about Captain Cuvio and the blueberries. "He picked them beside a mountain lake in a place called Kanata."

"Ka-na-ta," he repeated, letting the sound of that distant and exotic land dance across his tongue.

I didn't mention that I'd soaked the blueberry skins in pear vinegar to extract every bit of color. Nor did I tell him it was essentially a replication of a potion I'd previously given him, except instead of daisies I'd used butterfly pea petals. I also hadn't added Tullia's tear. A personal identifier was no longer necessary.

He drank the liquid. He told me that when his time came, he

wouldn't be in the banquet hall. "My mind will take me to that mountain lake in Kanata. I'll be picking blueberries when the axe comes down."

I somberly nodded, then glanced at Harwell. His executioner's expression hadn't changed one iota.

I didn't tell Pito the purpose behind the blue liquid. It would have been cruel to give him false hope. I didn't know if it would work, or, more importantly, even if it did, whether I would find the necessary courage. I was still the same coward who had failed Babette.

As I started to leave, he reminded me to take the two board games. That just about did me in. I shed more than a few heartfelt tears as I carried them back up the stone stairs.

FOR THE BANQUET, I WORE A LIGHT BLUE SILK SHIRT WITH SILVER buttons and my dark blue cape with a satin lining. Instead of my fancy long and pointed shoes, I chose a more comfortable pair. If I did find the courage to act, I would need to move quickly.

I arrived at the great hall more than an hour before noon. The room was already filled with people, many of whom had gathered around the enormous glass elephant. It had been placed in a corner of the room, so as not to get in the way.

Musicians strolled among the guests, strumming lutes and lyres. A woman with dark hair, so long it nearly reached her ankles, was playing the hurdy-gurdy. This too was a stringed instrument. The strings were plucked by the turning of a wheel. Still other musicians played various-sized pipes; the more narrow the pipe, the higher the pitch.

Women wore elaborate hats that were made from fabric fitted over wire frames. There was one shaped like a swan. Another was a huge and colorful butterfly twice as large as the head of the woman who wore it. As I made my way toward the glass elephant, I saw one hat that was a replica of a three-masted schooner. As the woman wearing it walked, the hat seemed to bob up and down as if on waves.

Men's clothes were equally showy and impractical. Long and baggy sleeves were in vogue, despite the difficulty they posed while eating. Many of the men wore shoes even longer than the pair I had left in my alcove. Some of their shoes curled backward at the front. Walking in these shoes was difficult and painful, but that was the point. Men of wealth and culture didn't walk the fields like peasants.

Having been ostracized for so long, I was surprised and a little disconcerted by the number of courtiers who stopped to say hello. Everyone was well aware of my new status, even if the reason behind it remained a mystery. A few made subtle attempts to find out, but as much as I would have liked to recount my glorious success, I couldn't speak of the potion.

I noticed people starting to take their seats, so I did the same. Such was my new status that I was seated at the head table, only eight chairs away from where the princess and prince would be sitting.

Lady Angelica sat across from me. I've previously mentioned her charm and wit but not her dark eyes, her smile, or how pleasant it felt to gaze upon her face. Her hat, a small bouquet of silk flowers, was simple and tasteful. I commented on how realistic they seemed, and she said if it were a June wedding, they would have been the real thing. "Apparently, twelve years ago, Prince Dalrympl's magician consulted the stars or whatnot and chose this as the ideal date for the wedding."

I could see the Oxatanian magician seated on a bench at one of the outer tables. He was easy to spot as he wore a tall, cone-shaped hat adorned with suns and moons.

When I pointed him out to Angelica, she smiled at me and said, "He didn't merit a spot at this table, did he?"

Next to Angelica was the considerably less pleasant face of Dittierri. He only glanced my way for a moment, then did his best to focus his attention the other way. Despite my rise in status, Dittierri still sat one chair closer to the head of the table than I did.

Gregor sat on the other side of Angelica, and an Oxatanian woman sat across from him, next to me. Blond curls framed a lovely face. She didn't wear a hat. Oxatanians wore hats for protection against the elements, not for adornment. I didn't get her name and probably wouldn't have been able to spell it for you if I had.

The elephant artist was on her other side. He was going on and on about his *magnificent masterpiece*—his words, not mine. He said he'd overseen a team of sixteen glassblowers and explained that the elephant was made from more than two hundred carefully crafted pieces of glass, all fitted together.

My height and the size of the women's hats had prevented me from getting a good look at the elephant, so I can't comment on its accuracy or artistic merit. It was nothing compared to my memory potion, which I couldn't mention, for obvious reasons. But then again, I'm not one who likes to boast.

Crumhorns resounded, heralding the entrance of the royal families. We all stood.

King Sandro of Esquaveta and King Lurtzk of Oxatania entered side by side. King Lurtzk walked bent over, with the aid of a cane, so it took them a long time to reach our table. Once they sat down, the two queens made their entrance.

The women could have been mother and daughter, with Queen

Corinna being the elder. King Lurtzk might not have been long for this world, but it seemed Tullia would have to wait a very long time to become queen of Oxatania.

The crumhorns blared again, and then everyone applauded as the handsome prince and his lovely bride-to-be strolled gracefully across the room. Tullia's gloved hand rested on the prince's forearm. Her head was held high, and when she directed her smile toward each table, it seemed to sparkle as much as the diamonds she wore around her neck, dangling from her ears, and in her tiara. My eyes filled with tears. It was hard for me to believe that this poised and beautiful woman was the same person who once played with mice in my workshop.

The prince's posture and his overall demeanor expressed strength and confidence. Though he appeared to be significantly older than Tullia, the difference in their ages seemed negligible when compared to that of the Oxatanian king and queen.

I didn't get a good look at the prince's face until he and Tullia reached our table. And when I did, it was like a kick in the stomach. His face was fuller, and his blond hair cut shorter, but he had the same protruding jaw I'd seen twenty-three years before, when he admired Babette's exquisite lace.

23

ENTERTAINMENT

TWO DOZEN ROASTED PEACOCKS in full plumage were paraded through the hall, held high by two dozen footmen. Queen Corinna explained to the table that the feathers had been removed for the roasting, but then each one had been returned to its original spot.

"They're just for the presentation," she said with a laugh. "You don't eat them."

Angelica winked at me and said, "I'm glad she told us."

I didn't respond or even acknowledge that she'd said anything. My attention was on Tullia and her prince. She smiled at me, but I couldn't bring myself to smile back. I had failed Babette. I resolved not to fail Pito.

I remember eating the peacock, but I can't report on its taste. The birds were followed with platters of fish and eel, and after that, wild boar, aurochs, lamb, and venison. There were heaps of greens and root vegetables, purple carrots and white beets. I only took a bite when I remembered it was expected of me.

I counted seven doors to the great hall, and my eyes kept darting from one to another. I didn't know from which Pito would enter, or when, just that it would be before dessert.

Each time I glanced at Tullia, I'd see her smiling at Dalrympl and touching his sleeve. My stomach turned.

Angelica, who excelled in the art of conversation, spoken and unspoken, eventually gave up on me. The pretty Oxatanian woman at my side made a few polite attempts at conversation, but when I failed to respond, she seemed all too happy to turn her attentions to the handsome Gregor, or to the bombastic elephant artist.

The strolling musicians gave way to other forms of entertainment. An area between the tables had been left open. There were singers, acrobats, and even a small acting troupe who put on a short play.

Tullia seemed thrilled by all of it. She had turned her chair around to watch the entertainment, and a juggler began his act by placing a glass bowl on the table behind her. The juggler proceeded to toss three brightly painted eggs into the air, probably falcon eggs by the size of them. Three eggs became four. Four became five. He kept pulling more eggs from the brim of his hat while keeping the others aloft.

When he reached seven, Tullia clapped and cried out in delight. She clutched Dalrympl's arm with both hands as the juggler caught the eggs, one after another, and placed them back on his hat. The seventh egg he didn't catch. It went over Tullia's head and landed in the bowl he had placed there. She squealed, then stood and held up the glass bowl with the yolk now swimming inside it, for all to see.

The applause that came from around the room was ostensibly for the juggler, but I think it was mostly for the delighted and most delightful princess.

A shrill whistle pierced my ears, and we all turned to see a skinny man leap and prance his way to the center area. He wore skintight and very colorful clothing. He blew into a very small and narrow pipe, often called a pip-squeak because of the awful sound that came out of it.

He stepped close to the princess, where the juggler had been, bowed, and loudly farted.

The room erupted in laughter.

He proceeded to tell a very vulgar joke, then blew into his pip-squeak.

Tullia laughed as she covered her ears.

The man pranced from table to table, bowing, telling crude jokes, blowing into his pip-squeak, and farting. With each fart the laughter grew louder.

So much for your most refined and cultured Renaissance man.

PEOPLE WERE STILL LAUGHING WHEN I SAW HARWELL COME through the door farthest to the left. He carried an axe in one hand and a chopping block in the other.

Behind him, two other guards held Pito. Pito's wrists were bound and his legs were loosely chained. He could only take short, shuffling steps. A dark hood had been placed over his head.

This was my moment to act boldly! I'd been preparing for it since the moment I recognized Dalrympl. But I couldn't act until I knew the potion had worked, and I wouldn't know that until I saw Pito's face.

Harwell set the chopping block down in front of Tullia, where the juggler had been. I saw the color drain from her face. "No, not here!" she sharply whispered.

"Yes, right here!" Dalrympl demanded, and then he put a hand on the back of Tullia's head so she couldn't turn away.

The guards pressed down on Pito's shoulder, forcing him to kneel. I could only hope he was picking blueberries in Kanata.

Voltharo stepped forward, unfurled a roll of parchment, and recited the charges against the prisoner: treachery, treason, and plotting to defile the princess's virtue. King Sandro asked Pito if he had last words.

"Yes," Pito answered, his voice clear and full of purpose.

The king made a gesture, and Harwell removed the hood.

The woman beside me gasped. I heard cries of alarm coming from all around the table.

Pito's face was blotched with blue welts.

And still, I didn't move. My courage had left me. My legs were too weak to stand.

Pito stared right at Tullia. "Are you the princess?"

Tullia's face trembled, but she bravely looked right back at him. "Yes."

"You have no virtue," Pito told her. "You defiled it with your lies."

And then he set his head on the chopping block.

I tried to shout, but my words got caught in my throat. All that emerged was a quaking whisper. "The B-Blue Death."

But that was enough. The Oxatanian woman heard me and undoubtedly misinterpreted the terror she saw in my eyes.

"Plague!" she shouted.

Others began shouting it too. Chairs were toppling over as people hastened to get away.

"Cut off his head!" Dalrympl demanded.

"No!" I shouted, finally getting both my voice and my legs. "You'll release the evil spirits!"

Of course, nothing Dalrympl or I said could be heard by Harwell.

I pulled a smoke packet out from the inside pocket of my cape. Grabbing a candle, I lit a corner of the packet and tossed it over the table. It landed between Pito and Harwell.

The rising smoke smelled like death.

"Stay clear of the smoke, and you'll be safe!" I shouted as I lit a second packet.

By the time I'd made it around the table, I'd set off five more, tossing them in every direction. By then our table was deserted. Even Dalrympl had fled.

Through the smoke I could see Harwell raise the axe. I yelled for him to stop.

The axe came down hard and swift, but not on Pito's neck. It snapped the chain that bound his ankles. The large brute turned and walked slowly away, disappearing into the smoke.

24

DISPOSAL OF THE BODY

H ELLO, FRIEND," I SAID.

Pito stared back at me. After spending the past month preparing himself for death, he must have been bewildered to be still alive. Or perhaps he thought he was dead and was in the smoky depths of hell.

The smoke began to dissipate. We were the only two left in the hall. The floor was littered with broken dishes, coats, scarves, hats, and quite a few of those pointed and curled shoes. Several benches lay on their sides, and one of the tables too.

Having never expected to make it this far, I had no plan as to what to do next. I found a sharp knife and cut the rope tying Pito's wrists. He didn't even blink.

I suggested he lie on the floor and pretend to be dead. I doubted anyone would return, but I needed to be ready just in case. I made sure I had a candle and a smoke packet ready. Pito gave no indication that he understood anything I said.

I went back to the head table and yanked out the cotton

tablecloth, letting everything crash down off of it. I cleared a space on the floor and laid the tablecloth out flat. Then I picked up all the scraps of meat and bones I could find and tossed them on top of it.

I moved on to the other tables. The ship hat had been squashed. The hurdy-gurdy lay smashed. A broken lute was held together only by its strings.

As I gathered more meat and bones, I glanced back to where I had left Pito. He was gone! After about twenty seconds of panic, I saw him by the glass elephant, staring up at it in apparent bewilderment.

Somehow, one small round table remained untouched by the chaos. There was an urn, an array of cups, and a bowl of thickened sweet cream.

I filled a cup with the warm chocolate, added a dollop of cream, and brought it to Pito. He took it without a word.

A short while later, as I was adding more scraps of meat to my pile, he appeared next to me and tossed in a plate.

"Just meat and bones," I said.

He smiled. The chocolate seemed to have revived him.

IN ALL WE MUST HAVE COLLECTED CLOSE TO EIGHTY POUNDS OF meat and bones, which was still only about half of Pito's weight. I couldn't carry any more than that anyway. We folded the corners of the tablecloth inward and tied them together, turning it into a sack.

Pito hoisted it up onto his shoulder.

Before leaving the hall, I lit a smoke packet and tossed it through the door ahead of us. "Keep clear for your own safety!" I called out.

My precautions were unnecessary. The corridor was deserted. People didn't want to be anywhere close to the Blue Death. Just the same, I set off additional smoke packets whenever we approached a corner or open door.

We made it to my curtained archway without encountering anyone, then pushed on through. Pito dropped the bundle on the floor of my workshop. He looked around in awe.

"This is where you make your magic."

I smiled.

"What a mess!" he said.

I told him I preferred it that way.

I gave him some of my clothes, and while he changed, I went down to the root cellar for my jars of blood. Besides yak's blood, I also had ox, pig, aurochs, horse, water buffalo, skunk, and weasel. There might have been more. It took me several trips.

Pito looked ridiculous in my clothes. His legs were too long for my leggings, and the waist was too wide. My tunic hung like a tent on his thin frame, but the sleeves were too short.

It didn't matter. If anybody saw him, we'd have worse problems than that.

I changed my clothes too. I didn't want to get blood on my silk shirt and cape.

We untied the bundle and stuffed the meat and bones inside Pito's old clothes. I drenched everything in blood, then retied the tablecloth around it all.

Pito helped me lift the bundle up to my shoulder, but I would have to carry it from here on out. I staggered a bit as he helped me find my balance, and then I headed out the door and past my iron stove.

Pito remained behind, a smoke packet and candle at the ready.

The castle grounds were bustling with people. This was where they'd fled.

That was fine by me. I wanted to be seen, as long as nobody came too close. And I knew they wouldn't dare.

My biggest concern was becoming overheated. It was a cool day, but the sunshine was bright, and as I struggled under the weight, I could feel my body temperature rising.

I made it to the fishpond and plopped down on a bench in the shade of an elm tree. The people who had been nearby scattered like birds when I approached.

I kept the bundle balanced over my shoulder, worried that if I set it down, I would never be able to get it back up. After a short rest, I felt ready to continue on.

With one hand holding the top of the bench, I struggled back to my feet. I stumbled and nearly fell, but regained my balance. People were staring at me from all sides, but they kept their distance.

I crossed the grounds and made it to the wall that encircled the entire castle complex. There was a series of narrow stairways and ledges leading up to the top. I started up the first set of stairs.

The steps were steep and set far apart. I had to raise my knee up past my waist in order to climb from one step to the next. The wall shaded me from the sun.

A soldier shouted down to me from atop the wall. I hadn't seen him. My eyes had been focused on the steps before me.

I called out my name to him, but I needn't have wasted the energy. He must have recognized my hairless head and was already quickly walking away along the top of the wall. Evidently the news from the banquet had already reached even this lone sentry.

I counted nine steps before I made it to the first ledge. There I leaned into the wall to rest. I felt a little queasy and waited for the feeling to pass before I started up the next nine.

I was determined to reach the top and continued past the second ledge without stopping. That was a mistake. I felt a rush of dizziness halfway up the next set of stairs, and when I reached the ledge I fell face forward into the wall, smashing my nose. I stayed like that for a good while while I let my body temperature cool. I could taste blood.

I continued from ledge to ledge, resting a little longer each time. When I finally reached the topmost ledge, I slid the bundle off my shoulder and onto the very top of the wall.

I could finally sit down.

Fire pits had been constructed at regular intervals along this ledge. Soldiers could shoot flaming arrows or pour boiling tar down on the attacking hordes.

As I rested, I thought about all I had done. I'd finally reestablished my reputation and court standing. A month ago, I would never have thought I'd have a seat at the head table. And here I was, putting all that in jeopardy. I imagined castle guards storming my workshop and taking Pito away.

Yet despite it all, I was glad I'd done what I'd done. For once in my life, I'd been bold and courageous.

I stepped up onto the raised rim of a fire pit, then hoisted myself up on top of the wall, where I was greeted with a brilliant orange and pink sky.

Despite my newfound courage I was still very much afraid of heights. The wall was wide enough that I could lie flat across it. I pulled and pushed the bundle from one edge of the wall to the other.

I wriggled closer to the edge, then gave the bundle one final push, knocking it off the wall.

I peered down at it.

It took only about five minutes for the tiger to come. It approached cautiously, and curiously sniffed the package. Then a sudden swipe of a paw ripped it open.

25

TIGER MICE

THERE WAS NO MOON. Even without my heavy load, going down the narrow and steep steps felt perilous, and all the more so because I didn't know what awaited me back in the castle. By the time I passed the iron stove, I was convinced I'd be arrested the moment I entered the workshop.

Instead, I found a giggling Pito. He was watching Luigi run through the obstacle course.

I could only smile and sigh. By playing with Luigi, he might have undone seven years of carefully recorded experiments.

"I made you some tea," he said.

I normally didn't drink tea that late in the day, but Pito seemed so eager to please I didn't want to disappoint him.

I looked at the obstacle course. Not only had he figured out how to release the latch on Luigi's cage, but he'd also rearranged the tubes and loops to make it more difficult.

Pito handed me a goblet of tea, then anxiously watched as I drank. I suppose the expression on his face was not too different from how mine had been in the dungeon when I first shared my tea with him.

The tea was cold and rancid. He must have brewed it when I first set out for the wall and then let the leaves steep for too long.

I set the goblet back down. "Very tasty," I told him.

He smiled.

I turned my attention back to Luigi, partly to assess the damage done by Pito but also to avoid drinking the tea. I directed Luigi back toward his cage, while I explained to Pito how every run-through needed to be well thought out in advance, with the results carefully recorded. "Luigi isn't a pet."

I also noticed there was no cheese at the end of the course.

"He doesn't do it for the cheese," Pito said. "The achievement is his reward."

"He's a mouse, not a philosopher," I reminded him.

Pito merely shrugged and moved on to the other cage. "Are these special too?" He wiggled a finger through the wooden slats.

"Get back!" I warned. "Those are tiger mice!"

He quickly removed his finger.

"Their father was a mouse," I explained, "and their mother was a tiger."

He believed me, but just for a short moment, then burst out with laughter. "That must have been some mouse!" he hooted.

It felt good to see him laugh.

I GAVE HIM A CANDLE AND A BLANKET AND LED HIM OUTSIDE TO the root cellar. As he headed down the ladder, I suggested he use a sack of dried beetles for a pillow.

He looked around his new home. "Almost as nice as my last place," he remarked.

I smiled, then closed the hatch and dragged the sacks of sand back over it.

After I dumped out the remainder of the tea, I noticed my logbook lying open on the table. I couldn't remember if I'd left it there, but I knew that if anyone could decipher my cryptic symbols, it would be someone who had taught himself to read ancient Greek.

26

A POTION FOR
THE PRINCE

INSPIRATION STRUCK IN THE night!

Very early the next morning, I put on my hooded and beaked plague mask and strode through the castle corridors as I headed to the kitchen. It would have been more direct to cut through the garden, but I wanted to be seen by as many people as possible. People needed to be reminded that it still wasn't safe to come near me or my workshop.

The kitchen was in an outbuilding. The risk of fire made it unsafe for it to be inside the castle.

The mask served its purpose. The kitchen staff kept their distance and let me take whatever I wanted without questioning the amount.

I prepared a plate for Pito. My thought was that he'd best remain in the cellar until I figured out a way to sneak him across the bridge. But when I opened the hatch, the dank and musty odor caused a change of heart. I invited him up.

I stacked three crates of mostly glassware next to the table, so

Pito couldn't be seen from the archway as we ate our breakfast. A tall and narrow beaker fell and shattered on the floor, but I hardly used it anyway.

The crates were just a precaution. I knew nobody would dare come anywhere in the vicinity of my workshop.

I poured us each a cup of tea, letting its warmth linger over my tongue and against the back of my throat. This was how tea was supposed to taste, not like the putrid brew Pito had served to me the night before. "You can taste the wildflowers, and the bees," I told him.

Pito chuckled but then realized I wasn't joking. He obligingly took a sip.

"Let it linger," I coaxed.

He swished it around in his mouth, then swallowed.

"Well?" I asked him.

"Tastes like bees," he said.

I shook my head and sighed.

He asked how long he'd have to stay here, hiding and sleeping in the root cellar. I told him that unfortunately he couldn't leave until after the wedding, a week away.

It seemed the wedding would still proceed as planned. Prince Dalrympl refused to be intimidated by fear of the plague.

An Oxatanian contingent was staying at the castle for the weeklong festival leading up to the wedding. In addition to the royal family and their attendants, there was also a large number of Oxatanian soldiers for their protection.

"No one will be able to cross the bridge without being stopped and interrogated," I told Pito.

He took another sip of tea and again swished it around as if he was using it to rinse his mouth. That was not *letting it linger*, but I held my tongue.

"Don't worry about me," he said. "The festival starts today. Go enjoy yourself."

I eyed him suspiciously. He seemed a little too eager for me to go. I told him I had no plans to attend the festival. I needed to work on a new potion. "For the prince."

That was my new inspiration.

The potion would be a variation of one of the modifications I'd given Pito in the early stages of our experiments. Everything about it would have to be greatly enhanced: shark scales instead of eel scales, sunflowers instead of daisies.

A personal identifier wouldn't be necessary. I had no interest in erasing Dalrympl's memory. I was after the *unintended consequences*.

I told Pito that it was Prince Dalrympl who, almost twenty-five years earlier, had forced Babette to clean his boot with her beautiful and intricate lace. "I can't let him marry Princess Tullia."

Pito merely shrugged and spread some soft cheese across a slab of dark bread. "Why not?" he asked. "They're the perfect couple. Each is worse than the other."

I was stunned.

"I'm sorry, Anatole," he said. "I know you care for her, but you seem to forget she made up lies about me and then was willing to watch me die."

I didn't know what to say. How could I tell him that the lies came from Voltharo without mentioning the time they spent together in the library?

"And you can be sure that her virtue had already been defiled," he added. "Probably many times."

I looked at him in horror. "You can be executed for saying that."

"They can't kill me twice."

He bit into a pear. "Think about it, Anatole. Clearly, she was worried that on their wedding night, Prince Dalrympl would discover she wasn't . . . intact. So she accused me of defiling her in order to protect her secret lover."

Admittedly, there was a certain logic behind what he said. "But why you?" I asked.

He shrugged. "I was convenient. Maybe I passed by at the wrong moment. I'm nobody to her. She could watch me die and still enjoy her chocolate."

We finished the rest of our meal in silence. Pito was right about one thing. She had been in love with somebody else.

Him.

IN SPITE OF HIS ENMITY TOWARD THE PRINCESS, PITO WAS WILLing to assist me with the new potion. I think he was glad to finally have something to do.

I gave him a length of sharkskin and asked him to remove the scales. I warned him that they could be sharp, having cut myself on them several times before, but his fingers worked deftly and carefully.

I reminded myself that he grew up butchering animals as a child and used harsh chemicals.

He naturally wanted to know what the potion would do, but I was superstitious when it came to new potions. I never talked about them until I was sure they worked.

Although for the prince's potion, I could never be sure, not until Dalrympl drank it. There was no way to test it.

I couldn't test it on Pito or myself. The effects were intended to be permanent. And my ears weren't sensitive enough to test it on a mouse.

I would have to rely solely on inspiration, instinct, and my innate genius. I was, after all, the greatest magician in all the land.

I had an even bigger problem than determining how to test it. How could I convince the prince to drink it?

I couldn't simply show up at his quarters the night before the wedding and offer him the potion. "He'd throw it in my face!" I told Pito. "And probably make me lick it up off the floor."

Nor could I try to slip something into his drink. Soldiers stood guard over him, and he'd brought along a food taster.

Pito was carefully scraping the sharkskin. "Then don't give it to him," he said without looking up.

I thought he was just being petulant, but then he raised his head and I saw the gleam in his eye. I'd seen that gleam several times before.

It meant I was about to be checkmated.

"Make Dalrympl come to you," Pito said. "He must ask for the potion. No, not *ask*. He must *demand* it."

27

THE UNCTION

I ONLY HAD DRIED SUNFLOWERS, so it would be necessary to let the petals soak overnight in sunflower oil along with a handful of dried wasps. In the meantime, I turned my attention to creating the unction.

It was hard not to feel overwhelmed by all that had to be done in less than a week. I had to create a potion that couldn't be tested, an unction so that Dalrympl would demand the potion, and finally, an antidote for the unction. Whenever I became too frazzled, Pito reminded me to focus on just one thing at a time.

He was adept at dissecting the Amazonian spitting spider without damaging any of its internal organs. Eight years earlier, Captain Cuvio had brought me a jar of these spiders preserved in formaldehyde. They'd remained in my root cellar ever since. I was able to resurrect the spider's potent saliva by adding a few drops of urine that I collected from . . . well, from me.

I could have created the unction from a less exotic source, but Dalrympl had his own magician, ridiculous as he was, roaming around the castle with his long silver hair flowing from beneath his cone hat. Still, he should know how to cure a common rash.

"Let's see how he copes with the Amazon spitting spider," I said to Pito.

Though Pito smiled at that and was eager to assist in all that had to be done, he constantly reminded me that he was helping *me*, and not the princess. He never called her *Tullia*. It was always *the princess*, said with a derisive tone.

I tried to tell him that it was Voltharo who had made up the lies about him, not Princess Tullia. "You weren't just his apprentice. You were his replacement."

Pito remained unconvinced. "Then why didn't she speak up? She had plenty of time to tell the truth. How long was I in the dungeon? A month? Why didn't she say I never touched her? I'd never even spoken to her!"

I didn't have an answer.

Using a thin blade and some tweezers, he carefully separated a spider's head from its torso. "Maybe Voltharo did make up the lies," he admitted. "But the princess was happy to go along with it."

I didn't dare tell him the truth. Even if he believed me, which I doubted, it could cause an endless loop of confusion inside his brain. For all I knew, it might turn him into an imbecile.

For the same reason, I couldn't tell Tullia either. It was ironic. She had urged me to use my magic to carry out a bold and daring rescue of Pito, and in the end, that was exactly what I'd done.

And she would never know.

"I never spoke to her," Pito quietly repeated, more to himself than to me. "I don't think I ever even saw her. It's odd, Anatole, but I didn't know there was a princess. I knew about the wedding of the century, of course, but I must have thought . . . I don't know what I thought."

"I remember when I first came to the castle," I said, pretending to understand. "It was overwhelming."

"Maybe . . ."

We returned to our work.

"Soon there will be no more scribes," he said as he dissected another spider. "Voltharo needn't worry about me. Gutenberg will replace all of us."

He went on to say that scribes would become like knights, only useful for pomp and ceremony. I couldn't believe that any more than I could believe that one day magicians would only be used for entertainment.

CONTRARY TO WHAT YOU MAY HAVE BEEN TAUGHT, GUTENBERG did not invent the printing press. Printing presses had been around long before he came up with his innovation. Like a lot of great ideas, that innovation now seems obvious in hindsight, but at the time it changed the world.

Prior to Gutenberg, artisans painstakingly carved raised and backward-facing letters into blocks of wood. One block of wood was used for each page of a book. These carved blocks then would be dipped into ink and pressed against the blank pages. They could produce multiple copies of a book, but a separate block was needed for each page, and it could only be used for that particular book.

Gutenberg's printing press used much smaller blocks, forged from metal. Each block contained just one letter or symbol. The letters could be rearranged to print any page of any book.

What was once an expensive and laborious process became

efficient and affordable. Literature, newspapers, and all kinds of radical new ideas became accessible to the *popolo minuto*.

UNLIKE THE PRINCE'S POTION, THE UNCTION COULD BE TESTED. Pito volunteered, but he was still recovering from the blue rash, and with everything else I'd given him over the past month, he wouldn't make a reliable subject. I would have to test it on myself, but first I had to conjure the antidote.

Still, even if the unction and antidote worked perfectly, it seemed to me that it just added an additional step without bringing us any closer to the ultimate destination. How was I to apply the unction to Dalrympl?

"What am I supposed to do?" I asked in frustration. "Create another potion, so he'll want the unction, so he'll want the antidote, so he'll want the first potion?"

This could go on forever!

"It's too bad, if what you say about the princess is true." Pito offered.

"How do you mean?"

"Well, if she were secretly in love with someone else, then she might be willing to help."

Guilt and regret flooded my heart as I looked at the remarkable young man before me. "Yes, that is too bad," I agreed.

28

THE FESTIVAL

W E WERE STILL WORKING when the curtains rattled. I shouted, "Keep out!" as Pito slid off the chair and onto the floor. "It's not safe here!"

I picked up a smoke packet and prepared to light it.

"I apologize for the intrusion, Master," said Ian, the page. He was standing inside the archway, between the two curtains. He bowed when I looked his way.

I was taken aback. Dittierri's nephew had never shown me such courtesy. I set the smoke packet on the table and walked slowly toward him.

"King Sandro requests that you accompany him to the opening of the festival," he announced. "The royal carriage will leave at noon."

I wondered if Dittierri had set some sort of trap for me, and it took me a moment to realize Ian was waiting for my response.

"I'd be honored," I said.

"The king will be pleased." Ian bowed and left.

"YOU VANQUISHED THE PLAGUE AND SAVED THE KINGDOM," PITO pointed out as I put on my cape. "You're a hero."

It took a moment for Pito's words to sink in. I'd been so worried that my one act of boldness would result in my ruin that it never dawned on me that the opposite might happen.

I forced my feet into my long and pointed shoes. If I was going to ride in the king's carriage, I had to dress appropriately.

"You'll have to wait in the cellar," I said.

He nodded.

COURTIERS AND SERVANTS OFFERED THEIR SMILES AND GREETings as I strode through the castle, then outside to where the royal carriage was waiting. The driver bowed and held the door open for me. It was all very dignified until I was climbing up into the carriage and one of the horses stirred. I fell backward onto the dirt.

I think my pointy shoes were more to blame than the horse.

The driver profusely apologized as he helped me to my feet. He handed me my hat, and then, continuing to apologize, he held on to my arm as I ascended into the carriage.

I must have been late. The kings and queens of both kingdoms were already inside waiting for me. I needed a new clock.

The Oxatanian magician was also inside, his long silver hair flowing beneath his ridiculous cone hat. I supposed that King Lurtzk thought he had to bring him, since he knew I'd been invited.

He was introduced to me as Gthrdr (pronounced something like *goat herder*).

"I'm very glad you two have finally met," said Queen Corinna. "You can learn from each other, and your shared wisdom will benefit both kingdoms."

I held my tongue. The Oxatanian magician was nothing more than a fortune teller with a talent for vagueness.

Everyone agreed it was a glorious day to begin the festival: cool, but not cold, and not a cloud to be seen.

"We can thank Gthrdr for that," said King Lurtzk.

Gthrdr feigned modesty. "I didn't cause the weather," he said. "I merely recognized the omens. I'm sure Anatole would have done the same," he graciously added.

"Anatole can't interpret omens," said Queen Corinna.

"Gthrdr selected the wedding date twelve years ago," King Sandro explained.

Fortunately, it was only a fifteen-minute ride. I don't know how much longer I could have listened to Gthrdr's wisdom. He was trying to teach me how to interpret the "whispering of the wind."

Soldiers on horseback rode alongside the carriage, and when we reached the festival, they helped clear a path through the throngs of people. I heard music coming from one of the pavilions that had been set up for the occasion. The flags of Esquaveta and Oxatania flew from atop the colorful tents.

The crowds must have spooked a horse as I was stepping down from the carriage, but this time, thanks to the coachman, I only lost my hat, not my dignity. My bald head was instantly recognizable to the people gathered around, and a spontaneous cheer rang out.

I noted that there was no cheer for Gthrdr when he stepped down. But then again, he hadn't vanquished the plague and saved both kingdoms.

A small girl picked up my hat and shyly held it out to me. I thanked her with a smile. She beamed, then quickly returned to her mother and hugged her around the waist.

WE WERE ESCORTED TO A RAISED PLATFORM OVERLOOKING THE jousting field. Princess Tullia and Prince Dalrympl were already seated. Dalrympl held half of a roasted deer leg in one hand and a large curved aurochs horn in the other. Between bites of deer meat and swigs of ale, he related the gruesome details of a wrestling match we had missed.

Tullia smiled at her betrothed. "I suppose I should cheer for the Oxatanians now," she said to me.

Dalrympl glared at her for even thinking she had a choice.

Crumhorns blared, and then King Sandro rose and waved to the cheering crowd. In a show of unity, he invited King Lurtzk to stand beside him, and they cheered again.

Unity only went so far, however. Once the matches started, their shouts and curses revealed the animosity that still lingered. Dalrympl yelled as loud as anyone, aiming his most savage insults not at the Esquavetians but at those Oxatanians who'd been defeated.

Fights broke out between the Oxatanians and Esquavetians. I don't think these had much to do with the jousting matches. Oxatanian women had always seemed especially alluring to Esquavetian men. While the Oxatanian women in attendance might have welcomed the attention, not so their male companions.

My own mind drifted to the Oxatanian woman who'd sat next to me at the banquet. I could see her soft brown eyes and blond curls. I wondered what she thought of me now. Surely, she must know that her seemingly innocuous tablemate had courageously saved both kingdoms from the devastation of the plague.

As the jousting matches continued, various foreign delegations came by to pay their respects to King Sandro and to congratulate him on the upcoming union. They all brought wedding gifts for the prince and princess.

We were well aware of the real reason they'd come to the festival. It was to assess the stability of Esquaveta and the strength of our alliance with Oxatania.

Tullia announced that she needed to take a walk and suggested I join her. Two guards accompanied us as we exited the jousting area.

We walked along a relatively deserted space behind a row of tents. The guards kept their distance, one a few steps ahead and the other a few steps behind. My shoes hurt my feet.

"I need your help," Tullia said, her face trembling. "He won't let me sleep!"

"Who?"

"As soon as I close my eyes, I see that hideous face! It's not just the buboes. His eyes are filled with pure hate."

I told her I'd bring her some moon moth tea that evening.

"Why did he hate me so much?"

"He was deranged from the plague," I said.

A roar came from the jousting area. Something very good or very bad had just happened.

"Will he harm the tiger?" Tullia asked.

It took me a moment to piece together what she was asking. "No," I assured her. "Tigers can't contract the plague."

I didn't know whether that was true, but I knew that this particular tiger wouldn't contract it from Pito.

"A girl would know if someone tried to violate her virtue," said Tullia. "Wouldn't she?"

29

WHAT A PRINCESS DOES

THAT EVENING, I PREPARED my special blend for Tullia.

"The poor girl screams as soon as her eyes close," Marta said as she let me inside her chambers.

Marta looked like she hadn't slept either, and I asked her if she wanted me to bring something for her as well.

"When she sleeps, I'll sleep."

I went on through to the princess's inner chamber. Tullia was sitting, not lying, on her bed. I handed her the goblet.

She thanked me and even managed a smile. "Did you know that the king calls you Esquaveta's Leonardo?" she asked, and took a sip.

"He's so hideous," she whispered.

"Don't worry about him. He's gone."

She gave me a questioning look. "Oh, him. I know that. He's merely a phantom. I meant . . ." She shrugged, and wistfully added, "I suppose I'll never experience true love."

She lay back on the bed. "It's my duty," she said.

I was confused. "Did you mean *Prince Dalrympl* is hideous?"

She murmured something I couldn't make out.

"But I've watched the two of you together," I said. "The way you smile and touch his hand. You seem enchanted by him."

"Oh, Natto," she said as she closed her eyes. "Sometimes I think you forget. I'm a princess. That's what a princess does."

BY THE WAY, WHEN THE PRINCESS SAID THE KING CALLED ME Esquaveta's Leonardo, he was referring to Leonardo da Vinci. Just thought I ought to point that out in case it slipped past you.

30

AN ANCIENT
GREEK RITUAL

TWO DAYS LATER, PITO'S welts had all but faded, while I had a series of small red blotches running down my left arm. I had yet to try the antidote. Once I did, I could no longer test the unction.

Any time I was tempted to use it, Pito tried to remind me that the itch didn't exist anywhere except inside my mind. Easy for him to say.

Now that his blue rash was gone, I could possibly test the unction on him, but it would be impossible for us to compare the strength of the itches he felt to those previously experienced by me.

The antidote was also derived from the Amazonian spitting spider. The hair of the dog that bit you, so to speak. For the antidote I used the spider's sucking stomach, whereas for the unction I was using its lungs and venom glands.

Outside there was a torrent of rain and wind. The door was kept shut, making it smokier and smellier inside the workshop.

Pito was actually glad for the dismal weather. It meant he could step outside without fear of being seen. He seemed to like the feel of the rain pouring down on him.

This was the third day of the festival, and I wondered what everyone thought of Gthrdr's omens now. The Oxatanian magician had probably spouted some gibberish about how stormy weather portended a productive marriage.

The biggest challenge I faced with the unction wasn't so much the creation of a powerful enough itch but delaying the onset of that itch so that Dalrympl wouldn't associate it with what caused it. The graph I drew in my logbook reflected an inverse proportionality between the length of the delay and the strength of the itch. The stronger the itch, the shorter the delay. This was the opposite of what I was after.

"What does this squiggly line mean?" Pito asked, looking over my shoulder.

I shut the book.

WE'D COME UP WITH A WAY TO GIVE THE UNCTION TO DALRYMPL. Actually, it was Pito's idea. Inspiration had struck in the night, not in the alcove, but in the root cellar.

"It's an ancient Greek custom," Pito told me in the morning. "Used to confirm mutual trust and cooperation."

He demonstrated. He had me stand and face him, about two steps away. Then he extended a hand in my direction and had me do the same.

"They called it a *handshake*," he said, then clasped my hand in his.

He admitted the texts weren't clear on exactly how it was to be executed, so we tried several different ways, altering both its duration and the degree of arm movement. We agreed it should be dignified, while also leaving each of the participants slightly vulnerable. That was part of the trust.

In the end we settled on a firm grip, and . . . Well, a detailed description is hardly necessary. You already know the proper method for shaking hands. But it could very well be that the modern handshake as you know it was performed for the first time that morning in my workshop.

"BUT WHY WOULD DALRYMPL AGREE TO SHAKE MY HAND?" I HAD asked Pito when he first mentioned the idea.

"Not yours," said Pito. "The princess's."

I had told him what Tullia had said to me when I brought her the moon moth tea.

Pito explained that the ancient Greeks had also used the handshake ritual as a way to seal a contract.

"A marriage contract?" I asked.

He smiled.

In Esquaveta there were two requirements for a marriage to be legal and binding. First, each party had to voluntarily consent to it, before witnesses. And second, it had to be consummated. (That part needn't be witnessed.)

On the day before the ceremony, Tullia and Dalrympl were to appear before a magistrate and publicly state their consent. No doubt there would be documents to sign as well, as their marriage was much more than the usual union between two people. It was an alliance between two kingdoms.

"And then she'll shake his hand," said Pito. "Unless she decides to betray you."

"Why would she do that?" I asked.

"Oh, Natto," he replied mockingly. "Sometimes I think you forget. She's a princess. That's what a princess does."

31

CARTILAGE

THREE DAYS BEFORE THE wedding, two days before Tullia and Dalrympl were set to appear before the magistrate, both my arms were covered with blotches. I'd yet to succumb to the antidote.

The door was open, and fresh air drifted into the workshop. Pito was pounding on cartilage. After the intricate work of dissecting spiders, he seemed to enjoy pulverizing it with a heavy mallet.

I'd determined that cartilage effectively delayed the onset of the itch. It was like the wall surrounding the castle. Cartilage acted as a protective barrier that first had to be demolished before the invading hordes could enter.

The challenge was to find the right kind of cartilage. Snail cartilage dissolved too quickly. The shark fin I'd tested the day before had yet to be penetrated.

That was when I was still testing one dab at a time. I no longer had that luxury. Both of my legs were dabbed with several different variants of the unction, each using a different type of cartilage. On one leg was octopus, pig snout, and swan's neck. On the other was rat snake, eel, and oxtail.

The rat snake I'd kept preserved in a jar. I was able to obtain everything else from the castle's kitchen.

I would have applied even more, but the dabs needed to be spaced far enough apart so I'd recognize from where the itch was emanating. That wasn't as easy as you might think. Itches had a tendency to move. Pito said that was because the itch didn't exist anywhere on my skin but solely in my mind.

Even *knowing* the dabs were there made me feel itchy. We played chess to take my mind off it.

I was commenting on the oddity of a mind trying to distract itself when the curtains rattled. Pito dropped to his knees behind the crates.

"May I enter?"

It was a voice I should have recognized immediately, but it was so out of the ordinary for Dittierri to come to my workshop that it took me a moment. The fact that he had, and had then asked for permission to enter, was a testament to my new court status.

He didn't actually wait for my permission, however. The regent was through both curtains before I reached the archway. It might well have been his first time inside my workshop.

He looked around disdainfully. "How can you tolerate the smell?"

I explained it was the tallow candles, and told him I'd prefer ones made from olive oil.

"I'll see what I can do," he said.

"Unscented," I specified.

He didn't acknowledge my additional qualification but walked to the pile of black sand. "Still sand, I see."

I moved in front of him to try to prevent him from getting any closer to Pito. "The potion took precedence over the sand," I reminded him.

"Oh yes, the great memory potion."

"I was surprised I didn't see you at the festival the other day," I said. "When I accompanied King Sandro."

He glared, then said, "Someone had to stay behind to manage the affairs of the kingdom."

He walked farther into my workshop, trying not to be too obvious about his search, while I tried not to be too obvious about getting in his way.

"So what's all this?" he asked.

He was looking at the dissected spider parts and mashed cartilage.

I moved between him and the chess table. "I'm working on a potion for the princess," I said. "To ensure a male heir."

"Well, you have a fifty percent chance of success, don't you?" he asked. "And if it doesn't work the first time, you'll just make some of your *modifications*. Sooner or later, she'll give birth to a son, and once again everyone will celebrate the magnificent Anatole!"

I would have come up with a clever retort, but at that moment the swan neck cartilage disintegrated. The wall was breached, and the invading hordes rushed in.

The itch was overwhelming. I could concentrate on nothing else. I scratched, but the more I scratched, the worse the itch.

"Fleas?" Dittierri asked, then took the opportunity to move around me and over to the chessboard.

"Did you have a visitor?"

"Princess Tullia," I said, still scratching my calf as I went after him. "I needed a urine sample for the potion, and while she was here . . ."

I glanced behind the crates and was relieved to see that Pito was no longer there.

"Where's his head?" Dittierri asked.

"What?"

"I walked all along the moat," he said. "Made the full circle. I saw his shredded clothes, some bones . . . but no head."

"The tiger must have devoured it," I suggested.

"The entire skull?"

I didn't know the strength of a tiger's jaw, but then again, I doubted he did either. I scratched some more. "Maybe if you went down into the moat, you'd be able to find some skull fragments."

"I have no desire to become acquainted with the tiger," he said. "But one day, you may get that opportunity."

I was still scratching as he left the workshop.

For the record, I never did receive a supply of olive oil candles.

32

THE INVADING HORDES

I WORRIED WHERE PITO MIGHT have gone, and in my search I momentarily forgot about the itch, but as soon as I found him, the itch returned.

He was outside, crouched behind the iron stove.

"I need the antidote!" I told him, and hurried back into the workshop.

"No!" he shouted, coming after me. "You can't yet!"

The antidote was in a jar on a shelf. He grabbed my arm as I reached for it.

"Try doing some push-ups," he urged.

"I can't do push-ups!" I shouted.

Pito might have been stronger than me, but the itch was stronger than both of us. I jerked my arm free and grabbed the jar.

"Scratch something else," Pito said. "Scratch the table."

It seemed ridiculous, but I set the jar on the table and scratched the surface.

It worked! Evidently the itch only demanded that I scratch *something*, anything!

But my relief was short-lived. The itch must have realized it wasn't being scratched and started complaining again. I tried scratching my shoe, which at least was close to my calf, and that seemed to fool the itch, at least temporarily.

But it was then that the rat snake cartilage gave way, and the eel shortly after that. It was too much. I dumped handfuls of sand down my leggings, then rubbed furiously while hopping from one foot to the other. Pito was laughing too hard to offer any advice.

More walls came tumbling down, including the shark fin from the day before. I was being consumed by the itch. I drank the antidote straight from the jar.

"I'm sorry," I said later. The itch had disappeared in less than ten minutes.

"I understand," said Pito.

My experiments were over.

"At least we know the antidote works," I pointed out.

WHILE PITO CLEANED UP THE MESS, I WENT INTO MY ALCOVE TO examine my skin. There were so many red marks on my otherwise white legs, it was difficult to distinguish the blotches from the scratches.

But I noticed one area where there were no scratch marks. It seemed that the oxtail cartilage had yet to be breached. With my leggings still dangling around one ankle, I stepped out of the alcove to show Pito.

I didn't see him, but I did see that he'd cleaned up more than just the mashed cartilage I'd knocked off the table. He'd swept most of the floor, and finally removed the pigeon-egg-encrusted sand.

"I felt like a fool!" exclaimed Tullia, pushing through the curtains.

She stopped when she saw me, and laughed. First she covered her mouth with her hand, and then she covered her eyes.

I shuffled back into the alcove and readjusted my leggings.

"Warn me the next time you plan to use me as part of some deception," Tullia said from just outside the alcove. "Chess game? Urine sample? Pregnancy potion? I had no idea what he was talking about!"

I made sure I was properly put back together and came out of the alcove. She was studying the chessboard.

"So, is this the game you and I are supposed to be playing?"

I shrugged a shoulder.

"Am I white or black?"

It was the game Pito and I had started. I'd had the white pieces.

"Black," I said.

She scowled at the board. "It doesn't look good for me, does it?"

Her comment surprised me, but when I looked over the board, I realized her assessment was correct. Somehow, I had achieved the superior position.

"Unless . . ." Tullia started.

She slid the black castle across the board and removed the pawn catty-corner from my king.

"You're sacrificing a castle for a pawn?" I asked.

She smiled.

As things would turn out, it wouldn't be the last time she'd make such a sacrifice.

"So, who are you really playing against?" she asked, and then her blue eye twinkled. "It's that pretty Oxatanian from the banquet, isn't it? I saw how she kept looking at you!"

She looked around the workshop. "It's cleaner, isn't it?" She gasped. "Is she still here? Is that why your leggings . . ."

She rushed into the alcove. When she came out, she was clearly disappointed. She walked over to the clay pot. It contained the prince's potion, but I had yet to attach it to the wires or set up the candles.

"Is this my fertility potion?"

"Not fertility," I said. "To ensure a male heir."

She made a face.

"But it isn't that either," I told her.

She looked at me curiously.

"What would you think if I told you it would postpone the wedding?"

"For how long?"

"Indefinitely."

She smiled.

I TOLD HER ABOUT THE HANDSHAKE, WHICH CONFUSED HER AT first because she thought "shaky hands" meant that the potion would cause Dalrympl to suffer an epileptic fit. I explained that it was an ancient Greek ritual used to express mutual trust and cooperation. But when I tried to demonstrate how it was done, she couldn't take me seriously. She'd laugh and try to swing our clasped hands down almost to our knees, and then way up above our heads.

"Keep it solemn and dignified," I told her. "Just a quick up-and-down."

"Like intercourse," she said, and then laughed again, not only at her joke but at my reaction to it.

Not just my face but my entire head must have turned red.

33

THE MAGISTRATE'S OFFICE

S HE TRADED A CASTLE for a pawn!" Pito protested, when he saw the chessboard.

"You can take it back," I offered. It was easy for me to be magnanimous as, for once, I was winning.

He studied the board a little longer. "No, I'll keep it." And then he snidely added, "Who am I to contradict *the princess*?"

I was checkmated six moves later.

BY THE NEXT AFTERNOON EVERYTHING WAS READY, OR, AT LEAST, as ready as it could be. I'd decided on oxtail cartilage for the unction. It held out longer than the others, although I had no way of knowing *how much longer*.

I attached the clay pot to the wires, being very careful not to drop it.

"Can I light the candles?" Pito asked.

I let him have the honor. Then he retired to the cellar, and I lay in my alcove, staring at the clock. While I didn't drop the pot that evening, I almost did the following morning. Tullia surprised me as I was taking it down. Once again, she'd slipped noiselessly into my workshop.

"You told me to come early!" she reminded me.

I'd also told her to bring a right-handed glove, which she was holding out to me. It looked like the one she'd worn to the banquet. The long white silk had extended past her elbow. I had to roll up its long sleeve so it wouldn't get in the way.

Tullia held her nose as she watched me fill the glove with the unction. "It looks like diarrhea."

I would have described it as more like vomit, but holding her nose was hardly necessary. The odor was very faint, even to me, and not unpleasant. I squished it into each of the fingers.

"I'm supposed to wear it?"

"Not until just before you enter the magistrate's office," I instructed. "And then, once you've given your consent, and signed whatever documents need to be signed, remove the glove and shake the prince's hand."

Tullia laughed.

"But first you need to drink this."

I filled a goblet with the antidote and gave it to her.

She took a small sip and recoiled. The antidote did have an unpleasant odor. "What's in it?"

"Just some spider stomachs with a few drops of urine."

She glared at me, then drank it all down.

"Remember, Dalrympl won't know anything about a handshake. Somehow you'll have to explain the procedure to him, and also persuade him to do it."

"I'm a princess," she replied. "I know how to get my way."

Just before she left the workshop, I reminded her not to laugh.

I was adding what remained of the antidote to the clay pot when she returned. This time she purposely jangled the curtains to warn me.

"What is it?"

She stepped close, looking me in the eye. Solemn and dignified, she said, "Mutual trust and cooperation."

We shook hands.

I WAITED IN CASE SHE CAME BACK AGAIN, THEN LET PITO UP from the cellar. I felt too anxious to touch my breakfast, and I think Pito might have felt a little nervous too, even though he cared little for *the princess*.

It felt strange after a very hectic week to have nothing left to do. I paced the workshop.

"The arrow has left your bow, Anatole," Pito said to me.

He told me something one of his ancient philosophers had said. The philosopher had described an expert archer who practiced almost unceasingly. He knew how to account for the wind and the movement of his intended target. He took careful aim and judged just how much to pull back on his bowstring.

"But once the arrow leaves his bow," Pito said, "there's no more he can do. The rest is up to the arrow."

Pito passed the time by cleaning up the workshop. I tried telling him that it didn't need cleaning, and that I liked everything just how it was, but he wouldn't listen.

"Where are you putting that?" I'd ask. "I need to know where everything is."

His answers were curt. "Someplace safe" or "Out of the way."

I did notice that the workshop smelled fresher. I suppose it wasn't just the tallow candles that had caused the foul odor.

I speculated that the Oxatanian contingent would leave the castle once the wedding was postponed. Then, once everything returned to normal, Pito should be able to hide himself among the multitude of workers who came and went every day.

"I could put together a suitable disguise for you," I told him.

He nodded and thanked me, but as much as he wanted to get on with his life, I think he also felt some degree of sadness. I know I did. We were both aware that once he left, we'd never see each other again. It would be too dangerous.

We set up the chessboard for what very well could be our last game.

"What time is she due at the magistrate's?" Pito asked me.

"One o'clock."

That meant Tullia wouldn't be able to shake his hand until one thirty, at the earliest. I worried the unction could become too dry and powdery by then.

I couldn't concentrate on the chess game but merely moved my pieces around without a lot of thought.

And suppose Dalrympl does come to me, I worried, *and asks me to relieve his itch. Then what?* It would seem odd to have the antidote already prepared.

I would need to do a bit of acting. Was I capable?

"Maybe I'll use leeches," I said aloud.

Pito stared, wide-eyed.

"Just to give it more credibility," I explained.

But Pito's look had nothing to do with me.

"That glove!" exclaimed Tullia.

I stood up as she came toward us, to try to obstruct her view of Pito, but if he'd seen her, then she probably saw him. My best hope was that she wouldn't recognize him without the blue welts.

"It felt like I was sticking my fingers into somebody's chamber pot!" she said, then stopped and stared at him.

Pito met her gaze without flinching.

She turned to me, confused. "I thought he was dead."

"Disappointed, *Princess*?" asked Pito.

Her blue eye flashed at him. "I'm neither disappointed nor pleased. Why should I care one way or the other?"

She was disappointed . . . in me. "What happened to mutual trust and cooperation?" she demanded.

Before I could come up with an answer, she walked away, toward the mouse cages.

"Did you know about this too, Luigi? I didn't think so. You would never have betrayed me!"

"I thought you weren't due at the magistrate's office until one o'clock."

"That's your excuse!" Tullia said. "You're not sorry about your lies. Just that your deception was discovered!"

"Pito didn't deserve to be executed," I said. "And besides, if it weren't for him, I never would have learned of the handshake. Pito read about it in an ancient Greek poem."

She walked back toward us and scowled at Pito. "Guess what? Dalrympl doesn't read ancient Greek poetry." Then she turned her anger on me. "Ten o'clock, Anatole, not one! Why do you think I came to your workshop so early?"

"Did he shake your hand?" I asked.

"No. I just stood there, holding it out for him to shake, while he stared at me as if I were deranged!"

She held it out for me now, demonstrating. "The poor prince knew I wanted something, he just didn't know what he was supposed to do."

I knew better than to mention that I'd forewarned her about this. *I'm a princess*, she had answered. *I know how to get my way.*

"It didn't help that Dittierri and Voltharo were as confused as he was," she added, still holding out her hand.

"They were there?" I asked.

"And the Oxatanian ambassador," said Tullia. "It had to be witnessed, after all, and recorded for posterity. It's the wedding of the century, in case you forgot."

"So, what happened?" Pito asked.

She gave him a disdainful glance, then turned back to me. "Mind you, I have no illusions, Anatole. Once I'm his wife, he won't care what I want. But for the time being, he thinks he has to please me."

Tullia's arm remained extended before me. "I stood there, staring at him," she said, "until at last he dropped to one knee and kissed my hand. It was all he could think to do."

"So maybe some got on his lips," Pito offered.

Tullia ignored him. "And then I gently ran my fingers down the side of his face." Her blue eye twinkled as she demonstrated this *loving* gesture.

34

LEECHES

I N THE SIXTEENTH CENTURY, any physician worth his salt kept a
ready supply of leeches. We used them to extract bad blood until only good remained. Before you start feeling smugly superior,
allow me to point out that leeches are still used in modern twenty-
first-century hospitals to prevent blood clots in some patients after
surgery.

Mine were kept in a large earthenware jar amid a layer of mud
and moss. I'd periodically add more moss and enough water to keep
the mud damp. A loosely knitted piece of fabric, which allowed
airflow, was tied over the top of the jar.

Pito brought it up from the cellar to me. I set the jar of leeches
in one cabinet and placed the clay pot in another.

"Anything else?" he asked.

My look said it all.

"Now?" he asked.

Considering that the unction was applied sometime around
ten thirty, I hoped I wouldn't see the prince until at least six, so he

wouldn't connect his rash with Tullia's fond caress. But there was really no way of knowing how long it would take for the oxtail cartilage to give way.

Pito sighed, then returned to the cellar. I watched him pull the hatch shut as he descended the ladder.

SIX O'CLOCK CAME AND WENT. I WAS TEMPTED TO WANDER THE castle to see if I could find out anything, but I didn't want to arouse suspicion. Whatever the prince was feeling, or doing about it, was out of my control.

The arrow had left my bow.

OUT OF MY CONTROL OR NOT, BY EIGHT O'CLOCK, WHEN HE STILL hadn't appeared, I was overcome with doubts and worry. Perhaps Tullia's gentle touch had been too gentle. I also had to admit to the possibility that in my frenzied haste to create the prince's potion, the unction, and the antidote, some of the antidote might have accidentally gotten mixed with the unction.

I watched as the clock in my alcove ticked past nine . . . nine thirty . . . ten . . . It was close to midnight when I finally lay down on my mattress. Still fully dressed, I pulled the blanket over me, closed my eyes, and listened as the promise I made to Tullia ticked further and further away.

A KICK IN THE RIBS AWAKENED ME. HARWELL MIGHT HAVE ONLY intended to nudge me with his foot, but when he kicks, you feel it.

Someone else was holding a candle, and it took a moment for my eyes to adjust and see who it was. "We need you, Anatole," said none other than King Sandro. "We have an emergency."

I was very much alert but feigned grogginess. "Is it the prin-cess?" I asked.

"Do I look like a princess?" barked Dalrympl from the darkness.

I could hear other voices coming from the workshop. There was more light coming from there as well.

I stood. The king didn't comment on the fact that I had gone to bed fully dressed down to my shoes. Perhaps he assumed it was just another of his great magician's odd quirks.

MORE THAN A DOZEN OXATANIANS AWAITED ME IN THE WORK-shop, most of them holding candles. I'd seen a number of them before, but Gthrdr was the only one I knew by name.

I could see now that Dalrympl was wearing mittens, and his arms were tied to his sides. Presumably, this had been done to keep him from tearing off his face.

I might have shredded my own skin if it hadn't been for the antidote. But I was in no hurry to give it to Dalrympl.

I took Gthrdr's candle from him and made a show of closely examining Dalrympl's bloody, bumpy red face and his swollen lips.

"Do something!" he demanded, spraying me with spit.

I calmly asked if he'd recently eaten anything unusual.

He angrily cursed his "useless" food taster, splattering me with more spit.

"Isn't there a potion you can give him?" asked King Sandro.

"Possibly," I said with hesitation, "but I have no understanding of the prince's physiology. It's better for his own magician to treat him."

"Gthrdr is an imbecile!" exclaimed Dalrympl.

I suppressed the urge to smile.

I admitted I did have a very powerful anti-itch potion, but that "without more knowledge of the prince's physiology, I can't guarantee there won't be unintended consequences." I suggested that the prince leave a urine sample, and in a day or two, I'd be able to prepare a potion specifically for him.

"Try not to think about it," I said to Dalrympl. "Remember, the itch exists only in your mind."

An explosion of words came from his mouth. I couldn't pick out any one particular word, but the overall meaning was clear.

"The wedding is in less than twelve hours," said King Sandro. "We don't have time for urine samples. Give him the anti-itch potion, as is."

"It may not be safe," I protested.

"Your objections are duly noted," said King Sandro. "No one will hold you responsible for any unforeseen consequences."

"I demand it!" barked Dalrympl.

I MADE A SHOW OF SEARCHING MY CABINETS AWHILE BEFORE finding the clay pot. Then I hung it over some candles and said it would be ready in fifteen minutes.

As if that was all it took to conjure up a potion!

While we waited, I had Dalrympl lie on the floor, explaining that I needed to remove his bad blood. With his arms tied to his sides, it took two of his aides to help get him in position.

I got the jar of leeches out of a cabinet and set it down beside him. One by one, I plucked the bloodsuckers from the mud and carefully placed them on Dalrympl's face, including one on each of his lips.

For the next fifteen minutes, I had the pleasure of listening to his whimpers.

———————

THE LEECHES HAD BEEN ABOUT THE SIZE OF MY LITTLE FINGER when I first removed them from the jar. They were about three times that size fifteen minutes later, when I put them back.

I unhooked the pot and poured it into a goblet.

Dalrympl was sitting up, his hands still tied by his sides. I held the goblet to his mouth and let him drink.

It didn't take long for the antidote to work. Dalrympl's ropes were removed. He threw the mittens at Gthrdr.

"I won't forget this," he said to me, though it was difficult to discern from his tone whether this was an expression of gratitude or a threat.

The unction had been necessary to create the itch. The antidote had been mixed with the potion.

The leeches had nothing to do with any of that. They were for Babette.

35

THE WEDDING OF
THE CENTURY

I SQUEEZED INTO MY POINTED shoes. My feet still hurt from the last time I'd worn them.

Once again, I'd been invited to ride in the royal carriage, although I expected that the wedding would be postponed before it ever left the castle. Even as I walked the castle corridors, wincing with every step, I doubted the carriage would be waiting for me.

Yet there it was.

The coachman greeted me with a bow and set down a stool for me to use. The king and queen were already inside the carriage; I lowered my head to each of them before sitting. The Oxatanians had taken their own carriage.

"Thank you, Anatole," said Queen Corinna. "Prince Dalrympl is most grateful, and so are we."

I thanked her for her kind words. They were the only kind words she'd spoken to me since I treated her for the sable scratch.

"I'm pleased the prince is feeling better," I said. I considered adding something about unforeseen consequences, but I didn't want to overplay it. I'd made the point in the night. My reluctance to give Dalrympl the potion was duly noted.

"He should have gone to you immediately," said the king, "instead of relying on his magician."

"The Oxatanian magician does seem to be incompetent," the queen agreed.

Well, not everyone is a Leonardo.

I thought it but I didn't say it.

We set out for the cathedral, but I still believed there would be no wedding ceremony. Word of its cancellation simply hadn't reached us yet. I expected we'd hear about it when we reached the cathedral, or, more likely, we'd be intercepted by a messenger before we made it that far.

NO MESSENGER CAME. TENS OF THOUSANDS OF PEOPLE HAD ATtended the weeklong festival, and by the look of things, every one of them had come to the cathedral. The soldiers who had ridden alongside our carriage cleared a path for us.

The people cheered as first King Sandro and then Queen Corinna stepped down from the carriage. The Esquavetians sang "Esquaveta Eternal." Not to be outdone, the Oxatanians broke into a song of their own.

The coachman set out a stool for me, which he hadn't done for either the king or the queen, then held my arm as I descended. It was somewhat embarrassing. Just because I fell *one time*!

By the time I was on solid ground, soldiers had already escorted the king and queen up the stone stairs of the cathedral. Meanwhile, the singing had devolved into a shouting match between the Esquavetians and the Oxatanians.

My shoes were too long for the stairs. I had to turn my feet sideways as I ascended the fourteen steps.

I HAD HOPED IT WOULD BE MORE PEACEFUL INSIDE THE CATHE-dral, but when I finally made it through the bronze doors, I found it just as raucous inside the cathedral as out. In fact, the reason there had been such a large crowd outside was that there was no more room within. I lost sight of the king and queen and feared I might be trapped in the back, shoulder to shoulder with the *popolo minuto*. Fortunately, one of the soldiers came back for me.

The pews only took up about the front third of the nave. My escort had to draw his sword in order to get the people to clear the aisle for us. I told him I was supposed to sit beside the king, but it was noisy and he must not have heard me. He stopped seven rows back and pointed out a place in the middle of the pew.

It was a row of mostly Oxatanians, and I heard grumbles as I maneuvered past them to the somewhat empty place in the pew. The two gentlemen on either side had to press against their neighbors to make room for me.

I escaped the tightness of my surroundings by gazing up at the high ceiling and the array of arches and columns supporting it. Despite being constructed of more than ten tons of stone, the ceiling seemed to be floating on air.

It had been a long time since I'd been inside the cathedral. When my grandmother was still alive, her magic was celebrated by the Church as a gift from God. But the current pope had deemed that all magic was satanic, and the bishop accused me of having made a secret pact with the devil.

I never thought much of church services anyway. This may

seem strange, coming from me, but even as a child I thought they were little more than ritualistic hocus-pocus.

I noticed the blond Oxatanian woman from the banquet in the row in front of me, just three seats over. Perhaps all of Tullia's talk about her being my *secret lover* had gone to my head. *I saw how she kept looking at you!*

Maybe she had given me a certain *look*. Perhaps I was too worried about Pito to notice. I reached across the people sitting next to me and tapped her on the shoulder.

She turned.

I nodded and smiled.

She immediately turned back around, but that might have been because the bishop had entered and was approaching the altar. He was followed by the prince and princess.

Shouts and whistles came from the rear of the cathedral.

"You are in God's house," the bishop said, quieting them.

While he had spoken sternly, the bishop hadn't shouted. It wasn't necessary. The thirteenth-century architect who designed the cathedral understood the many complexities of acoustics.

The prince wore a gold suit, and Tullia was in white. Her face was veiled, but I had the impression that her eyes were scanning the pews, searching for me.

I had promised her the wedding would be postponed, *indefinitely*. My arrow had missed its target.

Maybe I'd been too sure of myself. The greatest magician in all the land! Esquaveta's own Leonardo! *I'm a genius. I don't need to test the potion!*

The bishop gestured for the prince and princess to turn toward him, and then the service started.

In Latin.

I don't know if anyone around me understood it, but I didn't. As the bishop droned on, I slipped off my shoes. The man on my right gave me a disdainful glance.

The droning was interrupted only by the occasional waving of incense. After a while, the man who had glanced disdainfully at me had fallen asleep and was leaning against my shoulder.

A sudden silence seemed to startle everyone inside the cathedral. The bishop had stopped talking. My neighbor awoke. Sitting up straight, he gave me another disdainful glance as if his sleeping had been my fault.

The bishop placed his hands over Tullia's bowed head and blessed her. Then he recited the wedding vows for her to repeat.

I could see Tullia's head bob, but I couldn't hear her.

"Speak loudly," the bishop encouraged her, and then took hold of her shoulders and gently turned her around to face the congregation. "Let the words of your heart, and of your soul, be heard across two kingdoms!"

Tullia, head held high, boldly declared her eternal love for Prince Dalrympl, as well as her subservience to him.

That's what a princess does.

Dalrympl wasn't required to swear his subservience to Tullia, but rather to protect and guide her.

The prince stood tall as he faced us in his dazzling gold uniform. He repeated the vows loud and clear.

Everyone laughed.

The laughter came from those standing at the back, and from those of us in the pews. Even the bishop had laughed.

Prince Dalrympl's bold declaration had sounded as if it had

come from a five-year-old girl. It wasn't just the high-pitched tone. There was also the childlike breathless excitement in his voice.

"It seems our groom is a bit nervous," the bishop said, trying to make light of the situation.

"I do not get nervous!" Dalrympl shouted, his voice so shrill it squeaked.

The laughter that followed was even louder.

"Is he a man or a girl?" someone shouted from way in the back. Others shouted questions regarding the prince's anatomy.

You might think that Dalrympl would have stopped talking, but instead he only shouted louder, as if he was trying to out-shout whatever demon was living inside him.

The incongruity of his rage and the infantile voice only added to the merriment.

"I'm a man!" he shrieked.

Someone asked if the prince had what it took to consummate the marriage.

The Esquavetians laughed at that, but not the Oxatanians, at least not the Oxatanian men.

The prince, in a way, was representing all Oxatanian manhood.

A fight broke out in the rear of the cathedral. At first there were probably just two or three people involved, but with everyone packed so close together, it spread like fire. And like fire, the fight increased in intensity as it spread.

I found myself trapped in the pews as the fighting made its way down to the front. I saw people being dragged into the aisles and beaten. A soldier's sword was taken from him and used to slash his throat.

Some were climbing over the pews trying to escape, only to be met by others coming the other way armed with crude weapons. The man who had been seated next to me was clubbed on the head.

It seemed my best chance to escape was by way of the altar. I was climbing over the pews toward it when I felt a shove from behind. I fell over a pew and onto the floor. When I tried to rise, something cracked against my skull. I saw a jagged web of light as everything else turned black.

WHEN I REGAINED CONSCIOUSNESS, EVERYTHING WAS QUIET AND still. I didn't know how long I'd been out. I lifted my head and banged it against the bottom of a pew.

As I wriggled out from under it, I felt a sharp pain in the side of my chest. I must have been kicked in the ribs. If that was how I ended up beneath the pew, then the kick probably had saved my life.

Pulling myself up, I could see dead bodies in the pews and aisles. Among them was the pretty blond Oxatanian who had sat next to me at the banquet.

I staggered out of the cathedral, bouncing from one stone column to the next as I made my way toward the door. I didn't notice I wasn't wearing shoes until I was almost outside.

Halfway down the stone stairs, my feet slipped out from under me, and I rolled the rest of the way down. I lay there a moment as I tried to muster the strength to continue.

"Are you Oxatanian or Esquavetian?" a voice demanded.

I sat up. A group of five men were standing over me. Their clothes were soaked in sweat and blood. Each held a makeshift weapon.

I didn't know if they were Esquavetian or Oxatanian. I could see smoke rising from what remained of the pavilions.

I dug deep within, then stood to face them. "Do you not know who I am?" I demanded.

A couple of the men chuckled, but I saw one take a step back. He'd recognized my bald head.

"I am Anatole, the magician!" I boldly asserted. "I serve both kingdoms. Stand aside, or I will cast a spell that will make your eyes run dry!"

Even as the words left my mouth, I realized my threat had made no sense.

They stared at me, confused.

What I'd been trying to say was that I would cast a spell that would cause them so much misery, they'd run out of tears. Since I don't actually cast spells, it was the best I could come up with at the time.

As they stared at me, I thought of what I should have said instead. *Your genitals will shrivel.* Or *Your bowels will come out of your mouth!* But it was too late. I was stuck with dry eyes.

But then I realized that the enigmatic nature of my threat actually added to its credibility. I tried to imagine what they were imagining. *Eyes so dry they became like lumps of coal, crumbling into tears of black sand.*

A man holding what looked like a piece of a table leg took a step back. The man next to him, holding a length of chain, also backed away.

The others held their ground, but they made no movement as I indignantly strode past them.

IT WAS A LONG AND PAIN-FILLED WALK. AS THE SKY DARKENED, the air became frigid. I discarded my damp and ragged stockings.

All the while, I focused on the cup of hot tea I would enjoy when I made it back to the castle.

I eventually reached a village, the same village where I now sit, sipping my cappuccino. Dead bodies lay across these cobblestone streets, and every structure was burning.

If only Dalrympl hadn't gone first to his own useless magician instead of coming directly to me, the greatest magician in all the land, then none of this would have happened. I would have given him the potion sooner, and he would have become aware of the change in his voice *before* the ceremony, and not *during*.

The wedding would have been postponed until his voice returned to normal. In the meantime, the Oxatanians would have been obliged to honor the alliance.

But Dalrympl's voice would never return to normal. The potion was permanent. The postponement would continue indefinitely.

For the record, I never intended to ignite a war.

PART TWO

UNINTENDED CONSEQUENCES

36

ON LANGUAGE AND SPELLING

ESPITE HOW YOU MAY have seen it written elsewhere, Dalrympl is spelled correctly. History books often use an *i* instead of the *y*, and put a silent *e* at the end. Such a spelling not only is inaccurate but misrepresents Oxatanian culture.

Oxatanians were known for their severe austerity. They considered vowels to be frills, which they only used sparingly. A silent *e* would have been an abomination to them.

Pito once told me that in many of the ancient texts, vowels were never used. The making of parchment was too arduous and costly for these unnecessary letters. He also said there were no spaces between words.

THROUGHOUT THIS ACCOUNT, I'VE USED QUOTATIONS AS IF THE words inside were the actual words spoken. Of course, that couldn't have been the case. We spoke Esquavetian. Some linguists recognize it as a separate language, but most consider it to be a dialect of sixteenth-century Italian.

For members of the court, knowing English was essential, along with French and the various other Italian dialects. The English I knew would sound foreign to English speakers today. If you have doubts about that, I suggest you try reading *Utopia*, the book Pito and Tullia read together in the library, in Thomas More's original English.

Having lived mostly in the United States and Canada for the past three hundred years, I've become very comfortable with modern English. So much so that when I recall the events of 1523, a part of me hears Esquavetian, while another part hears twenty-first-century English.

I'M ALSO COMFORTABLE WITH METERS OR MILES, BUT I'VE MOSTLY avoided units of measurement because in sixteenth-century Esquaveta nothing was standardized. We sometimes spoke in terms of braccios. A braccio was the length of one's arm from the elbow to the wrist, but everybody's arm is different, and there was also the question of *where* on the wrist and *what part* of the elbow. Unlike in Esquaveta, Oxatanian weights and measures were standardized throughout that kingdom. The time of day, too, was the same in every Oxatanian town and village. This may have been the primary reason for its more efficient economy.

I'VE REFRAINED FROM THE USE OF COLLOQUIALISMS, NOT BEcause we didn't have slang but because to translate it word for word would make no sense to you. And if I substituted a more modern expression, it would come across as anachronistic. Also, while I'm comfortable with English, I have trouble keeping up with slang. I always seem to be about thirty years behind the times.

I've avoided profanity for similar reasons. It wasn't that people didn't use vulgar language in the sixteenth century. Indeed, present-day curse words sound childish and insipid in comparison.

Similar to today, much of it concerned fornication, the sexual organs, and human waste. There were also descriptions of pubic hair, with outlandish exaggerations regarding its length and what was living within it.

Today, people toss about offensive words so frequently, they've lost much of their meaning. Back then, they were used less but with more specificity. Just one small detail could greatly accentuate a vulgarity. It was an art form. Women and men, peasants and courtiers, could be equally creative and repulsive with these details.

37

RETURNING TO TIGER CASTLE . . .

THE CASTLE GATE WAS up when I reached it. A full moon silhouetted the soldiers atop the wall. I could see the glow of their fire pits.

I shouted to the gatekeeper, but my sore ribs left me gasping and bent over. I was priming myself for another attempt when I heard the creaking and cranking of the cable wheels. The gate-keeper must have noticed me after all. Barefoot and freezing, I staggered across the bridge.

A man accosted me. "Are you Anatole, the great magician?"

Well, I couldn't say no to that.

The left side of his face had been blistered by fire. I told him I'd help him after I had a cup of tea.

He grabbed my sleeve. It wasn't his burns that concerned him but those suffered by his child.

More people approached and I was quickly overwhelmed. I managed to extricate myself from them by saying I had to get my medical supplies, and I promised to return.

As I crossed the castle grounds, I could see more refugees everywhere I looked, and could hear their moans. I was quickly surrounded again by more sufferers.

"I need my supplies!" I shouted, then coughed and bent over from the strain.

A large man took hold of my arm. "Let him through so he can help you!" he commanded, and then he guided me the rest of the way to my workshop.

"I hope that wasn't an empty promise," he said when we reached the iron stove.

"Just a cup of tea," I said with a gasp, "and then I'll be back."

I was too weak to pull open the door to my workshop. He opened it for me, then respectfully closed it behind me.

Pito was at the table, ready with a candle in one hand and a smoke packet in the other.

PITO REMAINS THE SMARTEST AND MOST CAPABLE PERSON I'VE ever known. Unfortunately, the brewing of tea was not among his many talents.

There's a fine line between full-flavored and turbid. The muck Pito served me was well across the line.

As I sipped, I gave him a brief account of the wedding of the century.

"So are they married, or aren't they?" he asked.

I didn't know.

"Where is the princess now? With him?"

I didn't know that either.

He undoubtedly had a lot more questions, but he could see the state I was in, and to his credit, he didn't press me further.

The tea, turbid as it was, helped revive me, and with Pito's help,

I was able to prepare the various ointments, balms, and poultices I would need for those outside. Pito offered to assist me in their treatment too—"Nobody will know who I am"—but I couldn't risk it.

THE MAN WHO HAD ESCORTED ME TO MY WORKSHOP WAS STILL waiting by the stove. I handed him a candle and a pile of rags.

Though much stronger than me, he seemed a good deal older too. He may have been in his late fifties or early sixties. His face was scarred, but none of the scars appeared recent. He said his name was Carlo.

Carlo recruited others to gather wood for splints and tear the rags into bandages. He also determined who needed immediate care and who could wait.

We worked all night. More than Pito's turbid tea, I think it was the hard work of Carlo and the others that kept me going. That, and the trust and gratitude I saw on the faces of those I treated, and on the faces of their loved ones. After all the petty rivalries of the court, all the deceptions and mysterious potions, I'd forgotten what it was like to simply help someone in need.

I suppose guilt played a part too. I might have been partially responsible for their misfortune.

38

OBEDIENCE AND DEVOTION

THE SUN WAS ALREADY up when I returned to my workshop. I retired to my alcove but slept no more than a couple of hours before I was ready to get back to work.

I was dismayed to see that Pito had a pot of tea waiting for me. He watched me as I drank, and then asked me how I liked it.

"It has a subtle quality," I told him, and he smiled, quite pleased with himself.

It was so subtle, I could have been drinking plain water! As tired as I felt, I would have preferred the turbid muck he'd made the night before. At least that would wake me up.

I gave him a full account of the wedding and all that ensued. Pito laughed at the way I squealed, *"I'm a man."*

I was surprised that he said he remembered how his own voice had changed that day in the dungeon. But he hadn't been talking about Tullia at the time.

"How long before he dies?" Pito asked.

The question confused me.

"For the slow-acting poison," he said. "What'd you use? The venom of a snake from the deep, dark jungles of Kanata?"

"There is no slow poison," I told him. "I merely changed his voice, permanently."

Wasn't that enough?

I could see the concern on his face. "You've made Dalrympl more dangerous than ever," he said. "Haven't you read Machiavelli?"

I reminded him that Dalrympl had demanded the potion, and that I had strongly advised against it. There were lots of witnesses, including King Sandro himself. "My objections were duly noted."

"Do you think that matters?" Pito asked, slowly shaking his head. "You better hope the prince and princess are married. Only she can save you now."

OUTSIDE, I WAS SURPRISED TO FIND THAT MOST OF THOSE WHO had suffered less serious injuries had already been treated. The bandages had been changed on those from the night before. The villagers knew how to care for their own. They'd been doing it for years. However, there was still the danger of infection.

I headed to the kitchen, knowing full well that Philippe, the steward, would recoil at the very idea of moldy bread. He was as particular about his bread as I was about my tea.

Soldiers with longbows and muskets were spread out atop the full circle of the wall. The longbow was the more accurate weapon. There was no point in trying to aim those early muskets, but if there were enough soldiers shooting, and enough of the enemy coming toward them, some of them were sure to fall.

I passed a long queue of refugees waiting outside the kitchen, many of whom called out warm greetings as I passed.

"Save the bowl, you won't be given another!" admonished the woman doling out some kind of watery porridge. It looked worse than the gruel that Pito had been given in the dungeon.

I squeezed past her and into the kitchen. Philippe was offended when I asked for moldy bread, and then looked on, aghast, as I sprinkled water on several of his prized loaves. Nonetheless, he dutifully listened to the recipe I gave him and promised to prepare soup.

"A new pot every day for two weeks," I told him.

He grimaced as he nodded.

Carlo immediately called to me when I left the kitchen. "They've been looking for you."

I didn't know whom he meant. I was looking toward the door to my workshop when suddenly it opened. Dittierri, flanked by two guards, came outside.

I didn't know whether to go to them or flee. I did neither. I just stood there as they slowly came for me.

"You are wanted in the regency," Dittierri said. "King Sandro is engaged in negotiations with the Oxatanian ambassador."

I could detect neither threat nor smugness in his voice. He didn't mention Pito.

"WE HAVE A CANNON THAT WEIGHS MORE THAN TWO TONS," THE Oxatanian ambassador was saying as I entered the regency with Dittierri.

Only King Sandro and the ambassador were present. Even Voltharo had been excluded. The negotiations were secret. Nothing was recorded.

King Sandro gave me a brief description of our precarious position. The castle was under siege, completely surrounded by the large Oxatanian army. The cannons were en route and would be in place in three days. Prince Dalrympl was traveling with the cannons, and he would lead the assault.

"The prince has made two simple and reasonable requests," the ambassador said.

The first was that Princess Tullia should give herself to him when he arrived.

"*Willingly*," said the ambassador. "Gratefully. For everyone to see."

"She's here in the castle?" I asked.

King Sandro nodded, and it dawned on me why my presence had been requested. I was to give the princess a love potion.

A love potion really wasn't any worse than poppy tears, I thought. *She'll be glad to give herself to him*, I told myself. Better that than the slaughter of everyone inside the castle.

"I will need the prince to provide a tear," I told the ambassador.

He was shocked at my request. "Our prince does not weep!"

I didn't bother to point out that I'd seen and heard him do just that, beneath the leeches. Instead, I explained the necessity of a personal identifier.

"Otherwise, she might fall in love with the wrong person."

"Who said anything about *love*?" asked the ambassador. "The prince isn't interested in *love*! He demands only obedience and devotion."

I considered the implications. I would still need a personal identifier.

"Does the prince sweat?" I asked.

EVIDENTLY, THE PRINCE WAS QUITE PROUD OF HIS MANLY PERSPI-rations. I was to provide the vial. A horseman would take it to the prince, who was on his slow trek with the cannons. The horseman would be able to bring it back in time for me to prepare the potion, and for Tullia to drink it the night before the prince arrived.

I had started to leave the regency when I remembered that the ambassador had said the prince had made two requests. I asked what the other one was.

"To watch you feed the tiger," said the ambassador.

HIS WORDS WERE AS AMBIGUOUS IN SIXTEENTH-CENTURY ESQUA-vetian as they are in modern English, so it took me a moment to understand. He didn't want to watch me toss food down to the tiger. I was to be the food.

"I didn't want to give him the potion!" I protested. I turned to King Sandro. "You heard me. The prince demanded it."

"There was nothing wrong with the potion," said the ambassador. "It was your demon leeches. They drained him of his manhood."

39

TULLIA'S CHOICE

O NLY LATER DID IT occur to me that Dalrympl's *drained manhood* might not have referred solely to his voice. Perhaps other aspects of his manhood had also been drained. If so, then at least Tullia would be spared that indignity.

Conjuring the potion was easy enough. It was similar to a basic love potion, except that instead of daisies, for this, I did use roses—not the petals, but the thorns. I ground them into a fine powder. "So they won't catch in her throat," I explained to Pito.

Pito refused to help in any way. He just glared.

"You have no right," he said. "Free will is all we have. It makes us who we are! Everything else—health, wealth, prestige—is beyond our control."

"Do you think I should do nothing, and let everyone be slaughtered?" I asked.

"You're not God," he replied.

I HADN'T TOLD HIM ABOUT DALRYMPL'S SECOND REQUEST. THIS wasn't due to any sort of brave self-sacrifice on my part. It wasn't that I didn't want him to worry. To be honest, I could have used some sympathy.

Rather the thought of the tiger was just too frightening. I forced it out of my mind. If I didn't talk about it, or think about it, maybe it wouldn't happen.

I suddenly yelped and put my finger in my mouth. I had poked it with a thorn.

Judging from Pito's expression, I deserved it.

"I thought you didn't like her," I said.

"That makes no difference."

"If she doesn't give herself willingly to him," I argued, "he'll take her by force. And then he's likely to discard her and let others have their way with her. How is that better?"

"That's Princess Tullia's decision, not yours."

"What's my decision?"

We both turned. Behind her, the curtains hung still.

"I'm so glad you're safe, Natto," Tullia said, coming farther into the workshop. "I was very worried!"

"Then why didn't you do something to help him?" Pito demanded. "*Natto* was nearly killed."

She gave him a brief and disdainful glance, then took my hands in hers. "I never doubted you, Natto. Even while I was saying my vows, I knew you'd stop the wedding!"

I managed a halfhearted smile.

"What?"

I told her the castle was under siege. "In three days Dalrympl will arrive with giant cannons."

She merely laughed and said, "No Oxatanian soldier is going to risk his life for Prince Pip-squeak! As soon as they hear of his death they'll turn around and go home."

"He's not going to die," said Pito.

Tullia ignored him. "It was genius, Anatole. First turn him into a buffoon, and then let the poison kill him."

"There was no poison," said Pito.

She spun toward Pito. "There has to be," she told him, then slowly turned back to me.

"I just wanted to postpone the wedding," I said sheepishly.

I could see anger in her blue eye, and deep concern in the brown one. "Haven't you read Machiavelli?" she asked.

"That's what I asked him," said Pito.

She turned on him again. "Then why didn't you say something? You were here the whole time! His assistant!"

"I didn't know. You know how Anatole is with his potions," Pito explained. "He keeps them secret until—"

"Don't talk to *me* about Anatole!" Tullia snapped at him. "How long have you known him? A week? I've known Anatole my entire life." She possessively hooked her arm through mine. "He's like a father to me."

I was touched. I'd always thought of Tullia like a daughter, but I hadn't known the feeling was mutual.

"He risked everything to save your life!" she went on, continuing to assail Pito. "Maybe you'd be more grateful if you weren't so arrogant."

She let go of my arm and walked to the table. "What's all this?" She was looking at the thorns, and the mortar and pestle.

"Tell her," said Pito.

"Tell me what?"

"A potion," I said.

"Tell her!"

I did. I told her everything, that is, everything except Dalrympl's second request.

When I finished, she picked up a thorn and studied it. "Obedience and devotion," she said quietly, then dropped it back onto the table. "Or else everyone will be killed?"

I didn't know what to say.

"Princess Tullia's decision," she said. She walked to Luigi's cage and petted the eager mouse on the nose. "Make the potion, Anatole," she directed, then turned and headed back toward us.

"Once, for my birthday, Prince Dalrympl sent me a jeweled knife. It has a silver handle, lined with gold. Rubies, emeralds—"

She stopped, suddenly confused. "Did I tell you this already?"

"I don't know. Maybe, back when you were twelve."

My answer left her unsatisfied.

"Everyone must see me drink the potion," she said. "But it won't be the one with the thorns. By then you will have switched it with something else. When Prince Pip-squeak gets here, I will be just what he wants, devoted and obedient."

She turned to Pito and said, "I'm a very good actor."

I withheld comment.

"After he's had his way with me and falls asleep, I will remove the knife from under my pillow, Anatole, and finish what you started."

40

MARTA

TWO DAYS LATER, DITTIERRI delivered the vial to my workshop. The Oxatanian ambassador was with him, as was Gthrdr, the so-called magician. Gthrdr's purpose was to verify that the potion was properly prepared. I would have been insulted if it weren't so ludicrous.

I showed Gthrdr the rose stems, minus the thorns. When he asked about quantity and proportions, I made up the figures. I hadn't been very exact with the potion, since no one would ever drink it.

"And the purpose of the perspiration?" Gthrdr asked.

I was astounded that he had to ask, but perhaps I shouldn't have been. "Personal identifier," I said.

Gthrdr stared blankly, then nodded as if he understood. The ambassador asked him his opinion of my potion. Gthrdr sniffed the clay pot and confirmed its authenticity.

He likely would have reached the same conclusion had he sniffed my chamber pot! Not that I was complaining. Having earned the *great Oxatanian magician's* approval, I uncorked the vial of sweat and added it to the potion.

The ambassador asked me how I planned to persuade the princess to drink it. I said I'd tell her it was a fertility potion, and one that would ensure a son.

"But the purpose of the potion is to make her willing to consummate the marriage," Dittierri pointed out. "So why would—" He stopped himself. "Good work, Anatole."

This wasn't the time to accuse me of fraud. Dittierri might not have known what I was up to, but he knew that the safety of the kingdom depended on the potion, or rather on the ambassador's belief in its authenticity.

They watched me hang the pot and then light the star-shaped array of candles beneath it.

TULLIA STOOD STARING AT THAT SAME POT SEVERAL HOURS LATER.

"So, one sip, and I fall at his feet."

"Something like that," I said. I told her I'd replace it before nightfall. "You'll get something with lots of ginger and turmeric."

"No. Make it taste awful," she said. "I want everyone to see me recoil as I drink it."

I told her I'd brew a pot of stinkweed.

She laughed and said, "That's perfect!"

She had the same question as Dittierri. "Why would I want to drink a fertility potion if I wasn't willing to—"

"It was just the first thing that came to mind," I explained.

The chessboard was on the table. Pito and I had been playing when she came through the curtain.

She asked him if he needed any more of her help.

He scoffed. "Not if you think it's helpful to trade a castle for a pawn! Though I did figure out a way to take advantage of your blunder," he smugly added.

"Oh, *you* figured it out? Well, go ahead and finish your game. I'll watch."

"We don't have to," I said. "We only just started."

"Play," she insisted. "Whose turn is it?"

It was my turn. I placed a hand on a bishop, but Tullia gave a slight shake of her head. I tried the queen and got another head-shake. I then followed her eyes to a pawn, and when there was no reaction from her, I moved it forward one square.

Pito made his move, and then again, Tullia's eyes and head directed mine.

As the game continued, it didn't take long for Pito to realize who he was up against. His concentration grew more intense.

After a while I suggested to Tullia that she take my seat, but she kept up the charade. "I'm just watching," she said innocently. "I wouldn't want to make another blunder."

The position grew more complex. The pieces that remained on the board all had multiple functions, attacking one way and defending another. I couldn't predict what would happen once the pieces began to fall.

I placed a finger on a pawn, but Tullia shook her head. The moment of reckoning had come. It was time for the queen to enter the fray. I slowly moved the piece one square, then another, waiting for her signal to stop.

A shrill scream seemed to shake the entire room, causing me to knock over several pieces. I turned to see Marta, her trembling finger pointed at Pito.

Marta stepped back.

Tullia told her to stop and listen. "It's not what you think."

Her frightened handmaiden spun around and headed for the archway.

"Wait!" Tullia ordered.

Marta stepped on a pile of black sand and lost her balance. As she fell, she reached out for something to grab on to. Her hand found the clay pot, which crashed on the floor as Marta fell to her knees.

Marta used an archway curtain to help herself up and pulled that down too. Then she fled.

Tullia continued to shout for her to wait as she followed her through the archway, but then she came back to us. "She's gone."

Pito had remained in his chair.

"You have to leave, now!" Tullia told him.

He didn't move.

"Do you know what they'll do to Anatole if they find you?"

He had nowhere to go.

"If I can find the right clothes for him, he could hide among the refugees," I suggested.

"There's no time," said Tullia. She took hold of his arm. "Come with me." She pulled him to his feet. "There's a secret passage."

As she led him through the archway, Pito turned and gave me one last quizzical look.

The clay pot was in shatters, amid the puddle of the potion.

41

THE SEARCH FOR PITO

I COULDN'T FIND MY LEATHER gloves, and for that I blamed Pito. I had known where everything was before he cleaned up.

The potion was probably harmless. Nothing had been carefully measured. I hadn't bothered recording any of it in my logbook. Nevertheless, I was afraid to clean up the shards of clay without gloves. I didn't want to spend the rest of my life—however short it might be—devoted to Dalrympl.

I had other clay pots. I needed to get rid of the old one and hang a new one. I could fill it with anything. I could always stew the stinkweed later.

I finally found the gloves under a pile of dirty clothes. The fault, it seemed, was mine.

I stepped out of the alcove just as Queen Corinna came through the archway. "Where is he?"

With her were Dittierri and a half dozen or so guards who immediately began searching my workshop. One was going through a small cabinet, as if he thought Pito could fit inside.

"Who?" I asked.

"You're done, Anatole," said Dittierri. "Marta saw him."

"I don't know what or whom Marta thinks she saw," I said to the queen. "The princess and I were playing a game of queen's chess when Marta suddenly started screaming."

With a swipe of his arm, the guard knocked everything out of the cabinet, sending jars and glassware clattering to the floor.

Another guard was checking the mouse cages.

"Where's the princess now?" the queen asked.

"She hurried after Marta," I said. "We were both very worried about the poor girl. Marta was hysterical."

Two guards had gone outside. I could see them through the doorway as they looked around the stove.

"So this is the potion?" the queen asked, looking at the puddle and the broken pot.

"In her hysteria, Marta knocked it off the wires," I said. "She pulled down my curtains too."

There was a loud crunching sound behind me. I turned to see the guard stomping on the mouse cages.

I also saw that outside, the guards were opening the hatch to the cellar. I tried to think of anything incriminating Pito might have left down there but then reminded myself that everything he had was mine.

Inside the workshop, more cabinets and shelves were emptied. I couldn't understand the point behind their search. If Pito could hide in jars or mouse cages, then he would indeed be nothing but a phantom spirit.

"We found this," a guard announced, coming in from outside. He was holding a chamber pot. It didn't take an acute sense of smell to know it needed emptying.

"That's part of an experiment," I explained.

Dittierri laughed but not in his usual derisive manner. I think my explanation struck him as funny.

The queen bent down and picked up a long and jagged shard from the broken pot. She stepped forward and held it close to my neck.

"Prince Dalrympl will cross the bridge tomorrow at noon. The princess had better welcome him!"

Before I could reply, she suddenly yelped and dropped the shard.

The tip of a finger was bleeding. She instinctively brought it to her mouth.

42

OBSTACLE COURSE

I LAY ON MY MATTRESS, eyes open, staring at the ceiling. I didn't know how many hours I had left before I fed the tiger. The clock in my alcove had been smashed along with everything else.

Two guards had been stationed on the other side of the archway, and two more were out by the iron stove.

I couldn't even enjoy one last cup of tea. In their search for Pito, they'd dumped all my tins. The tea leaves were strewn across the floor, mixed with everything else that had also been dumped: fish scales, wasp wings, corpse flower petals . . .

Taking one of the empty tins, I stepped out of the alcove. "One last cup of tea!" I shouted. "Is that too much to ask?" Then I hurled the empty tin toward the archway.

It fell short and rolled sideways.

Both mouse cages had been crushed, and Luigi's obstacle course had been ripped apart. I didn't see any dead mice, so they must have all escaped unharmed.

I straightened up a chair and sat down. The table remained overturned.

I thought of Pito. I thought of the strength he'd shown in the dungeon, and the way he'd prepared his mind for his imminent execution. I had no such strength. I could have used some false hope.

Elbows on knees, head in hands, I wept.

I heard a noise outside. I lifted my head, and through my tears I saw the blurry image of Harwell coming into the archway. I wiped the tears away and saw that he was holding a cudgel.

"Come," he grunted.

I obediently stood up. Even in my misery, though, a part of me sensed that something was off.

"They're waiting for you," he said.

I followed him through the archway, where the two guards lay on the floor, either dead or unconscious. I gingerly stepped over them.

We continued down the corridor. Harwell stopped at a wall sconce, removed a candle, and handed it to me. Then he pulled down on the iron arm that had held the candle.

As the arm came down, a gap in the wall opened beneath it.

"Go."

I got on my hands and knees, unsure if I'd fit through the opening. Then the realization finally struck me.

"Can you hear too?" I asked.

The big brute smiled and said, "Not a word."

Holding the candle out in front of me, I wriggled through the gap.

I was inside a tunnel. My shoulders brushed against the sides and I had to keep my head down as I continued to crawl. I heard the wall shut behind me.

I followed a zigzagging path and wondered if this was how it had been for Luigi inside the obstacle course. Except Luigi had to make choices along the way. I could only go one way. I didn't even have room to turn around.

My knees were sore when I came to what looked like the end of the passageway. My path seemed to have led to nowhere. I was facing a wall.

It wasn't until I held the candle above my head that I discovered that the passageway continued upward. I cautiously stood up.

I was able to make out a series of steps going almost straight up. I held the candle in my teeth as I climbed. To get from one step to the next, I had to stretch my legs about as far as I was able, while pushing my hands against the side walls for support.

Upon reaching the top, I had to crawl again, though I had more room than I had before. My shoulders no longer rubbed against the tunnel, but I still had to keep my head low to avoid crossbeams.

There were more turns, and then another set of stone stairs that was more like a normal staircase. Then once again, I had to get down on my hands and increasingly sore knees.

After a while, I saw what looked to be the light at the end of the tunnel. Crawling toward it, I realized it was emanating from below, through a gap in the floor of the passageway.

The gap was large enough for me to fit through. I crawled close, then lay flat before peering over the edge.

I had hoped to see a set of stairs but instead found myself looking down at a room a good distance below me, with no obvious way to get down to it.

The room could have come straight out of *King Arthur and the Knights of the Round Table*. Except, in this room, the table was square, and there were only two knights. I could see various knightly regalia scattered about, including shields, staffs, and old-style weapons.

I must have made a noise, because the two knights turned simultaneously and looked up toward me. One of them waved.

43

NOON

ADMITTEDLY, IT TOOK ME longer than it probably took you
to realize that the knights were Pito and Tullia. But then
again, you didn't have a tiger to worry about.

"How do I get down?" I called.

Tullia lifted her faceplate and put her finger to her lips. "Use
the rope," she sharply whispered.

I couldn't see a rope, but even if there had been one, I wouldn't
have the strength or agility to climb down it. I was no acrobat.

"It's under you," Pito whispered, pointing.

When I eased my head down through the gap, I became dizzy
with fear. The room seemed to spin below me.

At last I saw the rope, hanging from the ceiling of the room,
directly below my stomach. There was no way I could reach it.

"You can do it," Pito said encouragingly. "It's easier than you
think."

I squeezed my shoulders through the gap. If I went any farther,
I was afraid I'd fall.

"Try saying some magic words," Tullia suggested.

I tried to pull myself back up through the gap so I could approach it from another direction, but I didn't have the strength. And what strength I did have was slowly draining away just from holding myself in place.

Closing my eyes, I pushed with both feet against the side of the tunnel. My stomach bent through the gap as I stretched out one arm.

I was falling.

Somehow my left hand found the rope. I felt the coarse fibers ripping at my flesh as I desperately tried to hang on. My other hand took hold, spinning me upright. My arms were nearly yanked from their sockets as my rear end slammed into the ground. My head banged against the floor, and I nearly did a backward somersault. Then I lay still.

Pito and Tullia hurried over.

"Can you get up?"

"Did you break anything?"

I sat up, raised both arms, and let out a loud and triumphant whoop!

Laughing, Tullia put her hand over my mouth. "We're directly above the regency," she whispered.

They helped me to my feet.

"Well done, Anatole," said Pito, and he extended a hand.

Tullia watched, bemused, as we executed the ritual of the handshake.

THEY HAD A SUIT OF ARMOR FOR ME TOO, WHICH I PUT ON OVER my clothes. This wasn't the stiff metal suit you sometimes now find in antique stores. My arms and legs were covered with interlocking metal rings allowing freedom of movement. A breastplate covered my vital organs.

Before gunpowder changed the world, wars were fought by knights who rode horses and engaged in hand-to-hand combat. Agility was just as important as protection.

Tullia said that she had discovered this secret room when she was a little girl. Sometimes, when she was upset, she'd hide out in here all day, so her parents would worry. "They never even knew I was gone," she said.

It was Pito who had suggested she ask Harwell to bring me here. Though he hadn't known for certain, he had long suspected that the keeper of the dungeon was neither deaf nor mute.

He's the king's spy, Pito had said.

Tullia had been skeptical. *Even if that's true, why would he agree to help you and Anatole?*

He likes us.

"That was even harder for me to believe!" Tullia said, only half joking.

I was putting on my helmet.

"I can understand that he might like you, Natto, but not . . ." She glanced at Pito.

Pito smiled at her.

I was given a staff with two banners attached to it. The Oxatanian flag, black and green with red stripes, was at the top. Just below it was the blue *X* of Esquaveta set against a yellow background.

Pito held a long sword. My only weapon was a small dagger, which I kept tucked into my belt beneath my armor. I could only hope that I wouldn't be called upon to use it.

I didn't know how I'd ever climb back up the rope, in heavy armor no less. My hands were raw and blistered.

To my great relief, I didn't have to. Tullia leaned her shoulder into a wall, which then swiveled open. Candle in hand, she led us into another passageway.

This one was just as narrow, but we didn't have to crawl. My greatest difficulty was maneuvering the long flagstaff through the many turns.

My helmet protected my head, but it also made it hard to see, and I would occasionally bang into low-hanging crossbeams. The fourth time this happened, I heard either Pito or Tullia snicker, maybe both.

We had to climb up more stairs, which wasn't easy in armor. Our passage crisscrossed other passageways, but Tullia always knew which way to go. She pointed out one passage that led to her bedchamber.

"Marta thinks I'm in bed, awaiting my *handsome prince*."

I REMEMBERED A TIME, WHEN TULLIA WAS MAYBE SIX OR SEVEN, that she had mentioned how she explored secret passageways. I probably smiled and nodded, without giving much credence to what she said. She'd also told me she was a knight and slayed dragons.

On the castle tour yesterday, the guide informed us that the castle was constructed during the eleventh century. Every stone had been cut to the architect's precise specifications. Archaeologists had found pages of his notes, which contained mysterious symbols. These same symbols had been carved into the stones. They'd only recently determined that the symbols indicated the precise location of where each stone was to be placed.

The guide said the secret passageways had been a part of the original design, but that over the centuries, the castle had been renovated and expanded, and this inner reticulum had been long forgotten. What the guide didn't know was that it was rediscovered by a very curious, brave, and lonely young girl whose only friend was a hairless man who studied plants and bugs.

WE WERE APPROACHING WHAT SEEMED TO BE NOTHING BUT A blank wall, but I wasn't concerned. By then, I fully expected the passage to continue one way or another. Either the wall would slide away, or the floor would open up to reveal a long descending staircase.

Yet once again, I was surprised.

Tullia held her candle between her teeth and then proceeded to climb, spiderlike, straight up the wall. Pito followed her.

I didn't know how they did that. Pito stopped midway up the wall and reached down to take my staff. He then handed it up to Tullia, whom I could no longer see.

There was hardly any light, so I had to feel around with my hands to discover the knobs and notches that had been carved into the stones. Most often, they weren't in just one stone. The stones had been fitted together, each in its designated location, to create these climbing aids.

I slipped the toe of my boot into a notch and grabbed hold of a smooth round knob. I couldn't see these grips or footholds, but thanks to the skill of the architect and stonemasons, they were always right where I needed them to be, making it surprisingly easy to climb the wall.

I was halfway up when light filled the area and I felt a rush of cold air. Tullia must have opened a window!

With my head close to the wall and helmeted, it was impossible for me to look up, so I didn't know I was close to the top until I was eye level with Pito's and Tullia's feet. Pito reached down and helped me up to their ledge.

I saw Tullia drop my staff out through what indeed was a window. A square of stone, the size and shape of the window, was propped against the wall. She climbed up to and then through the window.

Pito was next. He looked out the window and then back at me. His faceplate was down, so I don't know if he was scared, but I knew he'd never admit that *the princess* could do something he couldn't do. He swung one leg and then the other out through the window. Then he too was gone.

I tentatively approached the window. When I looked out, I most definitely was scared. I hadn't realized how high up I'd climbed.

I could look down upon our soldiers standing atop the protective wall, and the Oxatanian encampment beyond that. Dalrympl must have arrived, because a cannon seemed to be aimed directly at me.

That might have been an illusion, similar to the way the eyes on the faces in the portrait gallery follow me wherever I go. I pulled myself up to the window and sat on the edge, facing inward.

Holding tight with both hands, I slipped a leg out. A foothold was exactly where I needed it to be. My left hand found a knob to hold as I let the other leg through.

I could hear the pounding of my heart echo inside my helmet as I slowly worked my way downward. My breastplate and faceplate scraped the wall. My hands, still sore from the rope burns, became cramped from gripping the knobs so tightly.

I was thankful for the cold air. If it had been a hot day, I might have passed out. That I safely made it down wasn't due to either my acrobatic ability or magic. All the credit goes to an eleventh-century architect and the skill of some anonymous stonecutters and masons from the so-called Dark Ages.

Tullia welcomed me when my feet touched solid ground. We were at the back of the castle. Pito handed me my flagstaff. There was no time to rest. Dalrympl could cross the bridge at any moment.

Some of the refugees must have seen us climb down the castle wall. Others watched us as we made our way around toward the front.

As we passed the stables, I saw a crowd gathered by the gate, which was still up. We headed toward it. I held my banners high.

King Sandro and Queen Corinna were among those awaiting the prince's arrival. We stood at attention, a little off to the side.

Crumhorns resounded. Soldiers turned the great spools of cable as the gate slowly came down.

Soldiers on horses were the first to cross the bridge, followed by Prince Dalrympl and a contingent of guards and advisors.

King Sandro and Queen Corinna bowed before him.

He acknowledged them with a brief nod, then continued toward the castle. They followed after him.

As they went one way, three knights went the other, crossing the bridge in the opposite direction.

44

HERALDING THE NEWS

A LINE OF SOLDIERS POINTED their muskets toward us as we came toward them. Others had drawn their swords.

"My friends!" Pito called out. "War has been averted! Our two great kingdoms are united!"

I waved my flagstaff back and forth.

The soldiers didn't welcome the news with any more enthusiasm than they welcomed us. Their muskets weren't lowered.

A man, apparently their commander, stepped forward. "And the princess?" he asked.

"She welcomed the prince with open arms and an open heart," I answered. My faceplate was down, so I had to strain my voice to be heard.

The commander remained stern. The soldiers behind him came closer.

"And open legs!" Pito added.

Some of the soldiers laughed. The commander smiled.

"He give it to her good?" one of the soldiers asked.

"Good for the princess!" Pito replied. "Her pleasure moans could be heard throughout the castle!"

There was more laughter.

"I'm surprised you didn't hear her scream of ecstasy all the way out here," he added.

Their weapons were lowered as a few of the soldiers claimed they had heard her.

"She sounded like a cat in heat!" said one.

I listened to them extol the prince's great prowess, something that lately must have been in doubt. One of the soldiers pointed out that the Oxatanian flag on my staff was above the Esquavetian.

"Where it belongs!"

"Just as he belongs on top of her!"

I raised the staff higher and shouted, "It's a great day for Ox-atania."

There were shouts of "Hurrah!"

"And a great day for Esquaveta!" I called out, waving the staff back and forth.

A few of the soldiers even managed a mild cheer for that too.

"And the greatest day the princess ever had!" Pito called out, which elicited the loudest roar.

We continued our way through the encampment, heralding the news to one group of soldiers after another: archers, cannoneers, horsemen. They were receptive to us, having already heard the cheers of their comrades.

Pito repeated much of what he'd said before, incorporating the line about "a cat in heat" and adding, "But he soon had her purring like a kitten."

"She won't be able to walk for three days," he told another group.

"Walking isn't what's required from her!" someone called back.

The farther we moved through the ranks, the more slovenly and less disciplined the soldiers. If anything, they were too friendly toward us, insisting we drink with them in celebration.

Pito did his best to keep their attention on him by repeating what he'd said to the others. "But walking isn't required from her!" he said with a laugh, then took a long swig from the offered goatskin.

Back in the castle, they would have discovered that the devoted princess hadn't been waiting in her bed for her handsome prince. They would be searching for her, and for me, and possibly Pito too. I wondered if Harwell had gotten rid of the two guards he'd overpowered at my archway. He could have stashed them in the dungeon. But how long would it be before somebody remembered *those three knights?*

I drank stale ale from greasy goatskins, but Tullia didn't dare raise her faceplate. When some of the soldiers took offense at my friend's refusal to drink with them, I explained that "he had his fill last night and has been vomiting all morning."

A soldier with two swords, one curved and the other straight, approached Tullia. All I had was the dagger, and it would take some time for me to get to it.

The man insisted that a drink was exactly what my friend needed. He lifted her faceplate and shoved a goatskin toward her mouth.

He was, however, more than a foot taller than Tullia, so I don't think he was able to glimpse her face.

Everyone cheered as she took a surprisingly long drink.

"What did I tell you!" the man said, slapping Tullia's back.

Some of the others broke into song, and within minutes they were all singing.

I gave a final wave with my banners, and then we quickly headed away.

I felt hot and dizzy as we crossed a long and barren field. The strain and struggle had finally caught up with me. I removed my helmet, which helped. I carried it in one hand, while I still held the flagstaff in the other. I could hear the voices of the Oxatanian soldiers in the distance, singing their terrible song. I staggered from side to side as I tried to keep pace with Pito and Tullia, but I didn't stop until we reached the edge of the forest.

And then I collapsed.

PITO HELPED ME OUT OF MY ARMOR, AND THEN HE STASHED IT someplace along with his. I was lying on my back, gazing up at the forest canopy, when he returned, his clothes wet from sweat.

He sat down beside me, stretched his arms wide, and took a deep, satisfied breath of fresh air. "Tell me the truth, Anatole. Am I really out of the castle? Or am I still in the dungeon, dreaming?"

I laughed and then assured him he was free.

Tullia came toward us, also smiling. Her blue eye sparkled. She'd also taken off her armor. Her hair was matted against the sides of her face.

Oh, how I envied their sweat!

She stopped in front of Pito and bent her left knee toward him as she raised her right hand up to her shoulder. Then she slapped his face so hard, even I could feel the sting.

45

MUD DOGS

O F COURSE TULLIA UNDERSTOOD why Pito had said those disgusting things about her. But that didn't mean he didn't deserve to be slapped.

That's what a princess does.

And Pito understood that too.

I DIDN'T NEED TO REST FOR VERY LONG. THE AIR AROUND ME HAD become even colder, and I felt a lot better without the armor weighing me down. We needed to keep moving.

The forest would be the first place the soldiers would look for us, and their scouts would have little difficulty picking up our trail. While Tullia might be able to nimbly slip through the trees without leaving a trace, I was anything but nimble.

But I had one advantage. I knew every path and every creek in this forest. It wouldn't have been much of an exaggeration to say I knew every tree. When I was younger, I'd studied the plants, bugs, mosses, and fungi. This was the same forest where Babette and I shared our only kiss.

We headed east, toward Oxatania. They wouldn't expect that.

My plan was to cross Oxatania and then turn north, through France, and on to the *neder lands*. I'd heard that the citizens there had a great deal of freedom.

We were following a creek that was little more than a trickle, but I knew it would eventually lead to a fairly deep pool with even a small waterfall.

"I never should have left the castle," Tullia declared, and then she reached beneath her tunic and pulled out what had to be the most dazzling display of jewels I'd ever seen.

Pito could only stare.

It was the knife she'd told us about, the one that Dalrympl had given to her as a birthday present.

Embedded in the silver and gold handle were three large gemstones: a ruby, an emerald, and an onyx. A circle of much smaller gems surrounded each one: onyxes around the ruby, rubies around the emerald, and emeralds around the onyx.

"I should have stayed behind and slashed his throat," she said, then slashed at the air with the magnificent knife.

Pito put up his hands and backed away, but the blade hadn't come all that close to him.

"WHY DIDN'T YOU EVER TELL ME ABOUT BABETTE?" TULLIA ASKED.

It was sometime later. Pito had gone off to do his private business.

"That was before you were born," I said.

"You told Pito! If I'd known, I never would have agreed to marry Dalrympl."

I explained that I didn't know it was Dalrympl until I saw him at the banquet.

"You should have told me. I had to learn about it from *him!*"

I didn't know which upset her more: what happened to Babette, or that Pito knew about it before she did.

WE REACHED WHAT TURNED OUT TO BE NOTHING MORE THAN A shallow pool of muddy water. The waterfall was dry.

We stared upon it, disappointed.

I told them that I used to bathe there as a young child, which, for some reason, caused Tullia to laugh. She said she couldn't imagine me as a child.

"I had hair then."

She laughed at that, too, then turned to Pito and said, "You're right. I look like a princess."

I'd never heard him say that.

She set her priceless knife on a rock, then let herself fall with a splat into the muddy water.

She lifted her head and laughed.

Not to be outdone, Pito plopped in after her.

I watched them splash each other and throw handfuls of mud. They reminded me of two dogs rolling around growling and snapping at each other. It's hard to know if they're fighting or playing.

When Tullia came out of the pool, she no longer looked like a princess.

Pito came out behind her. She turned back to him and said, "Anatole is too clean, don't you think?"

"No one will think he's a peasant," Pito agreed.

They came at me with muddy hands and evil grins. I never stood a chance.

———

"I HAVE TO CUT MY HAIR," TULLIA DECLARED.

Pito happily volunteered to be her barber.

It was sundown. We were walking into a stiff wind. All that remained of the lush forest was a scattering of scrub oaks and junipers. The mud caked to our clothes was our only protection against the wind and the cold.

Tullia sat on a tree stump, and Pito stood behind her with my dagger. She winced as he grabbed a handful of her hair.

It took some time for the dagger to cut through it, and when she complained, he told her it was her own fault for not getting it cut before playing in the mud.

She suggested he use the jeweled knife, which was sharper, but Pito insisted that "Anatole's dagger works just fine."

I think he was afraid to touch Tullia's priceless knife.

He grabbed another hunk of hair, yanked it back, and hacked at it with the dagger.

"That hurts," Tullia complained.

"I'm so sorry, Princess," he said. "I hope you find it in your heart to forgive your most humble servant."

She didn't complain after that.

"I may be a princess," she told him, "but in a way, I was a prisoner too. Just because I slept in a feather bed with silk sheets doesn't—"

She stopped and squeezed her eyes shut as the dagger tore through the hair.

The suddenness caused Pito to lose his balance for just a moment. He grabbed another handful.

"You're enjoying this, aren't you?" she asked.

"Yes."

She couldn't see his goofy smile. He couldn't see the twinkle in her blue eye.

"There's a place . . ." Tullia said, then stopped, as if struggling to remember. "An island, where there are no kings or queens. Everyone is equal."

"Utopia," said Pito.

"You've heard of it?"

Pito seemed unsure. "I must have."

Tullia slowly pronounced the word. "U-to-pi-a. It sounds Greek. Maybe it was in one of your ancient texts."

Pito shrugged. "Maybe."

She asked me if I knew of Utopia.

As I tried to think of how to answer, Pito yanked another handful of hair, causing the princess to squawk loudly.

46

OXATANIA

W E STUFFED DIRT AND leaves inside our clothes at night but it was too cold to fall asleep. I lay on the hard ground, shivering, as I listened to the chattering of teeth.

We set out again at the first sign of light, before the sun came up. Walking at least generated some heat. The sun was a welcome sight when it finally appeared on the horizon.

All that remained of Tullia's hair were uneven clumps, cut close to her head. "Too bad you refuse to do anything about my eyes!" she complained.

I hadn't refused. I'd merely reminded her that I didn't cast spells and explained that I knew of no combination of leaves or bugs that would change eye color.

"Blue or brown," she persisted. "I don't care which, just so they're the same!"

We had crossed the border into Oxatania. The fields were long and narrow, each the same size and shape, neatly aligned one next to another. The cottages of the peasants who worked these fields were also in a straight line, perpendicular to the fields.

Esquavetian fields were more haphazard, in both their shape and orientation.

In those days, plows were heavy and very cumbersome to turn. These long and narrow fields allowed the Oxatanians to farm more efficiently. They could push their plows all day in just one direction.

If we had been in Esquaveta, we probably could have found a few scraps of food that had been passed over when the fields were harvested. Oxatanians never let anything go to waste.

Pito tried approaching several of the cottages, hoping to get us something to eat, but all he'd come back with were two soft carrots, wilted greens, and a crust of stale bread. Oxatanians prided them-selves on their self-sufficiency and expected the same from others.

To be fair, these peasants only kept a small portion of their harvest. The rest went to the overseer, who turned most of that over to the baron, who in turn gave the largest amount to the king. In this regard, Oxatania was no different than Esquaveta.

IT WAS THE MIDDLE OF THE AFTERNOON WHEN WE REACHED THE outskirts of a village. Despite our hunger, we couldn't enter. For all we knew, the news of the missing princess had already reached this part of Oxatania. Besides, we had no money. The only thing we had of value was the jeweled knife, and it was too valuable. If we tried to sell it, we'd put ourselves in even greater danger.

"Give me your knife," Pito said to Tullia. "And your dagger, Anatole."

He sat on the ground and laid Tullia's knife in front of him. Using my dagger as a chisel, he hammered on it with a stone until one of the small rubies pried loose.

Then he headed for the village.

"He's so arrogant," Tullia said as we watched him walk away. "It's his own fault if he gets robbed and murdered!"

Her tone softened more than half an hour later, when he still hadn't returned. "I suppose he was only trying to help."

And an hour after that, she acknowledged that he'd been brave to enter the village alone. "Stupid," she added, "but brave."

She was becoming more and more anxious, and so was I. "I'm going to look for him," she decided. "No one will recognize me. I'll keep my eyes closed."

Before I could begin to point out why that would be impossible, we spotted Pito heading not exactly toward us but in our general direction.

He stopped, looked around, and then headed the wrong way.

Tullia let out a short laugh and said, "The fool is lost!"

Pito stopped, looked around again, and changed direction.

I suggested to Tullia that he knew exactly where we were, but he was being cautious in case he was being followed.

She accused me of making excuses for him, "like you always do!"

Either way, he finally found us. Three goatskins hung around his neck, and he carried a loaf of dark bread and half a cheese wheel.

"Ooh, it's still warm," Tullia said as she took the bread from him.

"I also secured a room at an inn," Pito told us.

Tullia had already stuffed a hunk of bread into her mouth, and it took her a moment to swallow. "Imbecile!" she exclaimed at last. "We'll be murdered in our sleep! If there's one ruby, there must be more."

Pito smiled at her.

"What?" she demanded.

"I have no intention of sleeping there," he said. "Better to have the bandits wait for us at the inn than follow me out here."

He handed me the cheese wheel, and I used my dagger to slice into it.

Tullia didn't say another word for some time.

It probably would have been wise to save some of our food for another day. It would be a very long journey to the *neder lands*, and there were only so many jewels in the knife. But then again, the bread wouldn't still be warm tomorrow.

"There's no point in saving it," Tullia said. "It's the same amount of nourishment whether we eat it today or tomorrow."

Pito and I happily went along with her logic.

Our goatskins contained ale, which was safer than water. Villagers used rivers as sewers and garbage dumps. While we didn't know about bacteria, we understood the benefits of fermentation.

IT WAS ANOTHER VERY COLD NIGHT. WE LAY CLOSE TOGETHER, Tullia on one side of me and Pito on the other. "You could have gotten blankets!" Tullia complained.

I didn't stop shivering until late morning, and then by noon, I became far too warm. The sun was hotter in Oxatania. My lukewarm ale provided little relief.

We were walking single file on a narrow and dusty path through a rocky landscape of opuntia cacti and stinging nettle. I was in the rear, and I had to keep up a fast pace so as not to fall too far behind Pito and Tullia.

I could feel dizziness coming on, but rather than stopping to let my body cool down, I convinced myself that I could somehow save up the heat for later, when it became freezing again.

As I struggled to keep up with Pito and Tullia, I was once again reminded of two dogs. They each wanted to lead our pack. While trying not to be too obvious about it, whoever was behind the other seemed to be constantly waiting for an opening to step in front.

Tullia, who was currently leading, suddenly stopped. "What is that?" she asked.

Pito took the opportunity to slip past her, but then he, too, stopped.

I saw a vague dark shape in the distance, and by the time I caught up to Pito and Tullia, I could make out people and a wagon. They were coming toward us.

"You think they're soldiers?" Tullia asked.

We certainly didn't want to wait around and find out.

Pito remembered passing a gully a short way back. I had a recollection of it as well, but it seemed to me that it was more than just a short way.

Tullia had already started running, and Pito wasn't too far behind her. I hurried after them but continued to fall farther behind. I felt myself wavering from side to side as I became more and more light-headed.

Finally, Pito looked back toward me. He shouted something I couldn't hear. Tullia stopped and turned around too. Their shapes dissolved into blurry and spinning clouds.

I felt a sense of falling, but I have no memory of hitting the ground.

47

HOODED FIGURES

I<small>T WAS DUSK WHEN</small> I came to. I felt movement. I was surrounded by felt sacks and crates. I strained to raise my head, but the pain was overwhelming.

I realized I was in a wagon. A hooded figure was walking alongside. He must have noticed I was awake, because he offered his goatskin.

I managed a sip. It was water, not ale.

Beneath his dark hood, the man's face was so pale it seemed nearly transparent.

"I'm sorry about Babette," he said.

I was confused and decided I must be dead. The hooded figure was the angel of death, and he was carting my soul to the nether world. Although it did seem odd that he would apologize for Babette.

"Will I see her?" I asked weakly.

He didn't answer, and as I watched him drift away from the wagon, I wondered if I'd only imagined his apology. I took another sip of water, but a bump in the trail left me choking and sputtering.

THE NEXT TIME I AWOKE IT WAS DARK, AND THE WAGON WAS NO longer moving. My encounter with the angel of death seemed to have been a dream, but I wondered where I had gotten the goatskin.

I remembered that Pito had bought goatskins, but those had been full of ale. I took another sip. It was definitely water. I fell asleep again.

THE BUMPING OF THE WAGON JOSTLED ME AWAKE. I FELT SICK and only just managed to reach the edge of the wagon before vomiting.

"How do you feel, Father?" asked a voice I knew well. Tullia was dressed as the angel of death, in a dark robe and hood.

"Are you dead too?" I asked.

Tullia leaned close and whispered, "Your name is Galen. I'm Ippolita, your daughter. Pito is Marcus."

Another hooded figure came close. At first I thought it might be Pito, but it was neither him nor the angel of death.

This new person had a round red face and cheery smile. He looked to be in his midtwenties.

"Are you hungry, Galen?" he asked. "The pickled cabbage is just what you need to bring you back from the dead."

I think he meant it as a metaphor.

He introduced himself as Mortamus and explained he was part of a group of Capuchin monks returning to their monastery after a pilgrimage.

Some of the other monks had taken a vow of silence, and

Mortamus seemed delighted to have found someone he could converse with. He did most of the talking, and I was happy to let him.

Even if I hadn't been dizzy, I wouldn't have been able to follow everything Mortamus told me. He had a way of enthusiastically switching from one topic to another without so much as a pause. He also assumed I knew things I didn't, including, for instance, the tragic circumstances that led to my collapse. I think he attributed my confusion to the shock I must have suffered.

I did manage to piece together a bit of my *tragic circumstances*. My name was Galen, as Tullia had told me. I was a physician and had been called away to a distant village to treat an "epileptic imbecile." Evidently, I cured not only his epilepsy but also his imbecility.

I was on my way home when my two children, Ippolita and Marcus, met me on the trail. They informed me that our cottage had burned down, with my wife, Babette—their mother—trapped inside.

I had fainted from shock and grief.

There was also something about a witch. This witch was in love with me and jealous of Babette.

"Do you think she was the one who caused the fire?" Mortamus asked me.

"Possibly," I said.

I could almost hear Tullia and Pito adding one outlandish detail after another, each more preposterous than the last. It would have been impossible for them to work together and come up with a sensible story. Everything was a competition between those two.

I didn't know how Tullia chose the name Ippolita, but *Marcus* had clearly come from Marcus Aurelius, a Roman philosopher whom Pito had quoted many times in the dungeon. Marcus Aurelius had also been emperor of Rome, but Pito admired him for his philosophy.

Pito must have come up with my name too. Galen had been an ancient Greek physician, but his texts were still being used in the great medical universities in Salerno and Bologna. Pito probably had copied the text for a medical student.

You may already know that Aristotle believed the world to be made up of four elements: earth, air, fire, and water. You scoff, but Aristotle's elements are just as true and just as false as the modern periodic table. It is a matter of how one chooses to divide and categorize.

Galen taught that the human body was composed of those same four basic elements. Flesh and bone are the earth. Our breath, of course, is air. Blood, sperm, and bile are water. And our spirit, or will, is fire. According to Galen, illness occurs when those elements are out of balance. It is the physician's job to restore the proper balance.

While you may chortle smugly, remember that every generation believes themselves to be living in modern times. Future generations will be chortling smugly and rolling their eyes when they learn about the beliefs of the twenty-first century.

It wasn't some later historian who called my era *the Renaissance*. We named it that ourselves! And we named the previous one thousand years *the Dark Ages*.

How's that for smugness?

48

MY CAPUCHIN ROBE

I TOO WAS GIVEN A robe, although to say it was a gift isn't entirely accurate. Tullia showed me her knife. The large ruby had been removed, leaving only the circle of onyxes around where it had been.

She hadn't outright bought our robes. That would have been unseemly. She'd used the ruby to purchase an indulgence for Babette.

I wasn't sure which Babette she had in mind. Was it for my Babette, or to give credence to her preposterous tale? I think Tullia may have been thinking of both.

Selling indulgences was a common practice of the Church. Indulgences supposedly shortened the amount of time a soul was required to stay in purgatory before being allowed to enter the kingdom of heaven.

It was a great source of revenue for the Church. Child mortality was high. What grieving mother wouldn't scrape together every last cent to save her innocent child's soul?

———

I SLIPPED MY ROBE OVER MY HEAD. A LENGTH OF ROPE SERVED AS my belt. The wool was stiff and scratchy.

It would soften over time. Little did I know then just how long I'd be wearing it.

On the second day of the journey, I was able to leave the wagon and walk with the others, though with a limp. I must have twisted a knee when I fainted.

We were headed back to Esquaveta. The monastery was on Mount Clovis. The crates and sacks were full of supplies so they could make it through the winter.

There were a total of twelve monks, including me and my two children. A horse pulled the wagon, and a donkey carried more supplies.

We stopped every few hours for prayers, which Father Donovan, my *angel of death*, recited entirely in Latin. It still gave me chills to look at his pale face.

"A witch?" I asked Pito.

"Tullia's idea," he said.

"And the epileptic imbecile?"

"That was mine."

I told him that epileptics weren't imbeciles, but, based on my experience, tended to be more intelligent than most people, "just more sensitive."

For our meals we ate lentils along with the pickled cabbage Mortamus so loved. He was right. The combination of sourness and freshness had helped revive me.

"Delicious, isn't it?" he asked as he watched me eat.

I smiled and nodded.

Without asking directly, I tried to find out what he knew about a possible war with Oxatania. I got the impression he knew nothing about it, but Father Donovan must have overheard us talking. He came by and reminded Mortamus that "we don't concern ourselves with earthly matters."

On our third day, we had just reached the outer foothills of Mount Clovis when horsemen appeared on the horizon. I tried to convince myself that they weren't headed for us, but they kept getting closer and closer.

I'd kept my hood down as I walked, so as not to become overheated, but pulled it up as they approached. Tullia did the same.

There were no female monks. Her robe was meant for a man and was too large for her. She'd complained about that, but it helped conceal her now.

The horsemen dismounted. There were four of them. I pulled the dagger out from under my belt, the belt beneath my robe, not the one around it. I didn't know if they were soldiers or bandits, but it didn't make much difference. They all carried swords.

Father Donovan stepped forward to welcome the men and was immediately shoved out of the way. My dagger was in my fist, hidden beneath my sleeve.

As the men came toward us, Tullia turned her head, ever so slightly, away from the men. Her eyes were in the shadows of her hood.

One of the men approached the monk Diego and demanded to know where we were headed, where we had come from, and what we had in the wagon.

Diego met his gaze but didn't answer. The man raised his sword to the monk's throat.

"Diego has taken a vow of silence," said Father Donovan.

One of the men snorted, although hearing his laugh, I realized he was more of a boy than a man, fourteen years old at the most. "Cut out his tongue!" the boy urged. "Since he's not using it anyway."

Pito stepped up beside Diego and spoke with calm and self-assurance. "A vow is a promise made to Jesus Christ."

His words gave the soldier pause. He lowered his sword but then pointed it at Pito. "So why do you talk so much?"

"We each express our devotion to God in our own way."

"And what's your way?"

"Study and prayer," said Pito.

If I didn't know better, I would have thought he'd been a monk for his entire life.

"We're pleased to share our food with you if you're hungry," said Father Donovan.

The soldiers laughed. "Pleased to share!" one of them repeated.

While this was going on, one of the men was slowly making his way from monk to monk, studying our faces. He came to Mortamus.

I would be next, and then Tullia.

Mortamus smiled stupidly as the man stared.

I decided they were soldiers. Bandits wouldn't be looking so hard at our faces.

The man's stare moved slowly down Mortamus, stopping at his feet.

The other monks wore simple sandals. Mortamus's boots were crafted from fine soft leather. I could see the soldier's dirty toenails between the shredded leather of his own boots.

The other three men were busily stuffing their saddlebags with supplies from the wagon. Orders or not, they paid little attention to us.

When the four of them finally rode off, leaving us unharmed, Father Donovan led us in prayer. It was in Latin, so I didn't know if he was thanking the Lord for keeping us safe or asking him to have pity on those who threatened us.

Mortamus's bare feet were as pink and fleshy as his face.

"At least they didn't take the pickled cabbage," I said to him.

He laughed. He didn't know that his boots had saved the life of a princess.

49

A MIRACLE ON THE
MOUNTAIN

Aʟɪɢʜᴛ sɴᴏᴡ ʙᴇɢᴀɴ ᴛᴏ fall. I suggested to Mortamus that he might do better to ride in the wagon, but Father Donovan answered for him. "Suffering of the flesh purifies the soul."

It became colder and snowed harder as we continued up Mount Clovis. Our robes kept us warm.

Along the way I collected whatever might prove useful when we reached the monastery. The plants had lost their leaves, but I was able to find buckthorn bark, chaga, angelica root, and anisette seeds.

Pito spent a lot of time in quiet discussions with Father Donovan. Tullia helped me make it up some of the steeper parts, and I asked her if she knew where Pito had gotten the name Ippolita.

"Pito had nothing to do with it!" she replied, letting go of my arm.

I lost my footing and slid all the way back down the slope.

Tullia stared at me awhile, hands on hips, before coming down after me. "I think it's a pretty name," she said as she helped me back up. "Not everything has to be Greek or Roman!"

I agreed that Ippolita was a lovely name.

PITO OFFERED HIS SHOES, MINE ACTUALLY, TO MORTAMUS. "WE can take turns wearing them."

But Mortamus, who had been a monk for less than four months, refused. He wanted to prove his worth to Father Donovan. He did let Tullia rub his feet when we stopped for meals or prayer. I continued to scavenge for whatever roots, bark, or seeds I could use for frostbite, but I worried that amputation might be the best I could do for him.

To reach the monastery, we had to first climb above it and then circle around back down. The monastery was in a small mountain valley, surrounded by jagged, snow-covered peaks. Looking down, I saw two large gray stone buildings and several smaller ones. The snowfall had stopped, and the sky was blue and bright. Father Donovan had finally relented and allowed Mortamus to ride in the wagon.

As we headed down, I lost my footing and slid halfway down the slope. Evidently a vow of silence doesn't preclude laughter.

Other monks came out to greet us as we crossed a snow-covered meadow. I was so exhausted, and relieved to have finally reached our destination, that it took me a moment to grasp that these monks weren't celebrating our arrival. It seemed that disaster had struck the monastery two nights earlier.

Beneath the blanket of snow, the monastery was in shambles. It had been attacked by bears, drunken bears no less. It seemed that the bears had gotten into the wine barrels first.

From there they ravaged the cheese grotto, the barn, and the goat pens, and then entered the two main buildings. One housed the chapel and dormitory. The other consisted of the abbot's quarters and the library.

It was in the library where the biggest disaster occurred. A bear with a taste for sheepskin had eaten, or at least tried to eat, a rare fifth-century St. Augustine manuscript.

A monk named Hollister had been severely mauled when he tried to wrest it from the drunken bear's jaws. Hollister had already been given last rites when I went to see him.

I made some poultices from chaga and angelica root and applied them to his wounds. The bear rampage had also left a number of loaves of bread buried in the snow. Mold had already begun to sprout.

The monks also kept bees. They used the wax for candles and made mead from fermented honey.

As my bread mold soup simmered, I melted some wax in a pot. I added two types of tree fungus to the wax, along with ground bark, anisette seeds, and more of the angelica root.

Mortamus dipped his feet into the wax while it was still warm, then let out a pleasure-filled sigh.

"That feels really good."

The wax would solidify into a hard and therapeutic casing.

IPPOLITA HAD BEEN HELPING TO ROUND UP THE GOATS. SHE TOLD me later that although the animals ran away from all the other monks, they'd come to her.

"Maybe because I'm a girl."

I said I thought it was more than just that.

She smiled beneath her father's approval.

Two days later, as I was leaving the chapel, I overheard Father

Bartolomé, the abbot, speaking to Father Donovan. He said he didn't believe that they had just happened to find us by the side of the trail. We were a miracle, placed there by God.

The abbot hadn't been referring to my ability as a physician or to Ippolita's affinity with goats. The true miracle was happening in the library.

There, my son, Marcus, had begun the seemingly impossible task of collecting and organizing all the small shreds of parchment left by the bear, which he then copied onto new sheets of parchment.

When Father Donovan asked the abbot how Marcus filled in the parts that the bear had eaten, Father Bartolomé replied, "Divine inspiration."

50

THE POWER OF THE
ORDINARY

FATHER BARTOLOMÉ BELIEVED IN the transcendental power of mundane routine. It was the soil from which enlightenment flourished.

There were ten prayer services each day. The first, Mattens, was held just after midnight. The last was after sundown. We had two meals. When we weren't praying or eating, we worked.

My job, when I wasn't called upon to be a physician, was to tend to the garden. Though nothing grew this time of year, I had a lot to do to prepare for spring.

Ippolita, who remained with the goats, milked them every morning and assisted in making cheese. She would bring me wheelbarrows full of their manure.

Women weren't usually permitted at the monastery, not even as visitors. The large ruby had also bought her the right to stay. It also helped to have Marcus as her brother. Still, the abbot made it known that when spring came and the mountain passes were clear again, she would be sent to a nunnery. She was a hard worker, and in the dankness of winter, buried in her robe and smelling of goats, I'm not sure the other monks thought of her as female.

I remained on guard nonetheless. Ippolita's mat was in a corner, and I slept crosswise by her feet. If anyone dared approach her at night, he'd have to get by me. They might have been monks, but beneath their robes they were men.

We trudged down the stairs to chapel and tried to stay awake during Mattens while Father Bartolomé, or sometimes Father Donovan, chanted in Latin. I often heard the wind howling through the mountains.

Marcus didn't sleep in the dormitory but in a bed in the library, with sheets and a pillow. He wasn't required to attend chapel services either. According to the abbot, his work was "a form of prayer," and it was essential he be well rested and alert. A slip of a quill could spoil a week's worth of effort.

The main meal of the day was served after noon prayers. We'd have a stew of beans or lentils mixed with root vegetables, along with pickled cabbage or cucumbers. It was all served atop trencher bread, a round flat disk as hard as any plate. Ground acorns had been mixed with the grain. By the end of the meal, the juices from the stew made it almost soft enough to chew, if one was so inclined. I usually gave my bread to Mortamus.

My friend's feet had healed, minus one toe. Hollister's last rites had also been proven to be premature.

Marcus rarely ate with us but dined with Father Bartolomé and Father Donovan in the abbot's quarters. He didn't tell me or his sister much about these meals, especially after he complained one time about how difficult it was to remove sticky honey from his fingers. Ippolita just glared at him as he explained that his hands had to be immaculate. "It takes twelve precise strokes to properly make the letter *M*."

"Honey!" exclaimed Ippolita. "You're complaining about honey!"

I later learned he ate soft warm bread with goat cheese and apricot preserves. I didn't tell his sister.

One afternoon, I was warming my hands over Tullia's steaming wheelbarrow of manure. Her hands were buried down in the goat-shit, where it was even warmer. Our breath mingled in a small cloud beneath our frozen faces.

She never complained. There was a rosy glow to her face, and her brown eye shone almost as bright as the blue one. It had been a long time since I'd seen her so happy.

I was happy too. Father Bartolomé's dull routine might not have brought me enlightenment, but I did feel a kind of spiritual contentment.

Still, I would have sold my soul for a cup of tea!

"Here comes my brother," Ippolita said, looking up from the wheelbarrow. I could only detect a tiny hint of derisiveness when she said *brother*.

Marcus stopped at the garden gate, stretched his arms wide, and came through. "Nothing like a blast of fresh air to reinvigorate me."

"Don't you have more *M*s to stroke?" Tullia asked.

He said he needed a break, then asked if we wanted to join him for a brisk walk around the compound.

I might have joined him, but I had stepped on a shovel the day before and twisted my right ankle.

Tullia also declined. "I have to shovel more goatshit. You should try it. It's very invigorating!"

As we watched him walk away, she asked, "Now who's the princess?"

51

CHEESE WHEEL

W E BATHED ONCE A week. There were four barrels for forty monks. Each barrel was used three times before it was refilled with fresh warm water. Our soap was made from ash and lye.

Pito would always be one of the first four. I did my best to make sure I got clean warm water. I would appraise the queue, divide by threes, and then surreptitiously move forward or back one space in line, but somehow, I rarely figured it correctly.

Ippolita would always be last to bathe, usually in cold and dirty water, and only after the other monks had left the area. I stood guard. As the weather became warmer and her hair longer, I noticed more and more monks trying to sneak a glance back toward the barrels. As her father, I took some comfort in the fact that the smell of goats never completely washed away.

Her hair, though still quite short, had become soft and fluffy. Somehow it seemed to have evened out too, despite Pito's hacking.

Working in the sunshine, she kept her hood down, and I was forever telling her she needed to keep her hair hidden.

"They know I'm a girl!" she'd reply.

When I calmly told her it didn't help to call attention to her femininity, she replied with the same words sixteen-year-old girls have been saying to their fathers for centuries. "You can't tell me what to do!"

THE SNOW MELTED. GREENERY POKED UP THROUGH THE SOIL IN the garden. After toiling through the gloom of winter, it was heartening to know my hard work would soon bear fruit, literally. Blossoms began to appear on the plum, fig, and apricot trees. Grain and wildflowers would soon cover the same meadow where Ippolita had scrambled knee-deep in snow as she rounded up the goats.

I breathed a long breath of the sweet mountain air. But sadly, I knew I would never see the flowering meadow or any of the fruits and vegetables that grew in the garden. Once the mountain passes were clear, the monastery would no longer be safe for us. News of the missing princess would find its way up the mountain. And although Father Bartolomé hadn't mentioned the nunnery for some time, I had no reason to expect he would let Ippolita remain much longer.

I spotted her coming out of the cheese grotto. Her hood was down, and she was trying to balance a cheese wheel on her head.

Even from a distance I could see her intense concentration. She kept jerking her arms up toward her head, ready to catch the cheese if it fell, then slowly easing them back down again as she gained confidence.

I wasn't the only one watching. All around the compound, every hooded head was turned in her direction.

Marcus too was watching her. He must have taken a break

from his work in the library. He moved quietly toward the garden, then crouched low by the gate, ready to pounce.

Ippolita was slowly making her way to the kitchen. Her hands continued to move up toward the cheese, then down again. As she passed the garden gate, Marcus leapt up and roared.

Ippolita screamed. The cheese wheel fell from her head. It landed on its edge and rolled a surprisingly long distance before finally tipping over.

"You thought I was a bear, didn't you?" Marcus asked with a laugh.

Many of the other monks who'd been watching all this were also laughing.

Tullia wasn't. "No, I think you're a donkey!" she shot back. "How would you like it if I surprised you like that while you were making one of your precious *M*s?"

"It wouldn't bother me at all. I'm always in complete control of my emotions." He went to retrieve the cheese.

"And not all of the donkey," she shouted after him. "Just the rear!"

Marcus picked it up and started to bring it back, but stopped and then carefully placed it on his head.

Ippolita laughed. "You won't be able to take two steps!"

Marcus moved one foot slightly in front of the other. "That's one."

"Not even a half," corrected his sister.

He moved the other foot. "Two."

"One," said Ippolita, moving toward him.

"Three," said Marcus, inching closer.

"One and a half," said Ippolita.

"Four."

She stepped up and roared in his face. The cheese didn't even wobble.

"I am in control of my emotions at all times," he told her, as he took another small step.

"Five."

"I don't care," said Ippolita. She turned her back to him but then suddenly spun around and barked.

"Six," said Marcus.

She tried jumping around him, waving her arms, and screeching like a wild monkey.

"It's all about focus," Marcus said, unfazed by her antics. "Seven."

She leaned close, and I thought she was about to scream into his ear, but instead she gave it a quick kiss.

The cheese fell.

"I told you you couldn't do it," she said in triumph.

Marcus's face was even redder than Mortamus's.

LATER, WHEN SHE ARRIVED WITH HER DAILY WHEELBARROW OF goat manure, her hood was up. "You're right, Anatole," she said. "I need to keep it up."

Her change in attitude alarmed me. "What happened? Did one of the monks—"

"It's Pito," she said.

"Marcus," I quietly corrected.

"He's fallen in love with me," she said, and then sighed wistfully.

I asked her what he said, or did.

"He doesn't have to do or say anything. A girl knows. Poor boy. I just hope he can restrain his natural urges."

Her blue eye sparkled.

52

WHISPERS

THERE WERE TWO TRAILS that led to the monastery. We had come from the east. The western trail was supposedly much more treacherous. I was in the garden, stringing sticks and poles together in order to make a trellis for peas, when I noticed someone coming across the meadow from the west. He wasn't wearing a monk's robe.

This was what I'd been fearing. The mountain passes had cleared. He might have been the first to make his way up to the monastery, but I knew he wouldn't be the last.

When he got closer, I could see he was a simple peasant, and I tried to convince myself that he wouldn't know anything about the missing princess. His clothes were little more than rags, and he only wore one sandal.

I glanced toward the goat pen. Ippolita must have seen him too. Her hood was up, and she was turned away from him.

Father Bartolomé came out of his quarters and welcomed the visitor, warmly clasping his shoulders. The silent monk, Diego, who cleaned for the abbot and prepared his food, handed the man a goatskin.

The stranger took a long drink, swished it around in his mouth, and spat it out. Father Bartolomé escorted the visitor back to his quarters and Diego trailed a few steps behind.

Later, and even more alarming, the monastery's unalterable routine was altered. Afternoon prayers had been canceled. And then Hollister came to the garden and said the abbot wanted to see me in his quarters.

As I headed across the compound, I had the sensation that everyone was watching me and that they were whispering behind my back. I reminded myself that I was a pious monk, here in the service of Jesus Christ. Then I knocked on the door.

Diego let me in.

I could detect no sign of ill will or suspicion on Father Bartolomé's face as he greeted me. If anything, there was contrition.

"I'm afraid I may have exaggerated your abilities, Galen," he said, and then introduced me to Bruno, the visitor.

Bruno smiled at me and said, "I expect nothing less than miracles."

I'd been brought there simply to treat the many wounds Bruno had suffered while coming up the western trail.

"Only God can perform miracles," I said. "I am his instrument."

"Marcus is Galen's son," said the abbot.

Bruno glanced at what I presumed was the door to the library. "He's a very impressive young man. You must be proud."

None of Bruno's wounds were serious. I saw no indication of infection.

Throughout the winter, I'd been treating the other monks for mostly minor injuries and kept a supply of salves and ointments in the garden shed. I went to get them. Again, I had the sense that the other monks were watching me, and that as soon as I looked their way, they'd avert their gaze.

AS IT TURNED OUT, BRUNO WAS NOT A PEASANT BUT A WEALTHY shipping merchant from Torteluga. Every year he donned sackcloth and sandals and hiked up Mount Clovis to pray in the monastery chapel, "to cleanse the stench of money from my soul." I got the impression that he made a generous donation to the monastery as well.

He had so many scrapes and abrasions, it was hard to know where to begin. I started at the scalp and worked my way down. "*Galen?*" he asked curiously. "The Greek physician?"

I shrugged. "My parents gave me the name."

"And with it, your occupation, it would seem."

I LEFT THE ABBOT'S QUARTERS AND WENT STRAIGHT TO THE GOAT pen. Ippolita was brushing a goat. She looked up to see me attempting to climb over the wood-and-wire fence.

"There's a gate around the other side," she said.

I knew that. I'd thought this way would be faster, and it would have been if my robe hadn't gotten snagged on a knot of wire.

Tullia shook her head and laughed as she watched me try to wriggle free. "Careful," she said.

I managed to free my robe and immediately landed sideways on the dirt.

Ippolita hurried over and helped me to my feet. The goat she had been brushing lowered its head and glared at me.

"We need to leave," I told her.

I told Tullia that I'd formulated a new plan. It was foolish to think we could have hiked to the *neder lands.*

There was a well-known ratio: 23 to 7 to 1. If it takes you twenty-three days to walk to a place, it would only take seven days by horse-back. And you could travel that same distance in only one day by ship. Of course, people recognized there were variables that affected the accuracy of those numbers, but the general concept still held.

"We'll take the western trail to Torteluga," I told her, "and then we can trade some of the jewels for passage aboard a ship going to Antwerp." Antwerp was a port city in the *neder lands,* as vibrant as any of those on the Italian peninsula. I conceded that the western trail was reportedly steep and treacherous, but that also made it less likely that we'd encounter soldiers coming up the other way.

"Why?" she asked. "I like it here."

"The trails are passable. We're not safe anymore."

"He's just a harmless peasant."

I let her know that Bruno was one of the *popolo grasso,* but that wasn't the point. "Ever since he got here, the other monks have been staring at us."

She looked around the compound. "No one's staring."

"They won't look when they see you're looking."

She remained unconvinced so I reminded her what Father Bartolomé had said about sending her to a nunnery.

She just shrugged and said, "Maybe he changed his mind."

She returned to her goats. I left by way of the gate.

DURING THE EVENING MEAL, I HAD THE IMPRESSION THAT EVEN the silent monks were whispering about me, with their hands. Mortamus had explained that they had developed their own way of communicating using an elaborate system of arm, hand, and finger movements, everything from "please pass the salt" to petty comments about how some of the monks don't work as hard as others.

"They even tell jokes!" Mortamus insisted. He'd seen them gesturing with their hands and fingers and then erupting with laughter.

"What's the point of a vow of silence if you're still talking?"

I thought about Diego silently working in the abbot's quarters. From my experience with Harwell, I knew just how easy it was to ignore someone who never said a word. When I was with Pito in the dungeon, I'd sometimes forget Harwell was there, and he was sitting right next to me.

Perhaps Diego had overheard something Bruno had said to Father Bartolomé in confidence, something about a princess with one brown eye and one blue.

THAT EVENING WE RETIRED IN THE DORMITORY AS USUAL, AND then shortly after midnight Ippolita and I followed the other monks down to the chapel for Mattens. I hadn't slept in the interim.

There were only nine pews in our small chapel. Ippolita and I sat in the back. Marcus, presumably, was sleeping snugly between the sheets of his warm bed, his head on a soft pillow.

The first two prayers were led by Father Donovan. (I think it was two. I never knew for certain when one prayer ended and another one began.) Then Father Bartolomé rose from the seat and took over the service.

"We will say a prayer for the soul of King Sandro," he said, speaking in Esquavetian.

Ippolita, who'd been struggling to stay awake, suddenly sat up straight.

"I learned earlier today that our beloved king had died this past winter."

Ippolita's hand tightened around my wrist.

The prayer was in Latin, but when it concluded, the abbot returned to the vernacular. "We will now say a prayer for Queen Corinna."

It too was in Latin. Ippolita's trembling hand caused my arm to tremble too.

The queen, however, had not died. After the completion of the prayer, Father Bartolomé told us that "despite her enormous grief," the queen had remarried for the sake of the kingdom.

The abbot then led us in a prayer for the new king, a man whom he described as so humble, "he only speaks in whispers."

53

THE LIBRARY TABLE

I LISTENED TO TULLIA'S MUFFLED sobs throughout the night. From the moment of her birth, she had been a disappointment to her father, and continued to be so for the next sixteen years. As a child, she relished any rare kindness he bestowed upon her. Maybe she was remembering those kindnesses. Or perhaps she wasn't crying for him but for the father she always wished he would be.

By morning her tears had ceased. As the other monks filed out for the predawn service, she pulled me back and said the same words I'd said to her the day before.

"We need to leave."

We allowed ourselves to fall farther behind the other monks as we headed down the stairs. That none of them turned around to look at us was more revealing than if they had.

When we reached the chapel, we turned the other way, outside. In the darkness I kicked a pail and sent it clanging against a post, but it probably wasn't as loud as it seemed.

Nobody rushed outside after us.

I opened the door to the abbot's quarters. Light came from a single candle on the table. Through an open door I could see Father Bartolomé's meager bedchamber.

We went to the door that was closed.

Pito looked at us with surprise. He was already at work, seated behind a very long table. He had been holding a candle close to a small scrap of parchment and set both items down. "I'm sorry about your father," he said to Tullia.

"He wasn't my father," she answered, without any of the emotion I'd heard in the night. "He was King Sandro."

As I moved closer to the table, I saw that it was covered with hundreds if not thousands of bits of parchment, all neatly laid out, presumably in some kind of order. Some of the larger pieces might have been half a page, while others contained only one or two partial letters. There was also a stack of the new pages that Pito had already copied.

"What do you do about the parts the bear ate?" I asked.

"I try to put my mind into the mind of St. Augustine," he said. "If no words come, I get images."

I saw a small illustration on the page on top of the completed stack. No wonder Voltharo had worried about being replaced. Pito's drawing was a work of art, one that was deceivingly simple in appearance. It didn't look like a product of the Renaissance but seemed to come from an earlier era.

I told him our plan to sail from Torteluga to Antwerp. Tullia added plans of her own, saying we could use whatever jewels we had left to set up his own scrivener's shop.

He agreed it was a much better plan.

"We need to go right away," Tullia said. "It's no longer safe here."

"You should," he agreed.

She might not have noticed that he had said *you* and not *we*. Esquavetian pronouns were somewhat more ambiguous than modern English. But I also heard it in his voice.

"You're not safe here either," I told him.

"My work is too important," he said. "They won't be looking for me. Pito died from the plague."

"You're not coming?" Tullia said, finally understanding.

"I'll meet you in Antwerp, after my work is finished."

"How long will that be?" Tullia demanded. "Five years? Ten? Forty?"

"For the first time in my life, I have a purpose," he told her.

Tullia spun around and left the library, slamming the door behind her.

Pito came out from behind the table. "Thank you, my friend," he said.

We shook hands.

The door flung open and Tullia marched back in. She strode past us and then swept her heavily sleeved arm from one end of the table to the other.

Pito watched in silence as every last scrap fell to the floor, along with his candle, his quills, and two small jars of ink, one indigo and the other red.

Tullia left the library without even a glance in his direction.

54

THE WESTERN TRAIL

I TOLD FATHER BARTOLOMÉ I'D be taking Ippolita to a nunnery in Verona, and then I would return to the monastery. I didn't know if he believed me or just willingly went along with my deception.

"We don't concern ourselves with earthly matters," he said, and then he assured me that Marcus would be safe. "You can return Ippolita's robe when you come back. She'll need it to keep warm."

He handed me two goatskins filled with fresh water, a wheel of cheese, and two of the trencher disks.

THERE WAS NO GRAND SEND-OFF, NOT EVEN A CHANCE FOR US to say goodbye to the other monks. Father Bartolomé didn't want to disrupt the ordinary routine of the monastery any more than it already had been.

As we crossed the meadow Tullia only looked back once. When we reached the rocky mountainside, it became obvious to me that

I would need both hands free. I removed my robe, then slipped the cheese and the two disks of trencher bread under my tunic. I tied my belt tight around the bottom to hold everything in place.

Tullia had a look of disgust on her face, watching me. When I reminded her that I didn't sweat, she merely rolled her eyes.

She helped me maneuver the robe back over my head, and then we started up. I grabbed on to whatever would hold me, even if only briefly: branches, clumps of stalks, small cracks in the rocks.

Four months earlier, I would never have considered even attempting this climb. But that was before I boldly freed Pito, navigated a secret passageway, and climbed down first a rope and then the outside wall of the castle!

When we reached a relatively flat area, Tullia said, "You need to rest awhile."

I was breathing heavily but told her I was fine.

"I don't want you to faint and fall off the mountain!" she said, and insisted I let my body temperature cool down.

Annoyed, I sat on the dirt. I didn't feel warm. The sun wasn't up yet. But as we waited, I couldn't help but wonder if Tullia had another reason for wanting to stop. Maybe she still hoped that Pito would change his mind.

"Hah! I knew it!" she said haughtily.

The monastery was still in view, and I saw a hooded figure running across the meadow. He was waving his arms above his head.

"Well, if he thinks . . ." Tullia started to say, but she never finished her thought.

The monk was now below us. His hood had fallen back, and I could see Mortamus's round red face.

Tullia stood up. "We don't have time to dawdle," she said, then turned and continued up the trail.

I waved goodbye to my friend, then turned and quickly caught up to Tullia.

"I knew it wouldn't be him," she said. "You saved his life, but do you think he'd bother to say goodbye? His work is too important for that!"

I knew better than to point out that Pito and I had already said our goodbyes.

WE HAD LOST SIGHT OF THE MONASTERY AND VALLEY. THERE must have been an avalanche at some time, because we had to scale a series of very large boulders. Tullia often had to go up first and then reach down to help me.

She was pulling me up over an edge when she said, "I told you he was arrogant," and then let go of me.

Only a sudden surge of strength and agility kept me from tumbling backward.

"And selfish!" she added, as I pulled myself the rest of the way up.

Later there was a boulder so large, we had to tie our two belts together. These were the rope belts of our robes. My other belt was still in place, beneath my robe.

She lay across the top of the boulder and dangled the double rope down to me. A large crevice ran down the boulder, and I wedged myself against its jagged edges while I struggled.

"After all you did for him!" she angrily said down to me, almost as if I were to blame. I could only hope she wouldn't let go of her end of the rope.

It looked like the boulders continued all the way to the very peak of the mountain, but I was relieved to discover we didn't have to climb that high. Midway up we came to a break in the mountain.

We had reached the western trail and were finally able to head downhill.

The trail was so narrow, I had to watch every step, often finding myself pressed against the mountain on one side of me and a steep drop-off on the other.

Tullia seemed to have little difficulty, but then again, she was quite a bit thinner than me. "What's so *meaningful* about copying words someone else has written?" she asked.

I told her Pito was more than a copier. "He's an artist."

"That's what *he* thinks, anyway," she said.

BEFORE I CAME TO THIS CAFÉ, OR TOOK THE TOUR OF WHAT IS now called Tiger Castle, I visited the Biblioteca Capitolare in Verona, which may be the world's oldest library.

Included in their collection is a fifth-century St. Augustine manuscript, which is displayed inside a protective glass case. The manuscript was open to an illustration of St. Augustine himself, sitting at a desk, pondering. An anonymous sixteenth-century monk was given credit for the illustration as well as the manuscript's partial restoration.

"Hello, friend," I said aloud.

55

PITO'S BOOK

I F HE'S HALF AS smart as he thinks he is," Tullia said, "then he should write his own book, instead of copying something someone else has written."

We were sitting on the trail. Tullia's legs dangled over the side. I was afraid to sit that close and kept my legs stretched out along the trail.

She continued to insist on frequent rest stops, so I wouldn't faint and fall off the mountain. I was pretty sure that whatever dizziness I felt had been caused by my fear of heights and not by my rising body temperature.

Still, my sore joints and muscles could use the breaks. The biggest problem was that after each one, I found it more and more difficult to stand and start up again.

I didn't know if she was truly concerned about me or still held out hope that Pito would come after us. Of course, I didn't dare pose that question to her. Or else she might have pushed me off the mountain.

I wiggled my fingers and kept opening and closing my fists to keep my hands from cramping. I was feeling hungry but was afraid to remove my robe on this narrow trail to get to the bread and cheese.

"Not that I would ever read it!" she snapped, as if I had dared to suggest otherwise.

We continued along the trail. I remained focused on every step, while Tullia rattled off all the reasons she would never read Pito's book.

"Uninteresting . . . tedious . . . pompous . . . What makes him think he can write a book? How pompous is that?"

We came to a place where a large flat rock jutted out over a cliff. It was maybe three meters wide, and most of it was hanging out from the mountain. Tullia suggested that it would be a good place to sit and eat, calling it a "natural balcony."

I was scared to even look at it and told her I didn't think it was safe.

She stepped out onto it and continued all the way to its outer edge. There, she jumped up and down a few times. "Seems safe to me," she reported, and then laughed at my terror.

I sat down on the rock ledge, staying much closer to the mountain side of it. Tullia sat with her legs dangling above a vast forest, far below.

I struggled to remove my robe, having to pull it up over my head. My arms became caught in the twisted sleeves. The more frantically I tried to remove it, the more twisted it got. It might have been easier to do so standing up, but I didn't want to be stumbling around the rock, unable to see, if even for a moment.

I heard Tullia's voice above me—"Just stay still"—and then she yanked the robe free.

That was when I saw the bear.

It was lumbering up the trail toward us. Tullia dropped the robe. "Quick, put a spell on it," she whispered.

The bear stopped and stared at us. Then it roared so loud I thought I could feel the rock beneath me vibrate. More likely, it was my bones that were vibrating. I was looking at a mouthful of long sharp teeth.

I pulled the cheese wheel out from under my tunic and carefully set it rolling. It rolled off our rock ledge to the trail, then bounced a bit on a pebble, and turned down it, straight toward the bear, gathering speed as it went.

The bear watched it curiously, and then, when it came close, swatted it with its enormous paw.

The cheese skidded onto its side but somehow became upright again. It rolled off the edge of the mountain and down the steep slope toward the forest. The bear bounded after it.

"You did it, Natto!" Tullia exulted. "You enchanted the bear!"

Well, who was I to contradict a princess?

56

THE DEVIL'S MESSENGERS

D ULL, DIM-WITTED, REPETITIVE . . ."
We were off the steepest part of the trail and walking
in a gently sloping forest, probably the same forest we'd
seen from above. There wasn't a lot of light, and I wasn't sure we
were still on the right trail. Tullia didn't seem to notice. She was
too busy critiquing Pito's book.

"Original? What's so original about ancient Greek and Roman
philosophy?"

As long as we continued to head downhill, I knew we were ba-
sically going the right way. The problem was that ridges and ravines
crisscrossed the forest, so it wasn't always obvious which downhill
to take.

"If he thinks I'm going to wait in Antwerp for him to . . ." Tullia started to say. "Forty years? I wouldn't wait one day!"

I held out a hand, stopping her. I thought I'd heard something.

"Why would he want me anyway, if he's married to my mother?"

It took me a moment to realize she had switched from Pito to Dalrympl.

"She's prettier than me," Tullia went on.

I heard something crackle. Someone was coming through the trees.

"And both her eyes are the same color."

"Sh!" I whispered.

"What is it?"

I could hear more movement, and then voices.

Tullia heard them too. "Maybe they have food," she whispered.

We still hadn't eaten. The trencher was too hard to cut with my dagger.

The noises became louder. Tullia looked in that direction, then turned and shouted, "Run!"

She had already started, and I raced after her but then stopped. Tullia was fast enough to get away from whoever was chasing us, and the last thing I wanted to do was lead them to her.

I turned and ran in a different direction.

They could only kill me. They could do much worse to her.

My left foot kicked against something, probably a root. First my hands slammed the ground, and then my face.

It took me a moment to regain my bearings. When I looked up, I was surrounded.

"It's a monk!" one said, disgustedly, and then he spat on the ground next to me.

There were seven of them, but I was focused on the one holding an axe above my head. He might not have been as large as Harwell, but he was still a lot bigger than me.

He ordered me to give him anything I had of value.

"I've taken a vow of poverty," I said, and then, remembering Pito's words, I added that "a vow is a promise made to Jesus Christ."

The words didn't have the same effect coming from me. He raised the axe, but one of the others told him to wait.

"I want the robe. Without blood all over it."

The axe-man glared at him, then turned his glare on me. "Take it off!"

I'd had enough trouble removing my robe while sitting. It was even harder to do while lying on my back, not that I was in any great hurry.

"Anatole?" called Tullia.

She'd come back to look for me.

My head was caught inside my robe, but I was able to slip it back through the neckhole. I felt like a turtle poking my head out of my shell.

Only the man with the axe remained above me. The others now had ahold of Tullia, some distance away, and were struggling to remove her robe.

"Save some for me!" the axe-man shouted to them. He was done waiting, blood or no blood. The axe came down.

I felt the thump as it hit my chest.

And there it stopped.

My attacker and I looked at each other, both astonished that I was still alive.

A triumphant whoop resounded. The men holding Tullia had managed to remove her robe.

Thereby freeing her hands.

I saw just a flash of her knife. One of her attackers fell instantly; another gave an anguished cry as he slowly sank to his knees.

That's what a princess does!

Above me, the man raised his axe again, but then he gasped and dropped it. Pito was twisting a length of rope around his neck.

The man clawed at the rope until his life was squeezed out of him. He fell beside me.

"Gold, silver, jewels," Tullia said, taunting the men around her. "Come and take it."

There were four of them left. When one dared to make a move toward her, she'd whirl around, knife flailing, and the man would have to jump back.

Pito picked up the axe. I took out my dagger.

As we came toward them, I could see that the dead man's throat had been slashed. The one on his knees was clutching his hand and moaning.

The others took a step back when they saw us. "If we'd known you were monks . . ." one started.

"We're not monks," Pito answered. "We're Satan's messengers, sent here from hell."

All four men ran.

The one on his knees struggled to his feet and staggered after them, leaving two fingers behind.

57

ENCHANTMENT

Pito and i dragged the two dead bodies to a gully, and Tullia tossed in the two fingers. She and I attempted a prayer, piecing together whatever Latin words and phrases we could remember from the chapel services.

Pito, who actually understood Latin, just shook his head and smiled.

"Then you say the prayer!" Tullia snapped at him.

"The words don't matter," he said.

Pito had lunched with the abbot, Father Donovan, and Bruno, and Bruno had mentioned he'd be taking the eastern pass down the mountain, even though Torteluga was in the opposite direction. It wasn't just that the western trail was more treacherous. He'd said he'd been attacked by bandits, and was lucky to be alive.

"Anatole and I were just fine without you," Tullia said. "Go back to your library and make your precious letters."

Pito took hold of her hands and looked her in the eye. "I realized I couldn't leave you," he said.

All of Tullia's anger melted away. Her brown eye deepened, and her blue one twinkled.

"I couldn't do that to Anatole," Pito said. "You're such a pain in the ass."

He laughed.

≥◇≤

IF YOU'RE THINKING "A PAIN IN THE ASS" IS TOO MODERN AN EXpression, you're correct. Pito actually called her "an itchy hemorrhoid," but I worried that would come across as ugly and cruel, which wasn't how Pito intended it.

This is a good example of why I've avoided slang and vulgarities.

Pito had only meant "itchy hemorrhoid" as a joke. Regardless, Tullia wasn't laughing.

≥◇≤

WE CONTINUED DOWN THE SLOPING FOREST. THERE WAS A SMALL hole in my robe from the axe. It had sliced through one of the disks of trencher bread but only dented the other.

Tullia and I each kept a small piece of the bread in our mouths and eagerly waited for it to become soft enough to chew. Pito claimed he wasn't hungry.

Though it was very dark, we needed to keep moving. The bandits wouldn't forget the jeweled knife.

That didn't keep Tullia from insisting we stop so I wouldn't become overheated. When I said it wasn't necessary, she reminded me that these stops had saved my life.

"You don't know that," I told her.

"Otherwise, Pito would never have caught up with us."

I pointed out the fallacy in her logic. "My inability to sweat had nothing to do with being attacked by bandits."

She claimed that I was the one being illogical.

She glared at Pito when he laughed, but at least she was willing to admit that he had saved me.

We walked all night, and in the morning we came across a stream. We washed our feet and hands in the icy water. Since the source of the water was snowmelt, it was safe to drink. We refilled our goatskins.

Tullia acted out all the parts as she told Pito about our encounter with the bear. Sometimes she was me, sometimes herself, and sometimes the bear. She bent her fingers into claws, raised her arms in the air, and roared so loud that Pito flinched.

She recited a nonsensical incantation that I had supposedly said over the cheese before I rolled it toward the bear. According to her, this made the cheese glow. Then, still being me, she rolled it off the rock ledge.

Then she was the bear again, swatting the cheese. In her version, as soon as the bear touched the enchanted cheese, it was no longer a bear at all but had been transformed into a playful puppy dog. Tullia barked and yipped as she happily chased the cheese down the side of the mountain.

I kept expecting some snide comment from Pito, but he just sat on a rock by the stream, smiling his goofy smile and never once taking his eyes off her.

If anybody had the power of enchantment, it was Tullia.

"WHEN WE GET TO ANTWERP, YOU CAN OPEN YOUR OWN SCRIVener's shop," Tullia said to him. "Maybe someone will bring you another St. Augustine manuscript to copy."

She and Pito were walking side by side. I trailed behind, holding the axe.

I listened as Pito told her what he'd once told me, that the new printing presses would make scribes obsolete.

Tullia argued that machine-stamped paper would never replace the artistry of a beautifully handwritten manuscript.

"That's the princess in you talking," Pito said. "A book's art is its ideas, not the lettering."

Tullia didn't say anything for a while. I think she might have been insulted by the word *princess*, although I hadn't heard the usual derision in Pito's voice.

It was ten minutes later when she spoke again, but it was as if, in her mind, no time had passed.

"Then you should write your own book," she told him. "I said that very thing to Anatole yesterday." She turned around to face me. Pito also turned.

"Didn't I say that Pito ought to write a book?"

My bit of trencher bread was sufficiently soft. I silently chewed.

58

TORTELUGA!

W E'D FINISHED THE LAST of the trencher bread three days after leaving the monastery. It took another day and a half to reach the outskirts of Torteluga. During all that time I'd slept a total of seven hours at most.

We were beyond tired. There were long periods when Tullia seemed to disappear somewhere inside herself, only to emerge with a mysterious energy, giggling and spouting silly nonsense. Pito would respond with his own style of foolishness. I'd listen to their insane laughter with no idea of what they found to be so funny.

I could smell Torteluga long before we reached its ancient and dilapidated walls. This was more than just the stench of too many people living too close together: garbage, sewage, and rot. I could also smell the sea, and the treasures from far-off lands. I smelled adventure.

"I thought you were a mouse!" Tullia exclaimed.

"I'm not," said Pito. "I'm a rabbit."

This caused another laughing fit between them, but then Tullia, suddenly serious, asked, "Why were you experimenting on Pito?"

Pito recovered from his giggling fit too, and looked at me with earnestness.

I tried to mimic their silliness by saying I was trying to make his ears grow long, "like a rabbit!"

They weren't having it. They wanted the truth, but I didn't open that Pandora's box. Who knew what chaos would emerge from it?

Instead, I said I'd been working on a treatment for the plague. I explained that I needed to give Pito a potion that resulted in the visible symptoms of the Blue Death but was otherwise harmless.

"So you didn't do it to rescue him?" asked Tullia.

"No."

I could see disappointment in her blue eye and disillusionment in the brown.

THE ANCIENT WALL OF TORTELUGA LAY JUST AHEAD. PITO AND Tullia had yet to see it.

They'd been walking in opposing half circles. They'd bump against each other, bounce away, and then arc back toward each other and crash together.

"Stop it!"

"You stop it."

Then they'd bounce away, circle around, and do it again.

"Walk straight," Tullia ordered.

"I am walking straight. Your head is on crooked."

Tullia started to laugh, but then she noticed the wall too.

"Torteluga!" she called out, sounding something like a crumhorn, and then raced toward it.

Just before reaching the wall, she fell flat on her face.

Pito rushed after her, while I chugged along, trying to keep up.

By the time I joined them, Tullia was already sitting up and laughing. I set the axe down—monks don't carry axes—and then Pito and I helped her to her feet. We each continued to hold an arm, so she wouldn't fall again, as we went through the old gate.

The crumbling wall had been built in Roman times. For hundreds of years, Torteluga had been a sleepy fishing village, but the Renaissance had transformed it into Esquaveta's most vibrant and prosperous city. Much of the stone used for all the new construction had been taken from the old Roman wall.

We found ourselves atop a hillside, where we could see a pink and orange sky and the sun setting over the ocean. I didn't know if Pito or Tullia had even seen the ocean before. I'd only seen it once.

If we hadn't been so tired and hungry we might have stood and gazed until the sun sank beneath the sea, but we needed to find an inn before dark. Besides, a new and tantalizing aroma had drifted up to us from somewhere down below, one that didn't require my acute olfactory senses. Tullia and Pito were drawn to it as well.

We'd followed the smell down a winding tangle of steep and narrow streets. The buildings were the same colors as the sunset, and fitted together in odd ways. Someone's front stairway could be someone else's roof.

We came to a piazza, where we could see a crowd gathered around a street vendor and smoke rising from a metal basin. Tullia grabbed Pito's arm and whispered, "Potatoes!"

Pito looked at her blankly.

She described a potato as a very dense fruit, more like an olive than an apricot. She said they grew on trees in the mountains of South America.

"The potato is actually the root of the potato plant," I said, showing off my extensive knowledge of South American flora.

Tullia scowled at me. She didn't like to be corrected.

"Like a turnip?" Pito asked.

She perked up. "Just you wait," she promised.

There were statues of Greek gods along the outer edges of the piazza. Pito sat at the base of one as he tried to pry loose one of the small rubies. Tullia and I stood close, hiding him with our robes.

I think we knew we were being foolish and reckless, but we didn't care. It would have been better to find an inn where we could get a meal and a room to sleep, but we were too hungry to ignore the call of roasting potatoes.

The ruby popped free of the knife and rolled a good distance across the cobblestones. Tullia chased after it, then picked it up and took it straight to the potato vendor.

Yes, it would have been better if Pito or I had been the one who did that.

There was no organized queue. The people crowding around the vendor were holding out coins to him. They'd brought their own plates, bowls, and baskets.

We stood off to the side as we watched Tullia fight to get the vendor's attention. Using very long tongs, he would pluck four small golden potatoes out of the coals and place them in whatever dish the customer had brought. Then he'd sprinkle them with Spanish olive oil, some African salt, and ground peppercorns from the East Indies.

Tullia held out her fist. When the vendor looked her way, she opened her fingers, then quickly closed them again.

The vendor had seen what was inside. He happily provided his own basket, and filled it with as many charred and crispy potatoes as would fit inside it.

We devoured them beneath a statue of Adonis, laughing as they singed our fingers, lips, and tongues. It was the best meal I'd ever eaten, thence or hence.

59

THE WREN AND THE HUMMINGBIRD

THE SUN WAS DOWN by the time we set out to find an inn, and there wasn't much of a moon. A Tortelugan law required that all residents of the city keep a candle burning in any window that faced the street, so at least there was some light.

Having satisfied my hunger, I was now keenly aware of the riskiness of our actions. Tullia and Pito seemed oblivious to our danger, but I kept looking back to make sure we weren't being followed.

It was while I was being so vigilant that I slipped on a pile of what I could only hope was dog excrement. It would have been a very big dog.

Pito and Tullia had the courtesy not to laugh out loud, but I could see from the way they glanced at each other that they found humor in my mishap. They helped me to my feet and then held their noses as I scraped the bottom of my shoe on the cobblestones.

We would need to find a place to stay for at least a week, possibly two. Rather than risk approaching various ship captains, we decided it would be safest to wait for Bruno to return from the monastery. It would take him that long to hike down the eastern trail and then circle around Mount Clovis. We hoped to sail on one of his ships to Antwerp.

It was harder to find an inn than it should have been. The more we looked, the more lost we became. There seemed to be no order or logic behind Torteluga's layout, and whatever burst of energy we got from the potatoes was quickly fading into lethargy.

Pito remembered passing a church, and we decided we'd just sleep there for the first night, and look for an inn in the morning. It wouldn't be suspicious for monks to sleep on the floor of a church, or even in the doorway if it was locked.

When we tried going back the way we came, that too proved difficult. Tullia and Pito each had different ideas as to which way we should go.

"This is the way!" Tullia confidently declared, and we followed her down an alley that didn't look familiar to me. It led not to the church but amazingly to two inns, across from each other.

"I told you!" she said triumphantly, seeming to forget she'd been trying to get to the church.

Lanterns hung in front of each inn, illuminating painted signs. One was *The Wren*, and the other *The Hummingbird*.

Each inn appeared to be four stories tall, and they were much wider at their tops than at street level. The two roofs actually touched above the center of the alley. I had the impression of two drunkards, each holding up the other.

Pito and Tullia had another argument about which inn to choose. We went with Tullia's choice, since she had been the one who got us here.

Singing poured out of the Wren the moment Pito opened the door. The singers were fishermen, judging by their clothes and odor. They were seated at a long table, and when they saw us, their singing became louder, and, believing us to be monks, they put extra emphasis on the profane and vulgar.

One of their compatriots was passed out, his head on the table. Another lay on the floor amid puddles of ale and vomit.

Pito asked where we might find the innskeep. He had to shout to be heard above the singing.

One of the singers pointed at the man on the floor.

A rat scurried within inches of my foot.

"Try the Hummingbird!" another one suggested. "That's where the bishop goes when he's here!"

They all laughed at that.

I expected we would find more of the same, but perhaps the innskeep there would at least be upright. We crossed the alley and entered the Hummingbird.

The difference was striking.

The only singing came from a woman who was draped in colorful veils. As she moved through the tables, I caught a glimpse of a shadow of what was beneath the veils. Other women, also only in veils, were seated among the men, who were staring at the singer.

She swayed a little bit, which caused her red veil to momentarily cross with a blue one. The men whistled and hollered. Even more erotic than the glimpse of shadows was the illusion that this enchantress was wearing that most forbidden color, purple.

"Don't be shy," said a short, stout, and older woman stepping toward us. She was not in veils. "You're not the first monks in need of more than just spiritual fulfillment."

She recited a witty and brief couplet that rhymed in Esquavetian but unfortunately comes across as cumbersome and awkward in translation.

"The mouth of the hummingbird is incapable of making chirping sounds."

Your secrets are safe here.

"We just need a room for a week or two," said Pito. He opened his fist to reveal one of the small emeralds.

The innskeep seemed unfazed by it. "Two weeks!" she exclaimed, and some of the other women laughed. "You must have been at the monastery a very long time."

I saw more of these veil-draped hummingbirds seated at the base of the stairs. One rose and sauntered to me. She was tall and slender. When she stood next to me, the middle of her neck was level with my eyes. I smelled jasmine.

She ran a hand softly over my head, then down the front of my robe, and beneath my tunic.

"Like Adonis," she said, her hand on my chest.

A couple of the other hummingbirds laughed. So did Tullia.

While I would like to believe otherwise, I don't think she was referring to my godlike physique. Rather, it was my lack of hair, which made my skin as smooth as the marble statue in the piazza.

The innskeep was more interested in Tullia. "I never heard of a female monk," she said.

"We gave her the robe," Pito said. "She was cold and hungry when we found her."

The innskeep lowered Tullia's hood to get a better look. "Very pretty," she commented, fluffing Tullia's hair. "Perhaps you'd prefer to wear something a bit more colorful?"

"Keep your hands off her!" Pito ordered. He grabbed the innskeep's arm and yanked it back.

A man seemed to appear out of nowhere. He instantly had one arm around Pito's neck and was twisting Pito's arm behind his back with the other.

The emerald dropped and rolled across the floor.

The innskeep set her foot on top of it. "We don't have any rooms," she said curtly. "Try the Wren."

A loud shriek came from somewhere up above.

I turned to see a pair of bare feet and then very hairy legs come staggering down the staircase. As the man came down farther, the rest of him was revealed. He leaned over the banister, naked except for an orange veil wrapped around his waist. "Such a long, long time at sea," he lamented. "And just a brief moment ashore."

"That's mine!" a woman exclaimed, as she came down after him. Her disheveled veils no longer concealed much of anything. Laughing, she lunged for the orange veil around the man's waist.

The man jumped back, flailed his arms for a moment, then tumbled backward down the stairs.

His head banged against the floor.

I hurried to him.

He lay face up, with one foot still on the bottom step. The disheveled hummingbird watched with concern, a hand over her mouth, as I leaned close to try to detect if he was still breathing.

The innskeep came up behind me and dumped a pitcher of ale on the man's face, splashing some on me too.

The man sputtered and opened his eyes. He gazed at me, bewildered. "Anatole?"

I smiled at my friend, the great Esquavetian explorer Mario Cuvio.

60

MERMAID BOY

B EFORE HE PASSED OUT again, Cuvio effusively assured the innskeep, as only a drunkard can, that his friend Anatole was the "most exceptional bald man in the entire world!" He claimed he knew this for a fact because he had personally explored "every corner of the globe."

That was enough for her to allow us to stay in his room for the night. But her admiration for the famous sea captain only went so far. She kept the emerald.

I took his hands and Pito held his feet as we carried Cuvio up the three flights of stairs. The man who had knocked Pito down trailed behind us with three thin mattresses bent over his right shoulder.

We dropped Cuvio onto the bed, then tried to figure out where the three of us would sleep. The cramped room was barely big enough for the bed, a table, and Cuvio's large trunk.

"I'm so tired I can sleep standing up," Tullia said.

Pito's mattress was crammed between the trunk and the bed.

Tullia slept close to the window, and most of me was under the table.

"Your shoes are stinking up the room!" Pito complained.

"The odor exists only in your mind," I told him.

He laughed and said, "No, that smell is alive!"

It was only one of my shoes, but Tullia came and got them both and threw them out the door.

I AWOKE TO AN AWFUL RETCHING NOISE, AND WHEN I OPENED my eyes, the first thing I saw was Cuvio's hairy buttocks. He was leaning out the window. Sometime during the night, he'd shed the orange veil. Bright sunshine poured through the window.

He spat out the last of his vomit, turned, and stumbled over Tullia.

She stared up at him, eyes wide open.

He looked down at her, then over to where Pito was still sleeping, and finally at me. He covered his face with his hands and groaned. After a moment, he peeked out at me through his fingers. "Oh, Anatole, what have you done?"

An hour later the four of us were seated at the table. Tullia and I were in the only two chairs. Cuvio was on the edge of the bed, and Pito sat on the trunk.

The innskeep had sent up a breakfast of eggs, mutton, bread, and fruit. There was also a pot of tea, and that alone was worth the price of the emerald. It had been so long, I couldn't even recall the last time I had enjoyed a cup of tea.

I let its warmth linger in my mouth before swallowing. It had a smoky flavor, but unlike other smoky teas I'd tried, it was smooth, not harsh. The aftertaste was something like sage.

"Anatole!" Cuvio barked.

Apparently, it wasn't his first attempt at getting my attention.

"You can't talk to him when he's drinking tea," said Tullia.

"Do you even know how much danger you're in? You're not safe here."

"Where can we go that is safe?" asked Tullia.

He looked at her and slowly shook his head. "Nowhere."

The captain had recognized the princess the moment he saw those eyes staring up from the floor.

"But Dalrympl is married to my mother," Tullia said. "Why would he want me?"

There was no point in answering that question. We all knew why, and so did Tullia. *Revenge. Spite. The pleasure of watching her suffer.*

"Your mother won't protect you," said Cuvio. "It was she who murdered King Sandro, your father."

I saw Tullia's face quiver just a bit, but that was her only visible reaction.

I considered telling her that I might have been partially to blame. I had never mentioned the shard from the pot, which had pricked her mother's finger.

"I'm not surprised," she said to Cuvio, and then proceeded to tell him our plans to go to the *neder lands*. She showed him her jeweled knife.

After all he'd seen, it took a lot to impress the famous sea captain. He was impressed.

"Do you know the merchant Bruno?" she asked, and explained why we wanted to wait for him to return from the monastery.

"I know him well," Cuvio said, "well enough to know that he's the last person you can trust. Bruno will take the knife and then turn you over to Dalrympl in order to gain the favor of the new king. It would take more than a thousand treks to the monastery to clean all the stink off that man's soul."

Tullia's disappointment didn't last long. "You must know lots of other sea captains," she said. "Who can we trust?"

Cuvio considered before answering. "No one. I'm sorry. I wish I could help you."

"Then help us!" she shot back. "You have a ship. You can take us to Antwerp."

Cuvio groaned. He grabbed his head and asked me if I had any of my special morning-after medicine.

"We have nothing but our robes," I told him.

"I can't just pull up anchor and sail to Antwerp," he said, speaking to me, not to Tullia. "I'll be setting off for the Americas in two weeks, and it will likely be my last expedition. Dalrympl sees no reason to finance any more voyages, since I don't bring back sacks of gold or conquer territory."

"We don't have to go to Antwerp," said Tullia. "We'll sail with you to America."

Cuvio sighed. "She's persistent, isn't she?"

"Why not?" Tullia persisted.

It was Pito who answered. "Because it's too dangerous."

"It's dangerous here too," said Tullia. "He said so."

"I'm sorry, but I don't have room for passengers. The ship can barely hold the crew. As it is, there's only enough space for a third of them to sleep at any one time."

"You've done enough," said Pito, "just sharing your room. We're very grateful. We'll find our way to Antwerp."

"He didn't share his room with us!" snapped Tullia. "He was too drunk to know we were here!"

Cuvio laughed and acknowledged the truth of what she said.

"We don't have to be passengers," she told him. "We can join your crew."

"Ever worked on a ship, Princess?"

Her blue eye flashed at that word.

"No, she hasn't," said Pito. "None of us have. We'd just get in the way."

Tullia glared at Pito. "What's wrong with you?"

"Fear of the ocean," said Cuvio. "I've seen that look before."

"I'm not afraid," said Pito. "Just realistic."

"You weren't afraid to sail to Antwerp," said Tullia.

"It's not the same, is it?" Cuvio asked Pito. He turned to Tullia and said, "You can get to Antwerp just by following the coastline."

"So?" she asked.

"America is on the other side of a vast ocean." He turned back to Pito and asked, "What is it that frightens you?"

Pito shrugged and said, "Storms."

"It does get stormy," the captain agreed. "But even worse are the endless days when the wind doesn't blow at all. Which is why I need an *experienced* crew," he added for Tullia's benefit.

"And pirates," Pito said quietly.

"They're out there somewhere," Cuvio admitted. "But, as I said, it's a vast ocean."

"And giant whirlpools," said Pito, "that can suck a ship to the bottom of the ocean."

"Never encountered that phenomenon," said the captain.

"What about sea monsters?" Pito asked.

"Perhaps. The sea holds many mysteries."

"Mermaids?"

Tullia and I laughed, while the captain stared at Pito in astonishment. "Why are you afraid of mermaids?"

Pito looked down. "They lure sailors overboard with their beauty and sweet melodies."

"Not a bad way to go, if you ask me!" laughed Cuvio.

"He's read a lot," I said in Pito's defense.

Tullia left her chair, walked around the table to Pito, and placed a hand on Pito's arm. "Don't worry, I'll protect you from those wicked mermaids."

Pito shook her hand away.

I felt bad for Pito. I'd never known him to be scared or embarrassed. To take some of the pressure off, I admitted to my fears. "Not of sailing off the edge of the world," I explained. "I *know* the Earth is a sphere, even if I don't *understand* how that can be so." I also accepted the fact that there were people on the other side of our world walking around upside down. But they were walking on *land*. Land was solid. "But how can a boat sail upside down on *water*?"

This was one fear that Pito didn't share. "The cosmos has no up or down," he said. "Don't think of the universe as *a place*, Anatole. Think of it as *a process*."

That was beyond me, and I didn't know if Cuvio understood it either, but I detected a noticeable change in the way he looked at Pito.

Tullia must have also noticed the change, and she was quick to take advantage of it. "Pito's a brilliant writer," she asserted. "He can chronicle the journey. For hundreds of years, people everywhere will read about the adventures of the brave and heroic Captain Cuvio!"

"I have no need for a chronicler," Cuvio replied. "And I don't respond favorably to flattery."

"He's good at learning new languages," I put in. "He'll be able to help you communicate with the savages."

That, too, was the wrong thing to say.

"They're not savages!" Cuvio said angrily. "They understand mathematics, study the stars, build aqueducts . . ." He sadly shook his head. "We're the savages, Anatole." He rubbed his hands through his hair and groaned. "I could use a ship's doctor," he said to me. "I've lost too many good men to the scurvy. But you'll have to do other work too: cook, clean, cut hair . . ."

"And them?" I asked.

"These are very rough men, away at sea for a very long time," he said. "I can't protect her."

"I can protect myself," said Tullia.

"She can," I said. "And she was the hardest worker at the monastery."

"A ship isn't a monastery," said Cuvio. "And sailors aren't monks."

"Tullia's fearless. She'll climb the highest mast even if it's storming. And Pito's a quick learner. Whatever you need him to do—rig a sail, read a sextant . . ."

And then I finally said the right thing. "And he can beat you at chess too."

"Is that so?" Cuvio asked Pito.

Pito shrugged one shoulder and smiled.

Cuvio laughed, then said he kept a chess set in his cabin. He turned to Tullia. "If Mermaid Boy wins, you can join the crew."

61

TRIANGLES

N EVER WEAR THE SAME disguise twice," Cuvio declared as he paced his large body across the small room. Now that we were going to his ship, he'd taken charge. He'd arranged for a bath and a change of clothes for the princess.

"Go!" he barked at her.

She went.

My shoes were still outside the door, but they no longer stank. They'd been thoroughly cleaned. The emerald had bought that too.

Cuvio opened his trunk and looked for something suitable for Pito to wear. The bending over seemed to make him dizzy, so he sat down on the bed.

"There's a market on the way to the ship," he said, head in hands. "You should be able to find everything you need, Anatole, to conjure up your morning-after potion." He groaned and then added, "Get something for Mermaid Boy's seasickness too. We will both need to be sharp of mind."

"I'm not seasick," said Pito.

"Yet," said the captain.

"Maybe you should play against Tullia," Pito suggested. "She's better at chess than me." He quickly added, "Don't tell her I said that."

Cuvio laughed. "You can't squirm out of it that easily. It's you against me, Mermaid Boy. Chess isn't just tactics and strategy. It's about crushing your opponent's will. You have to be merciless. I couldn't do that to the princess."

"She's not a princess," said Pito.

From him, that was a compliment.

Cuvio gave him a red silk shirt with gold buttons. Pito started to put it on, but the captain told him to wait until after his bath. "It's my finest shirt, and to be honest, you're a bit rank." He also pulled a surcoat and a three-cornered hat out of the trunk.

He said he'd get some sailor togs for me at the market while I was getting what I needed for my potion. Until then, my monk's robe would have to do. Nothing else could conceal my hairlessness.

"We won't slink in the shadows," he declared. "We'll set out at fourteen hundred, when the streets are most crowded, and walk confidently along the esplanade."

There was a knock on the door.

Pito and I froze, but the captain calmly opened it.

Tullia entered, draped in veils. Pito couldn't stop staring.

"What?" she asked.

"Stop gawking and get down there!" the captain ordered.

Still staring, Pito started toward the door.

"Take the clothes!"

Pito's eyes remained on Tullia as he scooped up his new clothes from atop the bed. He walked sideways through the doorway, and then backward toward the top of the stairs.

Cuvio slammed the door shut. "So he doesn't fall down the stairs," he explained, then laughed. "Did she give you the green veil?" he asked Tullia.

She was clutching it in her hand.

The captain's eyes lit up. He flung open the door and raced to the top of the stairs.

"Be careful!" he shouted down below. "There may be mermaids in the bathwater!"

He came back in chuckling and quite pleased with himself. "I like him," he said.

"So do I," Tullia quietly agreed.

WE LEFT THE HUMMINGBIRD AS THE BELLS IN THE CHURCH TOWER tolled fourteen times. Cuvio walked ahead. Behind, and off to the side, Tullia hung on to Pito's arm. A green veil covered her face. I was farther behind, and on the other side of the narrow alley.

Cuvio had no trouble navigating the knot of winding streets that led to the waterfront. "That's the church we were looking for!" Tullia exclaimed.

Cuvio silenced her with a sharp glare. We weren't supposed to know each other.

Once we were on the esplanade, we were able to spread farther apart.

The men who passed us couldn't help stealing glances at Tullia, but it was Cuvio who drew most of the attention. Everyone recognized the famous sea captain. They'd shout his name and wave, and he waved back. Children ran up just to touch his coat, and then they'd run away.

One man asked him if Amazon women were truly eight braccios tall.

"Ten!" he replied, never one to disappoint.

Someone else wanted to know about flying monkeys.

Cuvio said they were small but "swarmed like bees."

I felt practically invisible. People tended to look the other way when I passed. They were all too aware of their sins and shortcomings to make eye contact with a monk.

I gazed out across the harbor and took a deep breath of the salt air. There were three great inventions that changed the world and brought about the Renaissance. The first two I've already mentioned: gunpowder and the printing press with movable type.

I was looking at the third. The ships in the harbor all had triangular sails.

During the Dark Ages, the sails had been rectangular. These were only useful when the wind blew from behind. The hulls of these ships were filled not with cargo but with oarsmen, who rowed their giant oars whenever the wind was blowing in the wrong direction, more than half the time.

The triangular sail, which could be easily shifted back and forth between port and starboard, somehow made it possible for a ship to sail *into the wind*. To me, that was magic.

62

A MOST IMPORTANT
DECISION

THE MARKET CONSISTED OF two permanent structures and a seemingly endless number of tents. Hundreds of tables had been set up inside and outside, and in no particular order. A pile of furs could be next to a bucket of fish.

This made it problematic to find everything I needed, but I didn't mind. I enjoyed wandering through the exotic sights and smells, and I had to keep reminding myself that there was some urgency to my mission.

Cuvio had given me a satchel of coins, and my first purchase was a burlap sack to carry everything else I would acquire. It took a long time to find a petrified robin's egg, but then anchovy paste was directly across from it!

I filled half of my sack with dried hot peppers. I only would need one pepper for the morning-after potion, and one for Pito's seasickness. The rest were for the scurvy that Cuvio had mentioned.

Scurvy was also known as the sailor's sickness. After being away at sea for long periods, sailors' gums would rot, their teeth would fall out, and their muscles would become weak. Many died from the disease. My thought was that the hot peppers would ward off the evil spirits, just as a fire in the night keeps wild animals at bay.

Twenty-first-century physicians would snicker at such a notion. They'll tell you that scurvy results from a lack of vitamin C. Then they'll shake their heads at those woefully ignorant sixteenth-century physicians who didn't know enough to give these sailors an orange or lemon to eat.

To listen to them, you'd get the impression that if you peered into a microscope—something we didn't have then—you'd see a bunch of As, Bs, Cs, Ds, and Es floating around, like soggy cereal in a bowl of milk.

Vitamins aren't the be-all and end-all. There are an infinite number of fractions between the numbers 1 and 2, and an infinite number of tones between what are now the accepted notes on a scale. Similarly, there also exist an infinite variety of qualities and benefits found between the vitamins A, B, C, D, and E. Most of my magic came from the stuff between the vitamins.

Oh, and by the way, it is now known that a hot pepper contains more vitamin C than an orange. Also, dried peppers are more easily stored aboard a ship and don't attract rats.

But what did I know? I was just a woefully ignorant sixteenth-century physician!

I PURCHASED SOME GINGER FOR PITO'S SEASICKNESS. THE VENDOR offered not only the ginger roots but also the sweet-smelling flowers, which are more potent.

I was determined to leave the market without any more dawdling. Cuvio, who was much more familiar with this market, had probably purchased the sailor togs a while ago and was growing impatient waiting for me.

But when I passed the tea vendor, I ask you, how could I not have stopped?

I still had a few coins left in the satchel. Who knew if they even had tea in the Americas? Surely, Cuvio would indulge me in this.

Various tins were lined up on a long table. In front of each tin was a small basket containing a sample of the leaves inside.

I went from one basket to another, sniffing the contents. I quickly identified the smoky tea I'd enjoyed so much at breakfast but wasn't sure I wanted such an unusual variety to be the one and only tea I would ever drink.

I rechecked the satchel and was glad to discover I had enough coins for two tins. However, instead of making my decision easier, it complicated my options.

I sniffed each basket again and narrowed it down to four, one being the smoky tea from breakfast. I sniffed those four baskets a third time, but then one I'd previously rejected caught my attention. When I sniffed that basket again, I decided it would definitely be one of my teas.

My hood jerked backward, and my collar rose up tight against my neck. "I found the hairless one!" someone shouted, as my arms were grabbed from both sides.

There were three of them. One held each arm, and the one who had shouted now brandished a knife. "Don't let him cast a spell!" he warned, and then a greasy rag was stuffed in my mouth.

They were young, none older than nineteen. One had a bad case of acne. If the circumstances had been different, I could have treated it with a few herbs and fungi from nearby tables.

A crowd was gathering and I spotted the innskeep from the

Hummingbird among them. She balanced a roll of blue velvet over her shoulder.

Other men came and took over. The one who appeared to be in charge asked where the other two monks were hiding.

I couldn't say anything with the rag in my mouth, but that didn't keep him from striking me with the back of his hand. Only after that did he order the boy to remove my rag.

"He might cast a spell," the boy warned.

"Anatole doesn't cast spells," said a voice I instantly recognized.

Dittierri, wearing a full-length white fur coat, strode through the market and came up to me. "On behalf of King Dalrympl, I'm arresting you for the abduction and murder of Princess Tullia."

Though he was ostensibly speaking to me, his pronouncement was made for the benefit of the onlookers. What started as gasps and murmurs soon became shouts and insults, all aimed at me. Various methods of execution were also suggested.

Dittierri let it go on awhile before holding up a hand to silence them. He announced he was still looking for two additional conspirators, possibly disguised as monks. He said that any information leading to their capture would be generously rewarded.

I looked at the innskeep, who was staring back at me. She eased herself backward away from the crowd, then turned and headed for the exit.

True to her word, the hummingbird did not chirp.

63

A LONG JOURNEY

MORE SHOUTS AND INSULTS followed me as the soldiers escorted me from the market. I could see soldiers on horseback patrolling the esplanade. There was no sign of Pito, Tullia, or Cuvio. I could only hope that the innskeep had warned them.

I was brought to a carriage, and despite having my hands tied behind my back, and jittery horses, I climbed into it without incident. Once I was inside the carriage, my ankles were also bound together.

Dittierri climbed in after me. "Where are they, Anatole?"

"Who?"

He laughed at my pretense. "Princess Tullia and the scribe, Pito."

I reminded him that Pito had died of the plague, and that from what I heard, the princess had been abducted and murdered.

We both knew why he'd had to accuse me of that. King Dalrympl couldn't let it be known that the princess was so repulsed by him that she'd run away with a lowly scribe.

"We have two tigers now," Dittierri told me. "The king considers it great sport to watch man against beast. But it's not really a sport, is it, since everyone knows from the outset who will emerge victorious?"

He left me to dwell on that while he joined the search for the others.

I REMAINED THERE FOR HOURS, WITH NO WAY OF KNOWING HOW the search was proceeding. My only solace was that every second I was there alone meant that another second passed without Tullia or Pito being captured.

I began to grow impatient. Bound as I was, with foul-smelling guards on either side, I just wanted to get going, no matter how many tigers were waiting for me.

It was dusk when Dittierri returned, and while I wouldn't say I was glad to see him, at least it signaled some kind of change. Without a word, he sat across from me, and then, at last, the carriage began to move. I could see soldiers riding along on either side.

IT WAS A THREE-DAY JOURNEY BACK TO THE CASTLE. DITTIERRI was surprisingly pleasant. Maybe it was because I was no longer a threat. Or he was simply bored and knew he was stuck with me for three days.

He filled me in on all I missed while I was away, almost as if I were a long-lost friend returning home. We were the last two left from King Sandro's court. Everyone else had either escaped or fed the tigers.

Dalrympl had made certain that no one loyal to King Sandro

would plot against him. Even Voltharo, who had been Dalrympl's spy, fed the tiger.

"If Voltharo was willing to betray one king," Dittierri explained, "he was likely to betray another."

Machiavelli would be proud.

I asked him why he'd been spared.

"My loyalty was always to Queen Corinna, and she's unquestionably devoted to Dalrympl."

"Devoted and obedient?" I asked.

He smiled.

I wanted to ask about Harwell but didn't dare call attention to him. For all I knew, he was still at the castle.

"You surprised me, Anatole," Dittierri said. "Monks buying potatoes with rubies? You're smarter than that."

"They were really good potatoes," I said.

He laughed.

After I fell asleep and leaned on one guard or the other, they finally changed seats so I could lean against the side of the carriage. I ate what the soldiers ate, and when we stopped so they could relieve themselves, I was on their same schedule.

I was jostled awake during the afternoon of the third day. The carriage had stopped. I recognized the sound of cables cranking. The gate was being lowered.

We crossed over the tiger moat. I was home.

64

THE WHISPERING KING

I HAD GOTTEN USED TO climbing in and out of the carriage with hands and ankles bound. The only reason I fell this time was that one of the guards shoved me. I think he wanted to impress the queen, who was waiting and watching.

She wasn't impressed. "Anatole is our guest," she told the guard, then ordered him to remove my ropes and help me up.

When I was back on my feet, she asked me if I would like a bath before supper.

I was too scared and stupefied to answer, but she didn't wait for my response. She ordered Marta, who was also there, to prepare my bath.

As I followed Marta across the grounds, two guards on either side, I wondered whose supper she had meant, mine or the tigers'.

The bathtub was in the laundry, which was part of the same outbuilding as the kitchen. I waited as Marta went back and forth, bringing pots of hot water to the tub. She seemed as fidgety as ever.

I didn't know if she was scared for me or *of* me. I wanted to reassure her that the princess was still alive, but I didn't dare say anything.

Clean clothes had already been laid out for me. I felt a warm nostalgia as I looked upon my cape and my favorite blue shirt with the silver buttons.

When the bath was full, Marta came close and gave me a quiet warning. "The king only speaks in whispers. But woe betide he who asks, '*What?*'"

She left while I bathed, but the guards remained.

AFTER MY BATH, I PUT ON THE NEW UNDERCLOTHES THAT HAD been set out for me. They were a little stiff and scratchy, and I didn't expect to live long enough for the fabric to soften. For whatever reason, I didn't want to die wearing dirty and shabby underclothing.

I chose not to wear my shirt and cape however, and put the Capuchin robe back on. I couldn't bear the thought of my favorite clothes shredded and covered in blood.

I silently made a vow, not to Jesus Christ but to Tullia and Pito.

I will not betray you.

MY GUARDS ESCORTED ME INTO THE CASTLE AND UP THE BROAD staircase. People I didn't know stopped and stared. It felt strange to be in such a familiar place with so many unfamiliar faces.

I'd been inside the king's chambers a few times before. They had been impressive but not garish. The former king had been a patron of the arts, and I had always appreciated the paintings and sculptures on display.

When the guard opened the door to these same chambers, the

difference was striking. It seemed as if everything in the room had been gold-plated, including the dishes and utensils on what I assumed would be the supper table. Even the tablecloth was embroidered with gold thread. All the lanterns, and wall sconces, and picture frames were gold. There was one massive painting of Dalrympl sitting atop a white horse, saber drawn. He was wearing the same gold uniform he'd worn at the wedding of the century. Two large silver mirrors hung on opposite walls, multiplying the opulence ad infinitum. So much for the Oxatanian ethics of austerity and utilitarianism.

A guard indicated where I was to sit. I was facing the painting of Dalrympl.

The king's chambers consisted of multiple rooms. Queen Corinna entered through one of three interior doors. She acknowledged my presence with a glance, then went to another door to await the king. The guard gestured for me to also stand.

I will not beg, I vowed.

The queen bent to one knee when the king entered. My legs were trembling, but I did not bow.

He wore the same gold suit. His saber was sheathed at his side.

I couldn't help but think of the sword that slashed Babette's arm.

He sat at the table, then waited a long moment before indicating with a nod that the queen and I could also sit. He whispered something. I couldn't hear most of it but I caught the word *monk*.

I didn't ask, *What?*

I told him I'd chosen to devote my life to the service of Jesus Christ. It was a cowardly thing to say. I suppose I was hoping for mercy. More effective would have been to say that I was devoting my life to the service of King Dalrympl.

A servant brought us each a plate of olives, cheese, and warm figs. The queen waited for Dalrympl to take the first bite, so I did the same. He bit into a fig and whispered, "Exquisite."

My stomach tightened at the word, the same word he had once used to describe Babette's lace.

He whispered something to Corinna, and then she turned to me. "Our most generous king is concerned that you aren't eating."

I obligingly took a bite from an olive. Swallowing was a struggle. My throat felt constricted. My legs wouldn't stop trembling.

Wine was poured. More courses were brought out. Whenever I looked up, I saw two Dalrympls: the one at the table and the one on the wall behind him.

The only sounds I heard from the king were his slurping and the smacking of his lips. He never spoke directly to me. If he had something to say, he'd whisper to the queen, who would then relay the message. It was always about the food.

"Our magnificent king hopes you are enjoying the smoked eel."

"Our most generous king wants to know what you think of the goose."

"Our wise and benevolent king wants me to assure you that there is plenty more goat leg, should you so desire."

My first thought was that he wanted to fatten me up for the tigers, but by the time we were on the fourth course, I began to wonder if he was recruiting me to be his personal magician. I was, after all, the greatest magician in all the land, whereas his magician could be described as at best inept. This realization was heartening, and I managed to eat some of the goat, but beneath the table my legs were still shaking.

Caramel custard was brought out for dessert.

"Our most glorious king would like you to understand that this isn't a special meal for him. He eats like this every day."

I nodded and obligingly took a spoonful of custard.

I knew what Pito would say. *You alone control your will, Anatole. Don't let Dalrympl take that away from you. Better to feed the tiger than use your talents to help him.*

And I knew what Tullia would say too. *Of course you should agree to be his magician. Earn his trust, and then assassinate him.*

A gold urn was set on the table. Dalrympl whispered to the queen.

She filled two cups from the urn and gave one to the king and the other to me.

"Our wise king knows how much you appreciate rare teas. This is Oxatania's finest."

That she didn't pour one for herself didn't arouse my suspicions. Nor did the fact that I'd never known of any tea grown in Oxatania.

If Dalrympl was willing to drink it, why shouldn't I? And besides, death by poison was certainly preferable to death by tiger.

He and the queen both stared at me while I sipped.

It was awful. Oxatania's finest tea tasted like swamp water.

Yet I couldn't have enjoyed it more. I smiled at the king. "Exquisite," I said.

Despite all this grandeur, *our most ignorant and boorish king* couldn't tell the difference between fine tea and stewed stinkweed.

My legs stopped shaking. Every sip of the terrible brew emboldened me more.

"Do you remember the girl who sold lace?" I asked.

"Lace?" he whispered.

"You forced her to clean your boot with it."

He stared curiously at me, and then he remembered. He whispered, "You had hair then."

"Her name was Babette," I said.

I could see the realization creep over his face, until he understood it all. The itch. The leeches. The antidote. His changed voice wasn't a result of his unique physiology.

It was the intended consequence.

I smiled at him. My revenge was complete, and I felt ready to face the tigers.

"Harwell," he whispered.

"Do you remember Harwell?" Queen Corinna asked me.

I took my time before answering. "The deaf-mute?"

"He wasn't deaf!" squealed Dalrympl, no longer whispering. "He was Sandro's spy!" His voice was so shrill, it could break glass.

"Harwell told King Sandro everything he saw and heard in the dungeon," said the queen. "And my husband told me."

"And she told me!" Dalrympl added, sounding very much like a five-year-old girl who had been promised some candy.

"But why spy on Pito?" I asked the queen.

"He wasn't spying on Pito," she answered. "He was spying on you."

Dalrympl giggled.

It didn't make sense. I could have reported directly to King Sandro.

"So, what ever happened to Harwell?" I asked, trying not to sound overly concerned.

"We don't know," said Queen Corinna. "He was put in charge of the search for the princess. And for you. He never came back."

So that explained why we were able to get away without being followed.

I kept my expression blank. Harwell would have been proud.

"You Esquavetians believe you are so superior!" Dalrympl

exclaimed. "Did you think Oxatanian mathematicians and linguists couldn't decipher your simple code?"

His absurd voice was so disconcerting it took me longer than it should have to figure out he was talking about my logbook.

"Do you think I plan to give you to the tigers?" He giggled a moment, then said, "That would be too quick. I want you to suffer for a very long time."

I stared at my empty teacup. It was my turn to come to a realization.

I'd been right about one thing. He had wanted to impress me, but not because he wanted me to be his magician. He wanted me to understand the difference between his life and the life that would be mine.

The tea hadn't just tasted like swamp water. It *was* swamp water, reconstituted.

We had drunk the Luigi potion.

"I will live forever!" Dalrympl shrieked. "I'll be king for the next ten thousand years! And you'll live below me, chained to the dungeon wall."

65

ETERNITY, DAY ONE

THE GUARDS CLAMPED A manacle to my ankle. They dragged me down the stone staircase while I pleaded with them to throw me to the tigers.

I was chained to the same bolt that had held Pito. I screamed when the iron door slammed shut. When they left, they took the light with them.

I prayed, piecing together a hodgepodge of Latin syllables and phrases I remembered from the monastery. *The words don't matter.* I wept until my eyes ran dry.

But then I realized that Dalrympl had been mistaken. The potion affected the aging process. It hadn't made us immortal.

I could still kill myself.

The chain was long enough to allow me to take three quick steps and then ram my head into the wall.

The darkness was my ally. I just needed to fool my brain into believing that the wall wasn't there.

How many times did I lower my head and take two determined

steps, only to abruptly stop? After each try, I'd touch the wall to see how close I came. Once my nose was less than two inches from the wall, but most of the time I had to stretch out my arm pretty far before I touched it.

My problem was that I wasn't yet desperate. It was only the anticipation of suffering that I felt, not the suffering. It was enough to know that I could kill myself when the suffering became unbearable.

And then I realized something else too.

I smiled.

If Dalrympl believed he was immortal, he was sure to do something dangerously stupid. And if he somehow survived that, he'd take more stupid and dangerous chances.

Ten thousand years? He wouldn't last one week!

I laughed out loud.

I LAY ON MY BACK AND TRIED TO GET SOME SLEEP. MY ROBE served as both my mat and my blanket.

I was curious if I needed to close my eyes. I tried to test it, but the longer I lay there, the more difficult it was to know if they were open or closed. I'd have to shut or open them to find out.

I thought about my friends back in Torteluga. I wondered who won the chess game, or if it was ever played. I liked to think that the innskeep had warned them, and they were safely aboard Cuvio's ship. Perhaps it had sailed away while I sat in the carriage, waiting for Dittierri to return.

Cuvio wouldn't have had a crew, but possibly the three of them could have maneuvered the ship out of the harbor. They could stop somewhere up the coast to hire a full crew.

My mind drifted out to the sea, where I saw a three-masted

ship bobbing over the waves. I had a vision of Pito tugging on a rope while the ocean sprayed his face. I didn't know what was on the other end of the rope.

I didn't have a clear idea of what Cuvio's ship looked like. I'd never seen it.

I envisioned Tullia high atop a mast. She was hanging on with one hand as the ship violently rose and fell. Her other hand was holding a spyglass as she looked out for pirates, sea monsters, and mermaids. I fell asleep not knowing if my eyes were open or shut.

I was startled awake by something crawling over my foot. Momentarily forgetting where I was, I tried to shake it off and nearly broke my ankle on the manacle.

The creature scurried up my leg, beneath my robe.

I lay still. I was thankful for my new undergarments as it crawled atop my genitals.

It continued up the hill that was my stomach, where it lingered awhile before descending to my chest. And then I didn't feel it anymore.

I anxiously waited, wondering where it might turn up next. I worried that perhaps it was the scout, and that there would soon be an army of rodents nibbling away at every part of me.

I heard a squeak.

"Luigi?" I whispered, then gently touched his head. He had nestled inside the axe-cut slit in my robe, just above my heart.

That was how we slept my first night in the dungeon, and every night thereafter.

PART THREE

A LONG AND DRAWN-OUT ENDING

66

MEMORIES AND
DELUSIONS

THE TOUR GUIDE SAID that the prisoner of Tiger Castle lived in the dungeon for one hundred years. I believe it was only ninety-two, but people prefer round numbers, just as they prefer the notes on the scale to the tones between them. It's why scientists and physicians focus on those lettered vitamins while ignoring everything else.

Ninety-two years is an estimate. I could be off by a year or two. I was delirious when I finally emerged, and it took me more than a decade and a half to recover enough wits to be able to function on my own. Most of my knowledge about what happened during those years comes from historical records. (I think you know my opinion of historians.)

Dalrympl lasted longer than the week I gave him. He died during my fourteenth year of captivity, although I had no way of knowing that.

Presumably, Queen Corinna became too old for him, and there were many younger women eager to take her place. From what I can surmise, most if not all of these unfortunate women eventually fed the tigers.

I never learned what the Oxatanian ambassador meant when he said that my demon leeches had drained Dalrympl's manhood, but I suspect the deaths of these women were connected to that. Either he blamed them for his inadequacy or was just making sure that they never spoke of it.

One girl was different than the others. She not only rejected his advances, but, according to two sources, she laughed at the king. You would think she would have been executed for such impudence, but as often happens in such circumstances, Dalrympl fell in love with her.

He set about to prove his manhood. On the sixth of September, 1538, a long ladder was set into the moat. As the girl watched from the bridge, Dalrympl climbed down, armed only with his saber.

I can only imagine what happened next.

It's not really a sport, is it, since everyone knows from the outset who will emerge victorious?

And imagine it I have! Thousands of times. Even now, more than four hundred years after his death, whenever I have trouble sleeping, I envision Dalrympl, dressed in his gold suit, confidently heading down the ladder.

More often than not I drift off before he reaches the bottom rung.

AS FOR WHAT OCCURRED *INSIDE* THE DUNGEON DURING THOSE ninety-two years, it's difficult for me to differentiate memories from delusions.

The servants who brought my food, emptied my bucket, and clipped my toenails were forbidden to speak to me. On the other hand, I remember long conversations with Luigi. Pito and Tullia also appeared from time to time, but their visits were frustrating because they never answered my questions.

Who won the chess game? Did you sail to America?

At some point my manacle was removed, and I was free to roam the dungeon. You would think this would have been a monumental moment, but I have no memory of the chain coming off.

THE CASTLE WAS CONQUERED AT LEAST NINE TIMES DURING MY imprisonment. Control mostly shifted back and forth between the French and the English, but the Venetians also held the castle for a few years, and the Hungarians, too, had it for a little less than ten months. The French Catholics and the French Protestants also battled each other.

To the conquerors, I suppose I was something like a bulky piece of old furniture that was too heavy to move. Like it or not, whoever took over the castle also got the tigers, the glass elephant, and the crazy monk living in the dungeon.

From what I was told, I eventually became something of a legend. People made pilgrimages to the dungeon to receive my blessings. I have only vague memories of that. I probably recited some of my garbled Latin.

THERE WERE ALSO TIMES OF INTENSE CLARITY, WHEN MY MIND burned so hot it felt like it was on fire. Inspiration struck in the dungeon. I recall waking up and shouting, "Not sand, salt!"

Or maybe I hadn't shouted. I never could be sure if I actually spoke out loud.

I conducted experiments inside my mind, mixing different compounds and substances with salt. Then I'd analyze the results and make modifications. I adjusted the size, shape, and array of the candles, and changed them when they burned too low.

Cat urine not only provided the color I needed but was the perfect catalyst to set the whole process into motion. Not just any cat piss would do. The cat would need to be kept on a diet of fresh crab and boiled asparagus.

The magic of salt had been known for a long time. There had been a period during the Dark Ages when laborers were paid with salt. That's where we get the expression "worth one's salt." The English word *salary* is derived from *salt*.

It seemed so obvious, I wondered why I hadn't thought of it before, while I was still court magician. If I had, Esquaveta might still exist today.

67

A NEW WORLD

DON'T WORRY, I HAVE no intention of dragging you through the next four hundred years of my existence but will keep to those instances that are relevant to what already has been chronicled. There was one particular instance that I think you'll agree was extraordinary.

An English duke eventually coaxed me up out of the dungeon. Apparently, he'd kept the dungeon's two doors unlocked and open since taking charge of the castle eight years earlier, but I'd been too frightened to leave.

That wasn't what was so extraordinary. I'd always been a coward.

He and the duchess patiently cared for me during the next fifteen years or so. Sadly, they were killed when the castle was once again overrun, this time by the French Catholics.

I was allowed to leave. No longer in my monk's robe but wearing a proper English suit, I crossed over the moat for the last time.

I had enough money in my pockets to see me through while I adjusted.

By then, the tigers were long dead. Tigers weren't brought back to the castle until late in the twentieth century, in order to attract tourists.

THE WORLD I ENTERED WAS NOT THE SAME ONE I'D LEFT. I WAS confused, but no longer deranged.

I tried to learn about Captain Cuvio's final voyage, but more than a century had passed and very few people had ever heard of the once exalted Esquavetian sea captain. Unlike his more famous contemporaries, he hadn't conquered territory or murdered and enslaved thousands of innocent people. As far as history was concerned, he was irrelevant.

All anyone knew about Princess Tullia was legend. A beautiful princess had been in love with a handsome prince. She was abducted and murdered on her wedding night, and the prince was so distraught he never spoke again. He only whispered. His sorrow only grew as the years passed, until at last he climbed down the ladder to the tigers.

I WENT INTO EVERY BOOKSHOP I CAME ACROSS, UP AND DOWN the Italian peninsula and then in America. I wasn't just looking for information about Cuvio but also for Pito's book. But the book had been Tullia's idea, not his, and if they did make it to America, he wouldn't have had the time for such an idle activity. It would have taken all of their efforts to survive.

I came to the New World in 1703. It was no longer new then, not that it ever was.

My travels brought me to Philadelphia, which, with a population of close to ten thousand, was the second-largest city in the colonies. There were so many carts and horses, I had to keep turning my head, first one way, then the other, to avoid being run down. I felt greatly relieved as I made it safely across a busy street, only to step in a fresh pile of horse manure.

There was nothing extraordinary about that either. It wasn't the first such pile I'd stepped upon, and it wouldn't be the last.

A man was laughing, but when I turned to glare at him, he immediately apologized. He was bald, but unlike me, only on top of his head. He had wide sideburns and a kind smile.

He introduced himself as Nathaniel and offered to treat me to a meal. And then he extended a hand.

I stared. It took me a moment to remember what I was supposed to do, and then I clasped his hand in mine and solemnly gave it a quick up-and-down.

"Then you're not a Quaker?" Nathaniel asked me later.

We were in the pub, sharing a pitcher of ale and a plate of fried fish. He explained that shaking hands was a Quaker tradition.

I told him that it had also been an ancient Greek custom.

"You're a scholar."

"No. A friend of mine was."

After we left the pub, he introduced me to his wife and three daughters. The youngest was no older than six. She was playing with a long stick, pretending it was a sword. She pointed it at me, inches from my neck, and demanded to know if I was an abolitionist or a slaveholder.

"If you're a slaveholder," she threatened, "I'll slash your wicked throat!"

Nathaniel and his wife were so busy apologizing to me, while at the same time scolding their daughter for her rudeness, that they didn't notice the tears streaming down my face.

The girl noticed. Her brown eye was filled with concern and curiosity, while her blue one flashed defiance.

68

FINAL THOUGHTS

THE PLANTS AND TREES in my garden sprout from seeds left by the plants and trees that came before them. Their roots run deep through the soil of history.

The Quakers would have had to learn about the handshake ritual from someone. They also believed in equality between all people. Nathaniel's family was a part of a peaceful and sharing community. No fences. No kings, queens, or princesses.

I choose to believe that Pito and Tullia not only survived but flourished in America. I doubt there was one big romantic moment when they passionately threw themselves into each other's arms. Despite Tullia's swagger and Pito's cockiness, I think they were both shy and nervous about their feelings toward each other. I suspect that there were a lot of awkward fumblings as they tentatively rediscovered the love I stole from them.

Do you think I'm being too presumptuous or vain to also think they may have had a son whom they named Anatole? And perhaps, somewhere along the family tree, *Anatole* was changed to the more American-sounding *Nathaniel*.

I'VE BUMPED AND STUMBLED MY WAY FROM ONE DECADE TO AN-other. I've fallen out of buggies, and off horses, rooftops, and ladders. I've stepped on banana peels, on rakes, and into open manholes. Yet, against all odds, somehow I'm still here, sipping a cappuccino while wearing jeans and a hoodie. I still find comfort in a hood.

Some people think it was the Capuchin monks who first created the cappuccino, but coffee was too great a luxury. My guess is that whoever coined the name was feeling whimsical at the time. Espresso is the same color as the robe I wore for such a long time.

I live on the eastern shore of Canada, in what used to be a very remote area. My cabin is about three times the size of my former workshop but just as cluttered, if not more so. Things tend to accumulate.

I still dabble in potions, but only for my own amusement. Five centuries too late, I finally conjured up a way to change eye color. These days, however, a person only has to insert a tinted contact lens, and she can have a different color for every day of the week.

My surrounding gardens cover more than six acres. I grow my own asparagus, which is more potent than what is sold in the new supermarket. From the cabin, it's just a twenty-minute walk to a rocky beach where I can usually find fresh crab. Salt, of course, is easily obtainable.

I have two cats, whom I haven't named. I need to remain detached and objective. While my sense of smell is severely limited, my eyesight remains strong. I can still distinguish twenty-four different shades of yellow.

I may have to move soon. The area around my house is becoming trendy. Whenever I venture into town, I see some new hotel or development being built.

I say that without complaint. I'm an observer of this world, not a participant.

There have been a few times in the past when I dared to form friendships. While these were nice at first, they gradually became awkward, and ultimately painful.

I've had two romantic relationships, and no, despite what you may think, these weren't the result of a potion. There have been two women over four hundred years who could love someone like me.

Neither relationship lasted more than three weeks. Though I didn't use a potion to instigate these relationships, I did use one to end them. It would have been unfair to allow these kind and lovely women to waste time with me. I have fond memories of them, but they were left with no memory of me.

For a personal identifier, I only have to think about the young girl in Philadelphia. Tears of joy are also heartfelt.

I take one last sip of cappuccino. I tear off a piece of croissant and place it inside the front pouch of my hoodie, where I feed it to my little friend and lifelong companion.

ACKNOWLEDGMENTS

Unlike Anatole, I respect and appreciate the work of historians. I listened to two series of lectures published by the Great Courses. *Renaissance: The Transformation of the West* contained forty-eight lectures by Professor Jennifer McNabb of the University of Northern Iowa. *Medieval World* consisted of thirty-six lectures by Professor Dorsey Armstrong of Purdue University. Those eighty-four lectures informed and inspired many of the ideas contained in this book. For example, Professor Armstrong told of a highly regarded minstrel who, according to the records of King Henry II, entertained the court "with a leap, a whistle, and a fart."

In chapter 6, Anatole refers to a remark by Angelica: "A woman may forgive a man who made an unwanted advance, but not the man who missed his chance." This was actually a variation on a quote by Charles-Maurice de Talleyrand-Périgord (1754–1838), who put it much more elegantly: "Women sometimes forgive a man who forces the opportunity, but never a man who misses one."

ACKNOWLEDGMENTS

I want to acknowledge and thank Ellen Levine, who has been my literary agent for more than forty years. Her combination of intelligence, integrity, and toughness has been invaluable to me and my career as a children's author. She was especially instrumental in helping to bring about *The Magician of Tiger Castle*, my first book for adults.